COLLEGE
TRUMPINGTON STREET
MASTER'S LODGINGS
DON'S GARDEN
LIBRARY QUAD
STAIRCASE 9
STAIRCASE 1
PATH
STAIRCASE 8
STAIRCASE 2
MILL LANE
STAIRCASE 7
EAST QUAD
STAIRCASE 3
STAIRCASE 6
STAIRCASE 4
PORTER'S LODGE
STAIRCASE 5
POND
COLLEGE BUILDINGS
WEST QUAD
PATH
TO BRIDGE AND RIVER
GREAT HALL

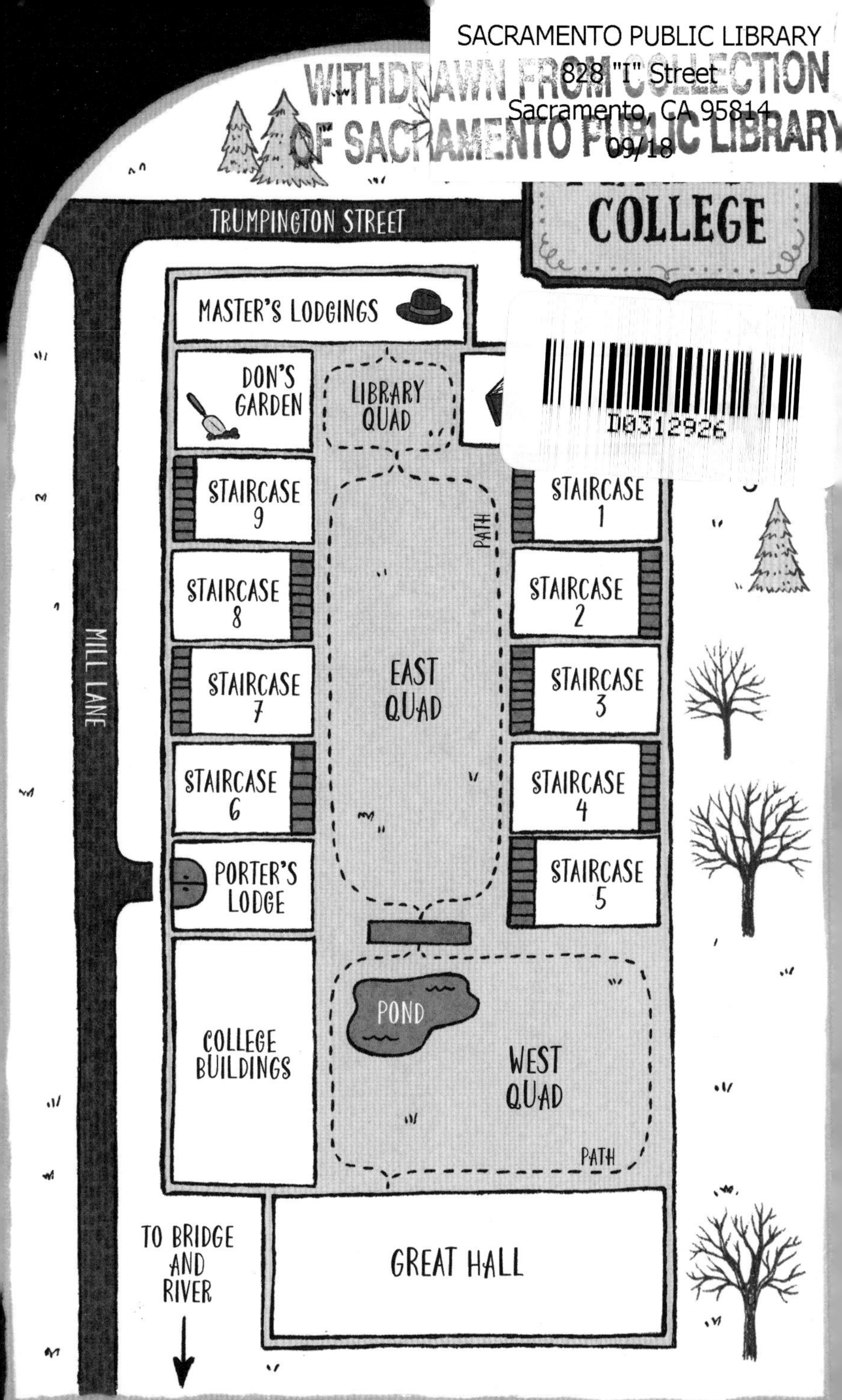

Mistletoe AND
MURDER

Also by Robin Stevens

Murder Is Bad Manners
Poison Is Not Polite
First Class Murder
Jolly Foul Play

Simon & Schuster Books for Young Readers

New York London Toronto Sydney New Delhi

SIMON & SCHUSTER BOOKS FOR YOUNG READERS
An imprint of Simon & Schuster Children's Publishing Division
1230 Avenue of the Americas, New York, New York 10020

This book is a work of fiction. Any references to historical events, real people, or real places are used fictitiously. Other names, characters, places, and events are products of the author's imagination, and any resemblance to actual events or places or persons, living or dead, is entirely coincidental.

Originally published in Great Britain in 2016 by Puffin Books.

Book design by Krista Vossen
The text for this book was set in Goudy Oldstyle Std.
Manufactured in the United States of America
0818 FFG
First Edition
2 4 6 8 10 9 7 5 3 1
Library of Congress Cataloging-in-Publication Data
Names: Stevens, Robin, 1988- author.
Title: Mistletoe and murder / Robin Stevens.
Description: First edition. | New York : Simon & Schuster Books for Young Readers, [2018] | Series: A Wells & Wong mystery | Originally published: London : Puffin Books, 2016. | Summary: "On a Christmas holiday to Cambridge, Daisy and Hazel get caught up in another murder investigation, and a competition with rival detectives."—Provided by publisher.
Identifiers: LCCN 2017042108 (print) | LCCN 2017053405 (ebook) | | ISBN 9781481489126 (hc) ISBN 9781481489140 (ebook)
Subjects: | CYAC: Mystery and detective stories. | Friendship—Fiction. | Murder—Fiction. Christmas—Fiction. | Chinese—England—Fiction. | Cambridge (England)—Fiction. Great Britain—History—George V, 1910–1936—Fiction.
Classification: LCC PZ7.S84555 (ebook) | LCC PZ7.S84555 Mis 2018 (print) | DDC [Fic]—dc23
LC record available at https://lccn.loc.gov/2017042108

To my grandma,

Phyllis Booth,

a truly formidable woman

Mistletoe and Murder

Being an account of
The Case of the Christmas Crimes,
an investigation by the Wells & Wong
Detective Society.
Written by Hazel Wong
(Detective Society Vice President and
Secretary), age fourteen.
Begun Monday, December 23, 1935

Cambridge University

ST. LUCY'S COLLEGE

Daisy Wells-Guest at St. Lucy's and president of the Wells & Wong Detective Society

Hazel Wong-Guest at St. Lucy's and vice president and secretary of the Wells & Wong Detective Society

Eustacia Mountfitchet-Mathematics don and great-aunt to Daisy and Bertie Wells

Amanda Price-First-year history student

MAUDLIN COLLEGE

Albert "Bertie" Wells-Brother of Daisy Wells and first-year history student

Donald Melling-First-year history student and older brother of Chummy Melling

Charles "Chummy" Melling-First-year history student and younger brother of Donald Melling

Alfred Cheng-First-year history student

Michael Butler-History don

Moss-Bedder for staircase nine

Mr. Perkins-Porter

ST. JOHN'S COLLEGE

Alexander Arcady-Guest at St. John's and co-chair of the Junior Pinkertons

George Mukherjee-Guest at St. John's, co-chair of the Junior Pinkertons and younger brother of Harold Mukherjee

Harold Mukherjee-First-year history student and older brother of George Mukherjee

A NOTE ON CAMBRIDGE COLLEGES

Maudlin College, Cambridge, is not a real place. I borrowed the sound of its name from Magdalen College in Oxford-Magdalen is pronounced Maudlin, which I always thought was very funny. St. Lucy's is not real either, though it is based on the women's colleges that existed in both Oxford and Cambridge at the time. St. John's College is real and so are most of the other places I mention in the book. Only the murder is entirely made up. . . .

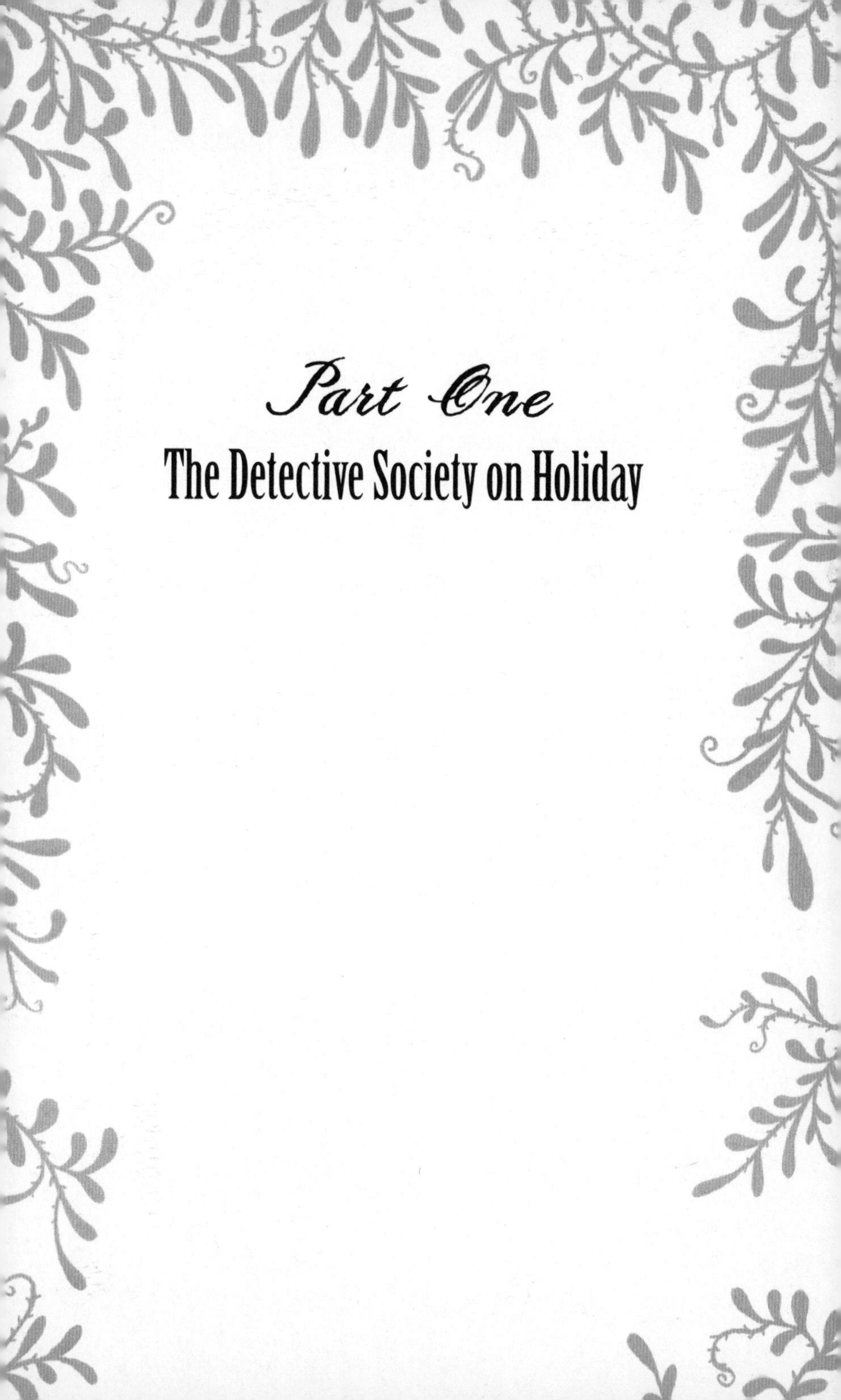

Part One
The Detective Society on Holiday

I

No one is dead—*yet*," said Daisy darkly.

It was two days before Christmas, and we were sitting in Fitzbillies tea rooms in Cambridge. It was just Daisy, Alexander, George, and myself, and as we sat there, I wondered if we would look odd to the grown-ups around us. Although Daisy is nearly fifteen now, tall and slender and with a most fashionable new fur-collared coat, my face is still round, and I am still disappointingly short. I suppose the grown-ups at the other tables thought we were only children, playing at being businesslike—but if they knew what we were really talking about, they would be terribly surprised.

"I admit that this case does not *so far* contain a death," Daisy went on. "But that may yet still change. And if it *does* come to murder, then Hazel and I will certainly have the advantage. We have investigated—"

"Four murder cases, we *know*," said George. "But that doesn't make you the better detective society."

"We'll see about that," said Daisy, glaring at him. "So. Let's discuss this bet."

You see, we are more grown-up than we seem because all four of us are detectives, members of two top-secret societies, the Detective Society and the Junior Pinkertons. Daisy and I really have solved four murder cases to date—and now it looked like we might perhaps be on our way to a fifth.

It was true that the information we had been given was slight, but as Daisy says, it is important for good detectives to seize every opportunity as it comes. In the day since Daisy and I arrived in Cambridge we have heard things and seen things that are highly suspicious. The fact that it is the Christmas holidays, and we are staying in a strange college in a strange city, will not be enough to stop us investigating. We are used to working in the most awkward situations, after all; we have done it before. Really, the most unusual thing about this case is that we will not be the only society investigating it.

You see, we have agreed to pit our wits against Alexander and George's society, the Junior Pinkertons, in the race to solve this new case. Daisy looks down on them for not having investigated any murders, but all the same I know that they are very good detectives. Alexander helped us with the Orient Express case last summer, and both Alexander and George assisted with the Bonfire Night murder only a month ago. Besides, I have heard from Alexander about some of the other cases they have solved—they are all quite hair-raising, and would have tested Daisy and me severely.

Of course, we have been up against opponents before as we have gone about our cases, but they have never *known* that we were in competition with them. Daisy and I have a very strict rule about keeping the Detective Society a secret from grown-ups. But I have the distinct feeling that working against Alexander and George will be far more difficult than outwitting Dr. Sandwich, the foolish amateur detective who tried (and failed) to solve the Orient Express case too. After all, grown-ups always underestimate children. Children never underestimate one another.

I ought to explain, I suppose, how we first heard about this case. It all began yesterday, when Daisy and I arrived in Cambridge and met her brother Bertie.

We took the train from Deepdean on Sunday morning. Mrs. Strike waved us off from Deepdean station nannyishly and handed us sandwiches wrapped in wax paper (we ate them almost as soon as the train had pulled away, and then regretted it when lunchtime rolled around). But, somehow, folding up the wax paper after our meal folded away the whole school term, the arguments and rivalries and especially the mystery we had investigated just after Bonfire Night. I breathed out, and felt all my school worries fading.

Daisy took out *Gaudy Night* from her bag, pressing it down so that the left-hand page touched my knee, and the right page hers. We were supposed to be reading it together—although really what happened was that Daisy turned the first twenty pages so quickly I could barely catch half the words, and then stopped and stared out of the train window at the bare, frosty hills we were galloping past. Of course, Daisy had taken the window seat.

I could tell that *Gaudy Night* was not turning out to be at all what she expected from a mystery novel, but I turned a few more pages myself, folding them under her hand as tidily as I could. Then I nudged her. She was very still, and I wondered if she was thinking about the book.

"I'm sure it'll improve!" I said.

Daisy turned to me, wide-eyed. "Oh, I wasn't thinking about *that*!" she said. "I was considering Cambridge. Imagine, Hazel. A whole city to ourselves, with no bothersome adults to tell us what we can and can't do!"

I smiled at her. A whole city to ourselves—a city (although I would never say this to Daisy) that had Alexander Arcady in it.

Daisy and I had met Alexander on the Orient Express over the summer. Since then, Alexander and I had begun to write letters to each other, and by now knew each other very well. I had not yet met his best friend, George, and nor had Daisy, but we both knew that he was the other half of the Junior Pinkertons. The boys had not been on the scene of our Bonfire Mystery—they had been at school themselves, miles away—but they had still written to us with suggestions and ideas for the case, and had been very useful indeed.

Alexander was already in Cambridge, spending Christmas with George and George's older brother, Harold, who went to St. John's College. They had both been sent by their fathers to see the place where they would go to university, and at the end of last term Alexander had suggested that we come as well.

The invitation came at the perfect time. I had been worried about where Daisy and I would go for Christmas this year. I cannot go back to my home during the holidays, for my family lives in Hong Kong, and it would take three weeks and several boats to get there. Last year I went to Daisy's house, Fallingford, for Christmas—but after what happened there at Easter, my father is not very willing to let me stay there again; and besides, Daisy goes very still and cold at the thought of visiting. Fallingford has changed, and it is hard for her to see it.

There was never any question about whether Daisy could spend Christmas in Cambridge. Her older brother, Bertie, is a student at Maudlin College. Daisy couldn't stay at Maudlin herself, of course—it is a men's college, and female guests are simply not allowed, not even little sisters. Luckily, she *could* stay with her old great-aunt Eustacia, a mathematics don at one of the women's colleges, St. Lucy's. (Cambridge is split up into lots of different colleges, you see, where students live and study. A don is just a university word for a teacher who looks after those college students, and apparently Daisy's great-aunt is a very important one.)

I was more of an issue. My father is not very happy about

the number of murders I have found myself part of recently. He thinks Daisy is mostly to blame, and so I worried about whether I would be allowed to stay with her in an unfamiliar city full of male students. But when I plucked up the courage to ask, he agreed at once. You see, my father studied at Cambridge, many years ago, and so all his memories of it are happy and scholarly, not dangerous at all.

He told me all about it down the telephone, and again in a very long letter, so I spent the weeks before we got on the train imagining what my life might be like if I passed my Deepdean leaving exams and was given a university place at Cambridge. I could not take a degree, for Cambridge does not let women have them (when I heard this I was rather indignant, but I suppose it is only one of the long list of things women are not allowed to do), but I could still study the same courses as the men. I saw myself walking across grassy quads in a black cap and gown, clutching learned books, bicycling past King's College Chapel, and taking tea with my clever university friends in a Cambridge tea shop. Here, at last, I could become truly English.

I thought at first that we would be chaperoned by Hetty, Daisy's maid from Fallingford, who had looked after us on the Orient Express, but Daisy managed that as well, in consultation with Bertie.

"What about my friend Amanda Price?" Bertie asked us on the telephone. "She goes to St. Lucy's, Aunt E's college, you know, and she'll be staying over the holidays. If we tell Aunt E that she's going to look after you, she'll let you go wherever you like."

"But *will* she look after us?" I asked.

"Do you *want* her to?" Bertie asked wryly down the phone.

I did not understand what he meant until Daisy, next to me, nudged me and beamed. "Oh!" I said. "So we'll be on our own?"

"You are clever, Bertie," said Daisy happily. "No one running about after us! We shall be able to have much more fun!"

I thought of Hetty, and felt a pang—but all the same I realized that I did love the idea of being free of grown-ups for once. Even on the Orient Express it had felt rather like we were still at school. But now we could really *be* almost fifteen. There would be no one trying to send us back to the nursery. It really is silly when adults try to protect children, as though we are not on our way to becoming adults ourselves. We need to understand the world, and they only have themselves to blame if we must creep about and lie to them to make sure we do it.

I stared out of the train window round Daisy's shoulder, and as the slender spires of the Cambridge towers came into view for the first time, elegant and fairy-like against the pale sky, I could almost feel myself getting older.

We stepped off the train at Cambridge, the train guard handing us out of our first-class carriage and arranging porters to take our trunks to St. Lucy's. It felt like the beginning of something important. I stared at Daisy as she stood gracefully in her fur-collared coat next to her pile of gold-monogrammed luggage, and realized after a moment that she was practicing her grown-up pose.

The station itself was hectically busy. As we began to make our way to the exit, people went shoving past us, their arms full of wrapped parcels and large books. I was pleased to see that everyone at Cambridge really did look as though they were clever.

Then Bertie came pushing through the crowd. His blond hair was longer than it had been last time I saw him, and he was wearing a new bow tie, but he still looked so much like Daisy that I immediately felt at ease. When he caught sight of her he waved his arms and beamed with the same expression she has when she sees something she is particularly pleased with. For a moment Daisy forgot the composure she had been trying on the platform. She jumped forward and flung her arms about Bertie's neck with a shriek. Then she stepped away, tucking her hair back in place under its hat.

"Hullo, Squinty. You've still got those awful green trousers, I see," she said lovingly.

"Hullo to you too, Squashy, Hazel," said Bertie, winking at her and bowing formally in my direction (I blushed, because it felt so awfully grown-up). "All right, both of you, come on!" He led us out of the station entrance, and we stood in the thin winter sunlight, shivering. "Amanda's late—I told her to meet me here ten minutes ago, but she hasn't shown up," Bertie told us. "She's been dreadfully forgetful lately, so I only hope she remembers!"

"How is Cambridge?" I asked, trying to say something polite. Daisy was staring about at all the cyclists flashing by, eyes widening to take everything in. There were lots of bicycles, which unnerved me—their bells were as loud as shouts, and they seemed quite precarious. I suddenly wondered if my vision of bicycling through Cambridge might have been rather wishful thinking. After all, I can barely balance on my two feet sometimes. Wobbling about on two thin wheels seems dreadfully advanced.

"Oh, it's excellent fun!" said Bertie. "Spiffing

food—meringues and fizz almost every afternoon in someone's rooms—and last week someone let a sheep into the quad."

"Oh," I said. The bunbreak sounded like my idea of Cambridge, but the sheep less so. "But how are your history lectures?"

"Oh, who cares about those?" asked Bertie, shrugging his shoulders. "I haven't been to one since the first week."

Daisy stopped looking at the bicycles. "Why aren't you going to lectures?" she asked sharply.

"Why should I? Amanda goes for us," said Bertie. "And anyway, no one cares about your first year."

"That isn't true," said Daisy, rolling her eyes.

"You don't know that, Squashy!" said Bertie quickly. "Look, it's perfectly ordinary. All the other fellows do it. Chummy does, and he's a good sort. You don't need to worry. I'm older than you, and I know what I'm doing."

"Hmm," said Daisy, still looking skeptical. "Who is Chummy?"

"My friend!" said Bertie. "Listen, I'll study when I need to. I don't see why I can't have a good time now, after . . . what happened earlier this year."

There are gaps in Bertie's sentences whenever he is thinking about Fallingford. He was hit terribly hard by the murder that took place in his own home, and by The Trial that followed.

I squeezed Daisy's arm. I could tell she was not happy, but I did not want her and Bertie arguing. I wanted this Christmas to be a merry one. "Oh, all right, then," said Daisy, breathing out and relaxing against me. "You can do what you like. Go on, tell me more about Chummy. Who would want to be friends with *you*?"

"You've heard of him!" said Bertie. "He's one half of the Melling twins, Charles and Donald. Their parents died in a car crash when they were young, remember?"

"Oh!" said Daisy. "The *Shropshire* Mellings."

I understood, after almost two years as Daisy's friend, that she was using English shorthand. What she meant was that the Mellings owned an estate, and were incredibly well off, and were absolutely English in every way. It never stops amazing me, the way the English all know who one another are, without ever needing to look it up.

"Donald's the older twin, isn't he?" Daisy went on. "Golly. I've always wondered—is Chummy cross about that? Only five minutes too late to inherit all that money."

"You're a ghoul," said Bertie, rather affectionately. "But—well, I suppose he is. It's a pity, really. Chummy seems as though he ought to be the elder. He's better-looking, and he *behaves* like an heir, you know. He's the one who speaks up and makes all the decisions. Donald's the follower. He just tags along with us."

"Chummy sounds just like me," said Daisy, smirking.

"Looks *and* brains and nothing for his brother. Poor old Donald—and Squinty."

"I'm ignoring that," said Bertie. "Anyway. Their birthday's on Christmas Day, and they're having a party for it in the Hall—supposed to be for both of them, but Chummy's invited almost all the guests. You'll be there, of course—I've had a word with Chummy about it. There are jazz bands coming, and Chummy's ordered a fountain of fizz. I think Donald's cross about Chummy taking charge of things, though he's trying to hide it. He's paying for all Chummy's friends. But really—who'd be friends with Donald, when Chummy's about? Donald does try, but he's like . . . a bad copy. He's not half so amusing. And he's unlucky too! He's always getting himself into the strangest accidents."

IV

"What do you mean, *accidents*?" asked Daisy, narrowing her eyes.

"Oh, there's Amanda at last!" cried Bertie, waving. "Hey, Amanda!"

I had been expecting someone as dandyish as Bertie himself, with his green trousers and slicked-back hair. But the girl swinging down from a rusty green bicycle and hurrying toward us was not well-turned-out at all. She was stocky, with pink cheeks and flyaway, frizzy brown hair that was escaping from a faded blue beret. Someone less like Bertie was hard to imagine.

"Bertie!" she panted, her face red and shining. "Sorry I'm late. I was at St. Lucy's working on an essay and I forgot the time, and then the Horse needed oil."

I looked about for a horse, but could see nothing of the kind.

"She means that bicycle of hers," said Bertie, grinning

at me. "Manda, meet my little sister, Daisy, and her friend Hazel. They're both far too clever for their own good."

"What rot!" said Daisy primly. She hates to let on how clever she is to anyone until she is quite sure they can be trusted.

"Hullo," said Amanda. She had her breath back now, and was assessing us both.

"Daisy, Hazel, this is Amanda," Bertie went on. "She's a brilliant historian. We'd all be lost without her."

He gave her a truly Daisy-ish smile, and I saw Amanda melt, exactly the way the shrimps do over Daisy. I understood why she was glad to give Bertie her lecture notes.

"Now," said Amanda, "have you told them how this is going to go?"

"Beginning to," said Bertie. "You can carry on for me, if you'd like."

Amanda turned to us, and I saw that underneath her soft, frizzy hair her eyes were sharp and determined, though tired. "All right," she said. "Listen up. Miss Mountfitchet's asked me to look after you while you're in Cambridge. She wants me with you all the time, but I've got far too much to do. So we're going to make a pact. I'll walk you in and out of St. Lucy's, and after that you're free to go wherever you like, so long as you tell anyone who asks that I was with you. All right?"

"All right," Daisy said quickly. I had known that this was

to be the agreement, but now I had seen Amanda I was curious about it.

"What are *you* doing while we're out?" I asked.

"Essays," said Amanda. "I've got a pile of them to finish before the end of the holidays."

"Manda's a workhorse," said Bertie, grinning. It should have sounded supportive, but there was something about the way he said it that made me feel uneasy.

"Bertie's going to give you the tour now, while I get some studying in," said Amanda. She brushed the hair away from her face—it seemed to hover about her cheeks and forehead like a cloud, coming back no matter how she pinned it or tucked it up under her beret. "Show you Cambridge, and Maudlin. If anyone asks, I was with you. I'll meet you outside St. Lucy's in an hour—we're all to take tea with Miss Mountfitchet before you have dinner at Maudlin."

"'*You?*'" Daisy echoed. "So you aren't coming with us to Maudlin?"

"No," said Amanda shortly.

"Why—" Daisy began, but Bertie elbowed her.

"Leave it," he said. "See you at four o'clock, Manda, just before the bridge to Lucy's."

"See you," said Amanda. She nodded at Bertie, and us, and then she swung herself back up onto the Horse and pedaled away. She went very fast, swerving in and out of the other cyclists, and I watched her go, feeling more curious than ever.

"What's up with her?" asked Daisy.

"It's not important," said Bertie. "She's staying away from Maudlin over the holidays, that's all you need to know."

Daisy turned and made a face at me. I knew what she meant. There was something odd going on here—something that I wanted to get to the bottom of as much as Daisy did.

"Come on, both of you," said Bertie. "I'll give you a proper tour of the place before tea and dinner."

"Will Chummy and Donald be at dinner?" asked Daisy. "Are they at Maudlin over the holidays?"

Bertie nodded. "They are," he said. "I told you, it's their birthday on Christmas Day. They turn twenty-one—they're older than the rest of us, you know—and Donald finally gets his inheritance. They'll be at dinner, and so will Alexander and George—they're coming with George's brother, my friend Harold, from St. John's College. By the way, Squashy, I knew Harold had a younger brother named George, but I didn't realize that he was *your* George!"

"George isn't mine! I've never met him," said Daisy. "Nor has Hazel. She's friends with Alexander, though."

"The American one?" asked Bertie.

"The *bothersome* one," said Daisy.

I flinched. It is true that Alexander was the cause of

a great deal of bother between us last term—almost our worst-ever row—but I was hoping that would all be over. Then I felt a burst of electricity through my body at the thought of seeing Alexander so soon. Today! I was not quite sure I was ready.

We walked up a long road away from the station. It was lined with white, wide-windowed houses, all set about with beautiful, bare trees. Bertie pointed out sights as we went.

"Look, over there—that's Parker's Piece! It's where they play cricket in the summer. It's awfully pretty."

I looked, and looked again, and could not help wanting to exclaim in delight. The whole of Cambridge was appearing before us, all stone and grass and statues. Everything was old, and everything was so beautiful I felt overwhelmed. We kept passing arches that seemed like doorways into another secret world—I caught glimpses of lovely lawns with fountains and pathways where men in black caps and gowns were walking.

It seemed that everywhere we passed had a story that Bertie wanted to tell us—an old oak doorway was where a second-year had hidden from a policeman; a high wall was the place Harold had lost his cap, and then had to crawl over to get it while the others stood watch; and a winding cobbled street with tree branches leaning close over it was a shortcut to a most *excellent* pub. We had to wait almost ten minutes, until we were standing below a soaring stone building fenced around with railings, to come back to the topic of accidents with an unexpected jolt.

"Blast!" said Bertie, peering upward. "They ought to be more careful! Someone's dropped a shoe on Senate House."

I thought he must be confused, but I was wrong. There, on a ledge twenty feet above us, was something that looked exactly like a tennis shoe.

"How did it get up there?" I asked.

Bertie looked awkward. "Squashy, Hazel, do you promise not to tell anyone what I'm about to say?"

"Of course," Daisy said, rolling her eyes. "We'll keep mum!"

"You're sure? This is important," said Bertie. "And if you blab after you've promised, I'll have you sent back to school."

It was a rather horrid threat, and Daisy went pink and white. Her nose wrinkled. "All—all right," she said. "I'm not a snitch. Neither of us are."

"I won't tell," I agreed. "Cross my heart."

"All right," said Bertie, lowering his voice. "Now. Some of us . . . climb."

“I know you do!” said Daisy. “You’ve told me about that.”

“Shush! I told you it was a *secret*!” hissed Bertie, lowering his voice even further. “All right. I’m a Night Climber. It’s a group—a deadly secret group—of students who go out at night and climb up buildings.”

I looked around at the spires and gargoyles and tall stone towers of Cambridge in amazement. They were so high above us—I could not imagine how anyone could manage to reach such high places without being killed.

“It’s all very hush hush,” Bertie went on. “If you’re ever caught, you’ll be sent down—that’s like being expelled, Hazel. All you’re ever allowed to know is who’s in your own section of the club—that’s so, if you’re caught, you can’t drop too many other men in it. There are five of us in our chapter—Chummy, Donald, another chap named Alfred, and I, all from our staircase at Maudlin, and Harold from John’s. We’re all history students, that’s how we met. We gather on the Maudlin roof, after midnight, and plan out our routes. It’s terribly exciting—even more so than mountaineering. All you can use are your hands and feet, and sometimes wire and rope if you really need to. Which reminds me, that’s how Donald’s latest accident happened—his worst yet, come to think of it.”

“Yes?” asked Daisy. “Go on!”

“Well, we all climb, but somehow it’s always Donald who gets into scrapes. It’s his rope that breaks, or the bit of wall he's leaning on that crumbles. It's become a joke among us all. Last week we were all going up Senate House, here—it's quite a difficult route, but it's well known. Everyone's done it heaps of times. There's one bit where you go up a drainpipe, and then you have to reach out and grab onto an overhanging bit of stone. Chummy was ahead, and Donald was below him—and then, just like that, an entire section of stone sheared away and came down on Donald.

"Luckily, he had his arms up, and they took the brunt of it, but it knocked him several feet to the next ledge. We all rushed over to him—his coat was ripped, and he was scratched all down his arms. His head got quite a knock too—he bled all over his shirt, and had to pretend he'd sent his bicycle into a wall when he handed it over to Moss to wash. Moss is our bedder, by the way—it means a sort of manservant. He looks after us all on staircase nine, keeps our rooms tidy and so on. You'll meet him later. But as I said, that's the worst accident Donald's had so far."

"And is Chummy always there for these accidents?" asked Daisy. I saw at once what she was getting at. Donald was the heir to an enormous fortune, while his brother Chummy would inherit nothing. Should anything happen to Donald, Chummy would inherit the Melling estate in his place. It seemed very interesting that Donald kept finding himself in danger, just before his twenty-first birthday.

"What?" said Bertie, frowning. "Oh . . . I suppose so. But you haven't understood. *That's* not Chummy's fault. The pranks he plays on Donald are quite different."

Daisy and I exchanged an incredulous glance.

"He plays pranks?" repeated Daisy.

"Oh yes," said Bertie. "Didn't I say that Chummy loves to joke? He's a great sport—always teasing us, especially Donald. I expect that sheep let loose in the quad was him, although he hasn't owned up to it. He switches our caps around so none of them fit our heads, and pins rude notices onto the dons' backs, too. But it's Donald who bears the brunt of it. Chummy will climb up to the Maudlin roofs and leave Donald's things there, or sew the sleeves of his jackets together, or put frogs in his bed. Why, only a few days ago he put a bucket of ice water on top of Donald's door. In the end, it was the whole bucket that fell on Donald's head, not just the water spilling out, and Moss had to bandage him up again! Chummy denied it, but of course we all knew it was him. Donald's expression was dreadfully funny!"

I felt a creeping sensation on the back of my neck. Some of this sounded rather more serious than simple pranks.

"Look at the two of you, Squashy!" said Bertie suddenly, laughing. "Come on, it's Christmas! It's all nuts and oranges and marzipan and presents this week. Don't go searching for trouble where there isn't any!"

"I never do!" said Daisy. "It isn't my fault if trouble simply finds me. And why doesn't anyone ever blame Hazel? She's been in just as many scrapes as I have."

"Not on purpose!" I said. It is true that trouble does follow us about, but not because we invite it—at least, I don't think we do. Had trouble found us again, here in Cambridge?

"Cheer up," said Bertie. "Look behind you—look at that view!"

We both turned—and there on our right was the great golden bulk of King's College Chapel. It rose up out of the grass, fringed with towers, its stonework looking delicate as lace. It felt somehow ridiculous that I should be so close to it after seeing it in pictures so often—as though I had suddenly come upon a dragon, or the Pyramids. I was amazed.

"It's quite something, isn't it?" asked Bertie. "You should see it at night, from the top of Senate House! You can see all the way across Cambridge—see King's Chapel up close. From high up it's magnificent. The clouds behind it, you know, and the spires."

He sounded so peaceful, as though just talking about climbing had soothed him. I thought I understood why. Being so high must give you a new way of looking at things. Bertie was looking at the chapel now and remembering his own secret view of it, a secret that he could keep long after the danger of the climb was over.

Cambridge really was beautiful, impossibly so. It almost

felt too large to take in. I tried to pull away from that dizzying vision of King's Chapel by moonlight and concentrate on things at eye level—the bicycles whizzing past us, the little warmly-lit beam-fronted shops selling sweets and cakes and students' gowns, and the group of carol singers striking up "We Three Kings."

Bertie stepped forward to drop coins into the carolers' upturned top hat, and while he was distracted, Daisy seized my arm. "Something's up!" she hissed. "Don't you think, Hazel? Something between Chummy and Donald!"

"You think—the accidents?" I asked.

Daisy nodded. "I've got a dreadful feeling that one day soon, something really awful may happen to Donald," she said ominously.

Once we were past the chapel, the road narrowed, high walls coming to hem us in on both sides. The buildings were all brick and stone, beautiful and old.

I was so busy looking at them that I was not paying attention to where I was going. My foot turned on a loose cobblestone and I stumbled out into the road. "Hey!" someone shouted. Daisy barely pulled me back onto the pavement in time before a man on a bicycle flashed past my right shoulder, just where I had been standing. He was hunched over his handlebars, with brown hair under his cap and a gown flapping behind him, and as I stood there gasping, he looked back at me, scowling. He had a rather round face and a snub nose—features that ought to have been nice, but somehow his expression made them unpleasant.

"Look sharp, Wells!" he shouted, stopping his bicycle and resting a foot on the ground. I realized that he was talking to Bertie. "Make sure your guests behave, or I shall have you written up! I nearly ran into her!" Then he kicked off again, pedaling away furiously down a lane to our right.

"What a horrid man! Do you know him?" Daisy asked Bertie after he had gone.

"That's Michael Butler," said Bertie. "He's a history don, quite a young one. He can't afford proper accommodation, so he lives at the bottom of our staircase and orders us about for extra pay. He can be all right, until he remembers he's supposed to be in charge of us. Then he comes over tiresomely dull, and tells us off for the smallest thing. He's part of the reason why we're all climbers—the drainpipe's simply the only way to get out after dark, with Butler guarding the downstairs exit. He locks the door to our staircase at eleven every night, and woe betide you if you're late!

"Now, up ahead's the museum," Bertie told us, pointing. "Looks a bit like a Greek temple. I've never been inside—though I did get up on top of it once. And there on the left—that's Fitzbillies. Absolutely the best Chelsea buns in Cambridge. You must go in another time."

I gazed in through the glowing plate-glass window of the little brick building as we went by. It was full of the most delicious displays, piled high with pink and white fancies, cakes piped with cream and scattered with nuts, and absolute heaps of swirled golden-brown buns. They were studded with raisins and dripping with syrup. My mouth watered. It had been hours since those train sandwiches, their cheese slightly warm and their chutney gluey. Beyond the buns I saw tables full of people enjoying splendid teas. My stomach gurgled.

But we turned away, along the narrow cobbled street Michael Butler had gone down, and perhaps it was just the high walls surrounding us, but the day suddenly seemed to darken, the shadows coming down around us. The air was chilly, and our breath steamed white.

"Now, we're passing Maudlin, but I'll take you back later. We must get to St. Lucy's. Keep along this road."

I looked up to the left as we passed high brick walls and a heavy wooden door set into the bottom of a narrow tower. Then we were suddenly out of the cobbled streets, into the open air. In front of us was an arched stone bridge, and below it ran a sleek, dark river. This was the famous Backs, I remembered from my father's stories. This was where the punts floated in summer, where the students lounged and ate picnics and studied for their exams. I marvelled, to see it. It was all so picturesque and English. Along it on our side rose the stone of the colleges, picked out in lit windows and decorated with curlicues and pillars. I felt that those lights were welcoming me in.

"Amanda should be along soon," said Bertie. "She's been working in town. Ah, there she is! On time for once. Hullo, Manda!" And there was Amanda, slipping out of the shadows behind us with the Horse beside her. She nodded to all three of us, and fell into step beside us as though she had been with us all the time. "And now we go over the bridge there."

I looked across the river to the other side—and saw a very different picture. The buildings there were raw, new brick, built very square and unromantic. Was this Cambridge University too? It could not be—surely this was where the people from the town lived, not the students! But Bertie was unmistakably pointing at the worst of them, a lumbering low building with several square red offshoots. "There's St. Lucy's. Manda's college, and Aunt E's. She'll be waiting for us—ah, there she is!"

The main door of the building was visible, and in front of it was a figure. It was a wisp of a person with a shock of white hair. The black gown it was wrapped in made it look like a bird, or a bat, and it turned its head in a birdlike jerk.

"Aunt E!" cried Bertie. "I've got them!"

"Hurry up, you silly boy!" shouted the old lady. As we came closer I saw that she had the same high, fine features and small nose as Daisy and Bertie, only sharper with age. "You must all be chilled. Daisy, my dear! And you're Hazel. Welcome to St. Lucy's College! I hope you're delighted to be here. Your trunks arrived some time ago—they have been taken up to your rooms. Come in, come in. Would you like some tea?"

One of the rules of the Detective Society is that we never say no to tea.

We were led into a room that was paneled in pale wood, with a bare white ceiling and a wood floor with a threadbare rug on it. Everything looked tattered and rather second-hand. This was not at all the grandeur I had been expecting from my father's stories.

"This is the senior common room," said Aunt Eustacia, as a maid in a much-mended apron brought in a pot of tea and a plate of scones. "It's a bit nippy, I know. I would take you into my study, which is always much more pleasant, but it is currently being cleaned. Radiators are on from eight to nine in the morning, and six to seven at night, so we have a few hours before our next burst of warmth. I'm told it's good for us. Good for the budget, more like. You'll learn soon enough that although half the brains at Cambridge belong to the women, the women's colleges have none of the money. Drink your tea, though, and you'll feel warm in no time."

She sat down in a worn green armchair and the rest of us perched on cane chairs around her. Amanda, who had a pen and notebook poking out of the sleeve of her gown and ink stains on her hands, took the seat next to Bertie, ignoring Daisy and me. I sipped on my tea, wrapping my fingers round my cup gratefully, and then picked up a scone. There was only jam to go on top, not cream—but it was warm, and as I cut it open it smelled lovely.

"There aren't many students staying with us over Christmas, so you've almost got the run of the place," said Aunt Eustacia. "I have put you in one of our first years' rooms. Trilling—I think you know her?—suggested especially that you stay in her rooms while she's at home for the holidays. She thought you might be pleased. Are you pleased?"

I had a moment of confusion—and then I realized. Henrietta Trilling was King Henry's real name, our Head Girl from the year before this. King Henry! She had been part of our first real case, the case of the murder of Miss Bell, our science teacher.

"Why yes, Aunt E!" said Daisy. "Of course!" We beamed at each other.

"Don't call me that silly name," said Aunt Eustacia. "I suppose you've picked it up from Bertie. Bertie, you are a most dreadful influence. Now, my nephew Felix tells me that you had some more difficulties at that school of yours last term. Quite shocking. Tell me everything."

In five minutes Aunt Eustacia had prodded out all the details of the Bonfire Night murder from Daisy (though not, of course, our own involvement). She looked quite fascinated, and I saw very clearly that if Daisy's Uncle Felix somehow turned into an old woman, this is what he would be like. Amanda was also listening in curiously, blinking and brushing clumps of hair from in front of her eyes. She looked tired, even more than I had noticed earlier.

"Now, Price!" said Aunt Eustacia to Amanda when we were finished. "I hope you'll look after the girls properly." She gave all of us a gimlet gaze. "And that you will all behave yourselves properly and be a credit to the family." I nodded, feeling myself blush.

"Yes, Aunt Eustacia," said Daisy.

"I hope you mean to obey me, Daisy," said Aunt Eustacia. "I can see you crossing your fingers. Now, you may dress and go to Maudlin for dinner. Price, look after them. I expect them back with no major injuries or defects. Goodbye."

We were dismissed.

"All right then," Bertie said to us. "I'm off to dress and meet the boys."

"I don't care about the boys," said Daisy, sighing.

"Of course you don't," said Bertie. "And Hazel's face is always that color."

I put my hands up to my cheeks in embarrassment.

"Anyway, hurry up and get changed—Manda, you'll bring them to Maudlin?"

Amanda nodded shortly. "Now come to your rooms," she said to me and Daisy. "Hurry up!"

We rushed after her, and I wondered again what on earth was up with her. Whatever it was, I had a funny feeling that the key to it lay in Maudlin.

King Henry's rooms were on the same chilly concrete-and-wood staircase as Amanda's, one landing below hers. They were small, and almost as faded as the senior common room—but there was a homely feel to them, as though we were back at Deepdean. King Henry's Deepdean cups and trophies were on a shelf in the sitting room, and her hockey colors were pinned to the edge of the small mirror, which was wound about with holly and ivy. In the bedroom a truckle bed had been set up next to King Henry's single bed (I was in the truckle, and Daisy had the real bed).

There was a note on the bed's coverlet. To Daisy Wells and Hazel Wong, it said. Daisy pounced on it, and I leaned around her shoulder to read what it said.

DEAR DAISY AND HAZEL,

WELCOME TO CAMBRIDGE AND ST. LUCY'S! I HOPE YOU'LL BE

SNUG HERE OVER CHRISTMAS—IT REALLY DOES REMIND ME OF DEAR DEEPDEAN! IT IS A JOLLY GOOD SCHOOL, YOU KNOW, AND I DO MISS IT, EVEN AFTER ALL THE THINGS THAT HAPPENED THERE.

I'M SO SORRY I COULDN'T BE THERE TO GREET YOU MYSELF, BUT I COULDN'T MISS CHRISTMAS WITH MUMMY AND DADDY. I DO WANT TO TELL YOU ONE THING, THOUGH. THOSE BOYS YOUR BROTHER LIVES WITH AT MAUDLIN, CHUMMY AND DONALD MELLING-BERTIE IS FRIENDS WITH CHUMMY, BUT REALLY THE TWINS HAVE RATHER AN UNPLEASANT REPUTATION. THEY SPEND FAR TOO MUCH TIME ENJOYING THEMSELVES. I DON'T BELIEVE THEY'VE BEEN TO A LECTURE SINCE THE FIRST WEEK. THEY'RE TURNING TWENTY-ONE OVER THE HOLIDAYS, ON CHRISTMAS DAY, AND THERE'S A REALLY SILLY PARTY PLANNED. I WAS INVITED, BUT I DIDN'T WANT TO GO. I'VE HEARD THAT DONALD'S GOT PLANS TO IGNORE CHUMMY—FOR THE FIRST TIME IN HIS LIFE—AND BLOW ALL THE MONEY ON A DIAMOND MINE, OF ALL THINGS. CHUMMY'S GOT WIND OF IT, AND HE'S FURIOUS—A FEW WEEKS AGO HE GOT IN RATHER AN EMOTIONAL STATE IN THE MAUDLIN BUTTERY AND TOLD A CHAP I KNOW THAT HE WASN'T GOING TO STAND FOR IT—THAT HE WAS GOING TO MAKE DONALD GIVE HIM THE MONEY.

YOU OUGHT TO BE CAREFUL—WATCH THEM, WON'T YOU? I DON'T WANT YOU MIXED UP IN ALL THIS AS WELL.

THERE'S BISCUITS AND COCOA IN THE TIN UNDER THE BED.

WISHING YOU A VERY MERRY CHRISTMAS,

KING HENRY

Daisy dropped the letter as though it was a hot coal.

"Hazel!" she said. "*Hazel!*"

All the thoughts I had been having about Donald and Chummy—I could tell Daisy had been having them as well—had suddenly been given backing, and from a source we both trusted.

"What shall we do?" I asked. "Get changed for dinner?"

"Get changed!" said Daisy. "I can't think about *that* when there's a mystery to solve!"

"But if we don't go to dinner we won't see Chummy and Donald," I pointed out, getting her pink taffeta gown out of the wardrobe where it had been hung and handing it to her.

Daisy sighed, but she put it on—and then she entirely lost interest in clothes, and sat down with a thump on her bed, eyes gazing off into the distance as she thought. I put on my green velvet dress, and peered at myself in the mirror unhappily. Next to Daisy, I felt rather a disappointment.

"Hazel!" said Daisy from the bed. "Oh, Hazel, it's another mystery!"

"Chummy and Donald!" I agreed, glad to turn away from myself.

"Exactly!" said Daisy. "Heirs having accidents and being the victims of so-called pranks is *highly* suspicious, even if my silly brother can't see it, and King Henry's letter proves that. Chummy is determined to inherit the money instead of Donald, and their birthday is only a few days away. Hazel, I think something is imminent!"

"I know!" I said. "And what about Amanda? Why doesn't she want to go to Maudlin? What essays is she writing—in the holidays—that Bertie doesn't have to?"

"Bertie," said Daisy with a sudden frown, "is not studying as hard as he ought. I know he does not have my natural intellect, but he isn't utterly stupid. He can't be allowed to throw away Cambridge. I shall have to talk to him properly. But yes, Amanda's actions—they are odd, and suspicious. Do they have anything to do with Chummy and Donald? Tonight will be the perfect opportunity to meet them, and watch how they behave around each other. We shall have to conceal what we are doing from the Pinkertons, though."

"Why should we?" I asked. "Alexander helped us with the Orient Express case, and we wouldn't have solved the Bonfire Night murder so quickly without the Pinkertons either. If we've noticed something, they might have as well. They might want to help."

"Well, they can't help, and that's that!" said Daisy crossly. "Aren't you ready to go yet?"

I tied my sash (it came out slightly lopsided, but I knew it was no good asking Daisy to fix it in her present mood). There was a smudge on my shoe, and I rubbed at it, which made it worse. I could not wait to see Alexander, but at the same time I was not sure I could bear it.

There was a sharp knock on our door—it was Amanda, a drawn look on her face. I put on my coat and followed her and Daisy down the stairs, into the stinging cold of the evening.

The stars were little pinpricks in the black sky, and our breath hung in the air in front of us. We went out of the lodge, over the still waters of the Cam, and I saw the most delicate mist hanging over it—over everything, in fact, blurring the light from the streetlamps and the figures pedaling past on their bicycles, wobbling on the cobbled streets.

Amanda wrapped her coat tighter around her and pushed her hat down over her ears. "Bitter!" she said. "It'll snow soon."

I imagined Cambridge in the snow, a picture postcard, or one of the paintings in my father's house. It was a lovely thought—warm as well as white. My heart fluttered.

"Now," said Amanda. "As you know, I'm taking you to the doorway of Maudlin but no farther. I will meet you at the end of the evening to take you back to St. Lucy's again."

"Why—" Daisy started, but Amanda glared at her ferociously and she stopped.

"As I've said, I've got essays to do," she said. "All right—there, up ahead, that's Maudlin's porter's lodge tower."

I squinted in the gloom. At first I could only see the high brick walls I had before. Cambridge really was dim—it felt as though the shadows had real weight to them here, or perhaps it was only that the streets were all so narrow, and the walls so very high. But yes—there was the tower I had seen earlier, with a massive, heavy wooden doorway set into the bottom of it, like the opening of a castle, only without the moat and drawbridge.

There was a tiny person-sized door set into the larger, grander doorway, light coming through it brightly, and Amanda motioned us toward it. She stood back, and then she turned away, melting into the shadows like mist.

Daisy and I walked through the door together and found ourselves in an arched stone space, lamp-lit, with a bank of pigeonholes on one side and a sort of hatch on the other. A man with a bald head and a thick walrus moustache was leaning out of it, and I could see that he was sitting in a little side room, bright and cozy. "Goodness!" he said as he caught sight of Daisy. "I know who this is! Why, you're Wells's sister!"

Daisy stood up as tall as she could—which, these days, is

really very tall indeed. "I am the Honorable Daisy Wells," she told him.

The man gave a chuckle of delight. "Of course you are!" he cried. "I'd know you anywhere! You're the spit of your brother."

"How awful!" said Daisy, though I could tell she was pleased. "I'm *much* better than he is."

"I'm Mr. Perkins," said the man. "I'm the porter at Maudlin. Been here over thirty years, you know—longer than any of the dons, even the Master himself. The college would collapse without me! I'm here from six every morning until I lock the gate at eleven at night. If I'm not here, you don't get into Maudlin. Nothing gets past me!"

"Pleased to make your acquaintance," said Daisy. "You sound most important. And this is my friend Hazel Wong."

Mr. Perkins looked at me, and I braced myself for the usual stare, or gasp, or angry look—the way English people usually behave when they see me for the first time. But for once I was surprised. Mr. Perkins took in my brown hair and dark eyes and round face and nodded in greeting, just as though I was not remarkable at all.

"A pleasure to meet you, Miss Wong. Now, I've been told that you are expected on Mr. Wells's staircase, staircase nine, in Mr. Donald Melling's rooms. If you go out of here and turn left, it's the last staircase on the left, before the Library Quad. The men are all waiting for you there—the Mellings, Mr. Wells, and their guests. Miss

Wells, a certain Mr. Arcady asked for you especially when he arrived. I think you might have made an impression."

He winked, and I suddenly felt as though I had swallowed a frog. Why was Alexander mentioning Daisy instead of me? It was not Daisy who Alexander had been writing to all term. It was not Daisy who was Alexander's friend. I was reminded once again of how very pink and white and pretty Daisy was, and how unfair that can be. I rubbed at the spot on my cheek and wished like anything that I was not so short.

We went out of the lodge and found ourselves in a grassy space, squared in with tall stone buildings. It was quite simply beautiful. This, I thought, was much more what I had been expecting at Cambridge; the sort of grandeur and specialness that I had heard in my father's stories. I loved it at once.

Only a few windows around us were lit—the college was quiet for the holidays. We turned left and stepped along the stone path at the edge of the green lawn, past several dark archways. Staircase six, staircase seven, staircase eight—and there, at the very end, was the entrance to staircase nine.

This archway was open and lit with lamps, and looked most welcoming. We stepped through it and I peered upward at a thin stone staircase that spun up dizzily, with only a narrow metal banister running around the outside edge. There were two doors at our level, one on the left, marked BATHROOMS, and one on the right, tucked in under the beginning of the staircase, with a sign on it that read

MICHAEL BUTLER. This door was next to a large notice board covered in bits of paper advertising plays and lectures and entertainments.

EMPIRE NIGHT!

COME DRESSED AS YOUR FAVORITE SUBJUGATED NATION!

MAUDLIN WINTER BALL—

DINNER TICKETS NOW AVAILABLE

THE OLEANDER QUARTET PLAYS BEETHOVEN—

1 P.M., THE MORNING ROOM

OVER THE HILLS AND FAR AWAY—NEXT MEETING, THE USUAL TIME, THE USUAL PLACE

I could hear voices farther up the stairs, loud male ones. "Come on!" said Daisy eagerly, tugging at my sleeve. I was suddenly more nervous than ever. I had been seeing Alexander in my head every day, frozen the way he had looked as he leaned out of the carriage when the Orient Express had pulled into Istanbul, his shirt cuffs up above his wrists and his hair untidy, down over one eyebrow. Would he be the same? What if he should be different?

Up the stairs we climbed. Each set was twenty narrow, steep steps high, with a landing at the top with one room on the left side and another on the right. By the time we reached the third landing, where the sounds of a party were coming from, I was gasping. But there, at last, was an open doorway, and there, inside, was a room lit and festooned with Christmas decorations—boughs of holly and ivy, sprigs of mistletoe and bits of tinsel.

Among all that brightness were several groups of men, all dressed in black and white for dinner. They were laughing and joking together, and it took me a moment, as we hovered in the doorway, to sort out exactly who I was seeing.

The first person I recognized was Bertie. He looked very debonair in his dinner things. He had put on a turquoise neckerchief, and it made his hair look bright gold. For a moment he reminded me very much of Uncle Felix. Next to him was Alexander. My heart shocked. I could not help staring at him. He was taller again, hair surprisingly darker blond and shorter, but he was Alexander still.

Next to Alexander were two other people. I barely looked at them at first, but then I did, and I felt everything in me stop short in confusion.

I had hardly given a thought to George, Alexander's friend. I had been expecting a small, round, fair-haired English boy, and his older but no less round and English brother—but the boys in front of me were none of those things. They were both quite thin, with big brown eyes, thatches of black hair, and brown skin. They were not little and round, and they were not blond. They did not look English at all.

"Daisy!" cried Bertie, seeing us. "Hazel! Hello! Come in! You know Alexander, of course—and this is my friend Harold Mukherjee, and his brother George."

I gaped. You see, it has been months since I looked at a face that was not pink and white. Now here were two. It felt almost wicked, how excited I was by it. It gave me a sort of hungry ache, although not the sort that I get over food. I realized my mouth was open, and closed it—but I saw the awkward expression on George's face. It was the same as the way I look when people stare at me.

But then George smiled. "You thought I'd look like Alex," he said to me. "People always do. He forgets to mention the fact that our father's Indian."

"I'm sure I did!" protested Alexander, turning to him. "Didn't I?"

"No!" I said. "I—he didn't—" I wanted to explain that I

was quite the opposite of upset, but I could not find the words.

"Well," said Bertie. "I suppose I ought to do the formalities. Daisy, Hazel, may I introduce you to Harold Mukherjee and George Mukherjee, sons of Sir Mangaldas Mukherjee, the renowned doctor? Alexander Arcady I believe you already know."

"Very pleased to meet you," said Daisy smoothly, taking Harold's and then George's hands as though she was not surprised in the slightest—although I had seen her pause at the sight of them, and knew that she was as amazed as I was.

Harold shook our hands with a smile and turned back to talk to Bertie, but George was another matter. He took Daisy's hand and caught her eye, a direct stare that was not polite, but bold and deeply assessing.

"Hello," said George gravely. "You must be Daisy Wells."

They both dropped hands and stepped back at the same time. Daisy took a small breath, and I saw the wrinkle appear at the top of her nose.

I knew that something rather unusual had happened. You see, Daisy always takes the measure of everyone she meets. It only takes her a moment to understand almost everything about them—what sort of person they are, what they want, and how they might be expected to go about it. I am used to her doing it. I am less used to the other person doing it to her in return. But—I looked at George—that is what had happened. George was seeing *her*, not the pretty, rather foolish Daisy she likes to show to the world, but the secret, clever, noticing Daisy. It was astonishing.

I was afraid of how Daisy would react. She is not used to being laid bare like this. But after a moment the wrinkle on her nose smoothed out. Her eyebrow went up, and a small smile quirked on her lips. "Hullo, George Mukherjee," she said. "I think I shall very much enjoy getting to know you better."

Then it was my turn. I found myself looking up into George's eyes, his hand in mine. "Hello, Hazel Wong," he said to me. "Pleased to meet you at last. I think I shall like you as much as Alexander does."

I blushed.

Then Alexander turned to me. I had been in agonies trying not to look at him properly. I was waiting for a polite greeting, or nothing at all—but I suddenly found myself caught about the shoulders, pulled forward, and squashed against a chest studded with shirt buttons. A bow tie tickled my forehead and my nose was full of a boyish smell that was both nice and very strange. I felt my whole body blush with shock. Alexander had hugged me! "Hazel!" he cried in my ear. "Why, Hazel, hello!" Then he pushed me away from him, just as violently as he had pulled me into the hug, and beamed down at me joyfully. His face was lit up with happiness, and I realized I should not have been worried at all about whether he was glad to see me. "You haven't changed a bit—no, wait, I do believe you're taller!"

"You're taller too," I said, my ears roaring. "You— Hello."

Then Alexander turned away from me. "Hello, Daisy," he said. "You look very pretty."

My stomach ached. Alexander might be glad to see me—but it was Daisy he had called pretty, Daisy that he wanted to admire. I knew my green dress looked garish next to Daisy's pink taffeta, and my hair dull and dark next to the glow of her blonde curls. It is not fair that I must stand beside her always. If the whole world was drowning, she is the person I would reach out a hand to save, but that doesn't mean that I do not sometimes wish that she were not so very perfect.

"Alexander," said Daisy—and there was something in her voice that told me that she had not forgotten the letters between the two of us last term. "How lovely to see you. Have you been here long?"

"Almost a whole week," said Alexander, his natural cheerfulness bubbling out and sweeping all the awkwardness away. "Weston broke up ages ago. It's been terrifically jolly, though—we've got wizard rooms next to Harold's at St. John's, and everyone's being so nice."

"Alex is being optimistic about human nature, as usual," said George. "It's all because they think our father might give money to John's for a scholarship if *both* his sons go to university here. They have good reason to be nice to us."

"Yes, but they like you too!" cried Alexander, as Daisy gave a small appreciative snort, which she quickly covered with her hand.

"Course they do, Arcady," said Harold, turning and clapping him on the back.

I heard the tone of his voice, and knew that there were some things blond, kind Alexander could never properly understand. It felt like a joke that only George, Harold, and I could be part of.

Then, at the other end of the room, voices were raised. I had been so focused on George, Harold, and Alexander that I had barely thought about the other people at the party—but of course, we were in Donald's rooms. Beside the drinks table stood the man who had shouted at me on his bicycle earlier, Michael Butler—and next to *him* were two young men who I realized must be Donald and Chummy.

Both were short and brown-haired, with small noses and blue eyes and rather red cheeks. They were not identical twins—one had a thinner face and the other had much richer brown hair—and the expressions on their faces made them look even less similar. The thin-faced, mousy-haired one had a petty, sour look, and a tightly pursed mouth. Next to him, his rounder-cheeked, chestnut-haired brother shone. He stood with his chest thrown out, his orange bow tie like a flame, and a confident, rather naughty look on his face. I saw at once what Bertie had meant. If this was Chummy, then he looked like a person who ought to be an heir.

"Three days to go, Donald!" he was saying to his brother. "You don't have enough champagne, though. I've ordered more under your name. And the music—haven't I told you I won't have Leslie Thompson?"

"*I* like him," said Donald, folding his arms defensively. He had two just-healed scars on his forehead, I saw—it must be where the bucket and the stone had hit him. It really did look like he had been hurt badly.

"I don't care what you think. I won't have a foreigner playing his trumpet at our party. So I've hired Nat Gonella instead. Someone English!"

"You can't do that! It's *my* money!" cried Donald.

"Not yet it isn't. And anyway, if it wasn't for an accident of five minutes, you wouldn't be getting it at all."

"It wasn't an accident! I *was* born first!" said Donald. He sounded shrill and furious. "And on the twenty-fifth all that money will come to me, and there's nothing you can do about it. You'll see—things will change. I'm just as good as you are, and everyone will see it!"

"Are you!" said Chummy. "I don't think so. You can't do a thing without me, and you know it. And anyway—well, just you wait and see."

Daisy kicked me, hard, with the toe of her shoe.

"Oh," said George, staring at us both. "So you think there's something going on as well."

Daisy turned white, and the crinkle at the top of her nose came back with a vengeance. "Whatever do you mean?" she asked George.

"It's quite obvious, isn't it?" he replied quietly, glancing over at Bertie and Harold. "Something's up between Chummy and Donald. Hasn't Bertie told you about Donald's 'accidents'?"

"We've been watching them almost all week," said Alexander, looking at both of us eagerly. "I'm glad you've seen it too. We were beginning to think we might be cracked."

"We've seen it now," I said—and then caught Daisy's enraged glare.

"George and I have decided that we're going to have a shot at investigating it," said Alexander. "Would you like to join in?"

"No!" said Daisy sharply. "I mean—there's nothing to investigate."

"Wait. You're only saying that because *you* want to investigate!" said George.

"Of course we don't!" spluttered Daisy, caught off guard. "We would never do such a thing!"

"Alex told me about the way you behaved on the Orient Express at first—trying to shut him out. You can't do that again."

"Oh, see here!" said Alexander, tugging at his cuffs awkwardly. "Daisy's a good sort."

"Look, we helped you with your last case," said George, sticking out his chin. I saw that he was not only noticing, he was bold, sure of himself, and able to carry a point. "Now you have to help us. Fair's fair."

"You helped *Hazel*," said Daisy spikily. I shifted awkwardly from foot to foot and tried not to look at her. It is true that Alexander's letters helped me—and also that they drove a wedge between me and Daisy that I can sometimes still feel the splinters from. "Look here. If anyone is going to be doing any investigating, it ought to be us. We have solved *four* murder cases, and so that makes this *our* mystery!"

"*Your* mystery? We were here first!" said George, crossing his arms. He was not giving an inch of ground to Daisy. I was rather impressed with him. Daisy is not an easy person to say no to.

"We're better detectives!" cried Daisy. "Have *you* solved any murders?"

"We once—" Alexander began eagerly, but George cut him off.

"No, but that hardly matters, as this isn't a murder either. Don't talk so loud! They'll notice something's up. Look. There's a way around this—a very easy one. We can *all* detect."

"But—" said Daisy. I knew she was about to say, *But it is still our case*—but before she could, someone came into the room behind us. We all went quiet, and pretended to be enjoying our glasses of cordial.

"Having a party, are you?" said a voice. "Give me a glass, will you?"

I jumped. There was something about those words that was both utterly familiar and completely out of place. It was not so much what the person had said, but the *accent* they had said it in. It dropped me like a stone back into the past, to being small in Hong Kong, and at another party.

Then I turned, and my heart began pounding. I had not been wrong after all when I remembered Hong Kong, for the handsome, well-dressed young man standing in the doorway had black hair, pale skin, and eyes as dark as mine. In fact, to most British people I am sure that this man would look exactly like me—that is what English people always think when they see more than one Chinese person together. I suddenly understood the reason why Mr. Perkins had been so calm when he met me. At Maudlin I was not unique.

And this was not just any Chinese person. I *knew* him.

His name was Alfred Cheng, and he was the cousin of Victoria Cheng, the girl whose father had sent her to a very prestigious girls' school in Cairo, and convinced my own father—a business rival of Mr. Cheng—to send me to Deepdean two years ago. Most unexpectedly, a piece of my Hong Kong life had appeared in the middle of polite, English Cambridge.

I remembered the first time I had met him, years ago. I had been at a party, very small and shy, and Alfred had come up to me in his padded silk suit and said, "Give me your cake."

I had politely done so—I had been taught never to say no to boys, especially older ones—and then watched as Alfred had worked his way round the room, taking cake from every plate. That was the sort of boy he had been. I wondered if he was still used to getting the things he wanted.

"Hazel, Daisy, this is Alfred Cheng," said Bertie, coming up to us again. "Lives on this staircase as well. Here, Hazel, he's not related to you, by any chance? Cheng, do you know Hazel Wong?"

"I know her father," said Alfred, at the same time as I said, "I know his cousin."

"We aren't related," I added in a hurry. Really, I should not have needed to say it—Alfred is quite tall and well-built, and his face is much squarer than mine.

Chummy looked over and saw Albert—and then his eye fell on me. "What's this?" he asked in a loud voice. "Another Chinese? Isn't it a bit much? Why, we English will begin to feel outnumbered soon!"

I froze.

"Hazel is my sister's friend," said Bertie.

Chummy stared at Alfred, Harold, George, and me rather accusingly, as though it was unreasonable of us all to be alive, and so close to one another. I felt embarrassed, as though I had made a mistake without noticing it—like eating with the wrong fork, or wearing the wrong sort of hat.

Then I saw George's chin tip up again, and remembered that I had made no mistake at all. It really is not rude to exist, whatever anyone else says. I decided I did not like Chummy at all.

"Do be quiet, Chummy, you prize idiot," said Alfred

fiercely. I looked at his hands, and saw they were shaking—Chummy's words had got to him, just as they had me. "Your *brother* may be coming into money soon, but my father could still buy and sell you both."

Chummy looked furious. "How dare you!" he snapped. "You jumped-up—"

"Don't, Chummy," said Bertie quickly. "Don't be like that. Come on. We're having a party." I saw that he looked embarrassed, and wondered how he could stick up for Chummy when he spoke to other people like that. I felt sick.

"Oh, I suppose," said Chummy, still angry. "Port! How about some port? Donald, you've been saving a decanter, haven't you? Let's drink it."

"No, that's my best vintage!" cried Donald, but Chummy ignored him. He pushed him aside and picked up a crystal decanter, uncorking it with a flourish that made its stopper gleam in the lamplight. As Donald grumbled and looked helpless, Chummy began to pour dark-red, sweet-smelling drink into tiny little glasses. They reminded me of a doll's house tea set.

"None for the children," said Michael Butler sternly.

"Oh, let them!" said Harold. "Father always gives George a glass."

"Certainly *not*," said Michael—and I saw what Bertie had meant about him taking his role as a don seriously.

Everyone else was a student, loud and silly, but he was behaving like a proper grown-up.

Daisy, George, and Alexander sighed, and I made sure to sigh too—although my father would never allow me to drink, and would have been quite furious if he knew I had even been offered it.

Then Chummy, Donald, Alfred, Michael, Harold, and Bertie all raised their glasses.

"To Christmas!" said Bertie.

"To holidays!" said Harold.

"To birthdays," said Chummy, with a glare at Donald. They all drank, and Chummy made a face. "Sour," he said. "I believe it's corked, Don. I shan't be having any more."

"It's perfectly all right," said Donald—though I could see his mouth purse, and knew that he had not liked the taste either. The others all politely finished their drinks, but Donald drank his glass down, and poured himself more. It was as though he was trying to spite Chummy, to show him that he could ignore him if he chose—but he did not do it very well.

Donald was just drinking his second glass when a distant bell rang.

"Ah!" said Bertie, straightening his bow tie. "Dinnertime! Come on, I'm starved!"

He went on a headlong dash out of the room and down the stairs, and the rest of us followed. I was glad—I had been feeling so uncomfortable in that awkward party.

Somehow Alexander managed to get himself just behind Daisy. My stomach clenched. Then George was at my elbow, and I turned to him, glad of the distraction. "Hello again!" I said.

"Hello again to you, too," said George. "It really is nice to meet you at last. Alexander has told me a terrific lot about you. He thinks you're terribly nice."

Terribly nice, at that moment, did not feel good enough, so I said, "*Oh?*" wanly.

"Yes," said George. "Of course, Alexander thinks everyone's terribly nice. He says the same about Daisy, although she clearly isn't nice at all."

I laughed.

"I can tell she's far cleverer than she lets on," George went on. "I think she might be cleverer than me. Don't look like that—I don't mind. Not many people are, but she is."

He said it so casually, as though he was saying an obvious truth. I was more fascinated with him by the minute. Like Alexander, he said what he thought, but he was more forceful—more, I realized, like Daisy.

"She's my best friend," I said.

"Lucky her," said George with a smile. "Now—I've got an idea about detecting this case."

"Is it to do with us working together?" I asked uncertainly. "Daisy won't like it."

"If you say yes, she'll come round," said George. "But listen. Why don't we—"

Chummy suddenly came clattering down the stairs behind us, and I knew we could not talk further.

"No good here," said George. "Tomorrow. Meet to discuss in Fitzbillies at noon?"

I nodded, feeling very brave and grown-up. I had made a decision on behalf of the Detective Society, and I knew it was a good one. I suddenly saw that this holiday might be very interesting indeed.

Out we went into the blue dark. We walked back along the path, past the porter's lodge, and through an archway into another, larger quad. This one had not only a square of dark grass, but a large pond, black and still, with a little metal statue in the middle. It stood up like a paper cutout against a set of grand, lit windows.

"That's the Great Hall," said Bertie in my ear. I breathed out in amazement. Maudlin really was like a castle, I thought; a castle out of a romance. Here was even more of the magnificence of Cambridge my father had described. I imagined the food, the warmth, the gowns and silver plates, and I stepped forward gladly.

My foot slid on a patch of ice. I stumbled, gasping, and two pairs of hands steadied me. Daisy was on my left, and on my right was Alexander. "Careful," he said.

I was so pleased and embarrassed that I shook him away,

tucking my arm instead closer into Daisy's. As we walked into Maudlin's Great Hall, I was in a turmoil of emotions.

Even up close, the Great Hall was astonishing. I had never been anywhere so very large and oak and stone. It felt like England itself, all its privilege and history bearing down on us. If I had not realized before how much better off Maudlin was than St. Lucy's, I knew it now. The windows were tall stained glass in Maudlin reds and yellows, and there were glossy wooden tables shining with silverware, around which small groups of students were standing. The Hall was half full—many students must be staying for the party on the twenty-fifth, I realized. Up on a dais at the far end, under the largest stained-glass window, was one more table, laden with even more gorgeous silver and glass.

"That's where the dons sit," said Bertie to Daisy and me. "High Table. There's the Bursar, and there's the Master himself. He's dreadfully distant, though—if you're lucky he'll never even speak to you."

Michael Butler peeled off to sit with the other dons and the Master, and we were led to our places by men in red-and-gold livery. I almost sat down before I realized that no one else had—we must be waiting for a signal. I stood in the candlelight behind my appointed chair and looked around at our group. I was next to Alexander, I saw with pleasure, and across from Daisy and George. Bertie was next to Daisy, with Alfred on his other side. Harold was opposite him, and Chummy and Donald were facing each other next to me and George. I wondered whether Alfred and Chummy sat as far apart as possible on purpose.

A bell rang, and up on High Table the Master suddenly said something thunderous in Latin. Then there was a tremendous shuffle of chairs. I had to scramble to be seated, and I bumped into Alexander as I did so. I could not seem to stop being clumsy around him.

As drinks were served, Chummy and Donald began to talk about the party again. It was clear that they both had very different ideas about it—and very different ideas about what would happen to the money Donald was about to inherit.

"I've always wanted a racehorse," said Chummy. "And a yacht—or two. I think I shall buy one in the New Year."

"Well, I don't want a boat," said Donald angrily. "It's *my* money, so I choose what I do with it. I shan't be giving any to you. I don't know why you can't understand that. I'm buying a diamond mine, I told you."

"You are not!" said Chummy, and I heard the bullying tone of his voice.

"I am!" said Donald. "On Christmas Day!" He was trying to sound firm, but his chin quivered. I saw that it would not be easy for him to go against his brother.

A starter was put in front of me: dressed crab, dropped down by a hand that seemed oddly disembodied in the candlelight. I ate it, but all the same I did not really taste it. Daisy, George, Alexander, and I were all sitting forward, watching Chummy and Donald—and that was why, I think, we were the first to notice what was happening.

It struck Donald first. He began to blink and touch his forehead, as though he had a headache. He took a forkful of crab that did not quite reach his mouth—his hand swerved away, and he had to stare at his fork, as though moving it was difficult. Then he put his cutlery down on his plate.

"Dim in here, isn't it?" said Bertie.

"*Isn't* it?" agreed Harold, and I saw that he had gone pale. "And I've got a dreadful headache."

"Whatever's wrong with you all?" asked Chummy, staring around. He seemed the only one unaffected—even Alfred was clutching his head and looking ill. There was a groan from High Table, and when I turned to look, I saw that Michael Butler looked positively green.

"Goodness knows," gasped Bertie. "I do feel awfully dizzy and queer. Did we all eat something, up in Donald's rooms?"

Alexander nudged me, and I jumped. "Are you all right?" he whispered, and my world was suddenly narrowed to the three inches of air between our cheeks.

"Yes," I breathed back. "I feel perfectly well!"

"So do I!" said Alexander. "Do you think . . . someone did something?"

"I don't know!" I whispered. "But if so—they all drank

the port, didn't they? The special port that Donald was saving."

"All of them but Chummy!" whispered Alexander. "He only had one sip, didn't he! D'you think it's important?"

I did. I felt that we had the next clue to our mystery—and again, it pointed to Chummy.

I felt a kick under the table, and looked up to see Daisy widening her eyes at me in excitement. There was something she was aching to say—something to do with detection. But, of course, she had to stay silent. It would have to wait.

The men suffered through two more courses, eating hardly a bite of the roast beef or the pear crumble in a lake of custard that came after, until at long last a gong went and everyone rose from the tables. It seemed, luckily, that whatever had been in the port was not strong enough to make any of them seriously ill, although they were all weak and wretched.

"Walk you all out," said Bertie unsteadily, wiping his lips. He had barely touched his food—if we had been back at Deepdean, I would have asked him to pass along his crumble, but I was not sure whether the same rules applied in Cambridge. "Come on, then. Daisy, Hazel, Manda'll be waiting for you outside."

Chummy, coming past him as he said this, clapped him on the back. "Good work keeping her away," he said. "I'll get to the bottom of it!"

That gave me an uncomfortable feeling. What did

Chummy mean? It sounded as though he knew why Amanda would not come into Maudlin—what did he and Bertie have to do with it? Daisy glared at Bertie, but he would not meet her eyes. He hustled us out of the Hall door into the quad.

We came out into the cold, and Bertie took a few deep gulps of fresh air. He was still unwell—perhaps that was all there was to his silence. Behind him both Alfred and Donald staggered and could not walk in a straight line. Everyone shivered and huddled against the wind—and it was funny how all the students' and dons' black caps and gowns made them blend together like a flock of crows. There was darkness all around us, Daisy's pink taffeta and my green velvet the only bright things I could see.

My eyes had not yet adjusted to the night, and the lamps outside the buildings seemed to burn very small in the distance. I thought we were following closely behind Bertie, but somehow we lost him. I clutched at Daisy's hand—we were suddenly alone, with voices echoing around us. Someone knocked against me as we came out of the West Quad, and I stumbled, but when I looked around I could not see anyone.

Then I heard a splash and a cry behind us. It was quite a small, surprised one, and I almost thought I had imagined it. But I turned, and saw the surface of the pond shining and rippling.

"Daisy!" I said. "I think someone's fallen in the pond! Quick—help!"

People came running from all directions.

"Who is it?"

"Chummy!"

"No, it isn't, it's Donald! Hey, Donald!"

But there was no response. I remembered Donald's pale face at dinner, and how his hands had shaken as he took a sip of water. He was already ill and dizzy—too weakened to climb out of the pond himself.

Was this another "accident"?

"He can't get out!" cried Bertie. "He could drown!" He jumped into the pond with a splash. The water came right up to his chest, and he stumbled—it really was quite deep, and he was still not well himself. There was another splash of water, one that caught me like dashes of ice, as Michael Butler jumped in, looking pale but determined. Daisy squealed (we were all kneeling on the lip of the pond, staring down at the scene). Together Bertie and Michael hauled Donald upright and more or less flung him out onto the gravel of the quad. Donald made a sort of *umph* noise and then was very sick all over the ground.

"Ugh!" said Chummy. "Donald, you oaf! You almost got my shoe!"

He was behaving as though it was all a joke, but I knew it was not—Donald really might have been in serious trouble. Was everyone else too unwell to realize what had happened? This did not seem very accidental. I remembered the person who had shoved against me in the dark. Was that a clue? Had Donald been *pushed*?

"I'll get him to his rooms," said Michael. "Wells, take the guests out of college. Don't just stand there! Hurry up!"

I knew all four of us were burning to follow and find out more, but we could not argue with a don. Bertie waved us all through the porter's lodge, and as Harold, Alexander, and George hurried away in the direction of St. John's, I caught sight of Amanda. She was waiting in Mill Lane for Daisy and me, arms folded. I wanted to turn to Daisy and discuss what had just happened—and also to ask Amanda about what Chummy had said to Bertie—but Amanda looked so tired and fierce that I quailed. She led us back over the bridge to St. Lucy's, and hustled us back to our staircase. The door to our rooms shut, and at last we were alone.

The room was chilly—St. Lucy's radiator policy was obviously very strict—and as we undressed I shivered. I wrapped my dressing gown around me and turned to Daisy.

Of course, she was ready. "All right!" she said. "There are two things we must do. First, we should make cocoa. And second, we must have a Detective Society meeting."

I was afraid that the electric kettle would not work, but miraculously it did, and we had soon heated up water for our cocoa. I poured out steaming mugs of it, and Daisy and I both picked biscuits from King Henry's tin—chocolate bourbons for me, and squashed fly biscuits for Daisy. Then we were ready to begin.

We sat cross-legged on the carpet. Daisy leaned forward over her cocoa, her cheeks pink with the steam, and said, "Now, Hazel. There have been several important developments in the case!"

I know!" I said. "We saw one of Donald's accidents—and it didn't seem accidental at all. Daisy, I think someone poisoned Donald's port, and then pushed him in the pond while he was weak!"

"Yes," said Daisy. "And that's not all. I've worked out exactly what was put into that port. You see, that setup in Donald's rooms made me remember something that happened one Christmas at Fallingford, when I was very little. Do you remember what decorations were hanging on Donald's walls?"

I thought. "Holly and ivy," I said. "Mistletoe and tinsel."

"Yes!" said Daisy. "*Mistletoe*. Now, what happened at Fallingford was that Mrs. D put the mistletoe too low, and I thought the berries were pretty, and ate them. Mistletoe berries are poisonous, you know, and I was frightfully ill because I was so small—she had to give me ipecac to make me be sick. But, see, I remember the symptoms. I was dizzy, and my vision went all blurred. It was exactly what was wrong with all the boys at dinner. And, if that wasn't enough, while we were in the room, I happened to notice that some of the berries were missing from the mistletoe branches. I didn't think anything of it until later, of course—but it backs up my theory. Hazel, I believe that someone put *mistletoe berries* into the port decanter! And who was the person who didn't drink much, and was almost unharmed?"

"Chummy!" I said. "It's what we suspected, isn't it? But—wait. Chummy told everyone to drink from that bottle! It made everyone ill, not just Donald. Why would he do that, if he was just targeting Donald?"

"Perhaps he wanted to cover his tracks, so it didn't *look* like he was just targeting Donald," said Daisy. "And remember, it was Donald's special bottle. Donald felt he had to drink more than the others did, and that made him more ill than everyone else. He was the perfect target by the time he was pushed into the pond."

"Remember when that person pushed past us?" I asked. "What if that was Chummy?" I shivered. The case seemed suddenly so clear.

"I think that is a very likely assumption," said Daisy. "Chummy is the younger son, but we know that he's been saying that he deserves to inherit the money, not Donald. You can see that Chummy's used to telling Donald what to do—he's pushing him to hand over part of the inheritance—but imagine what would happen if Donald died within the next two days. Chummy would get it all! He wouldn't have to take Donald's leftovers. What if that is his plan? To kill Donald and make it look like an accident?"

"What if it is? Can we stop him?" I asked.

"Of course we can!" said Daisy. "If we uncover proper evidence of what he's doing, we can show it to the Master, and get Chummy sent down. Donald will be safe, and the Detective Society will have solved another case!"

Her saying that reminded me of what George had said to me. "Daisy," I said. "The Pinkertons haven't been put off by you. They're detecting as well—they want us all to work together on the case."

Daisy made an exasperated noise.

"Why *can't* we, though?" I asked. "They've helped us before! And . . . I said we'd meet George and Alexander in Fitzbillies tomorrow to talk about it."

I said that in a rush, and then took a large bite of chocolate bourbon.

"Hazel!" cried Daisy. "It is really unfair, how bold you've become! Not a thought as to what your president might want! We are far better than the silly *Pinkertons*."

"If we are, then I don't see the problem. We'll solve the case quicker than them anyway."

"That is true," said Daisy, though she still sounded

reluctant. "After all, we do know things that they don't. What about Amanda, for instance? She's behaving awfully suspiciously. She's working all the time, and she won't go near Maudlin—and I'm quite sure that it has something to do with Chummy and my idiot of a brother. Didn't you hear what Chummy said earlier?"

"What if she knows something about the accidents?" I asked. "What if Chummy's bought her off? And Bertie knows about it?"

"It can't be that," said Daisy. "Bertie's pally with Chummy, but he isn't stupid enough to be part of actually trying to bump someone else off. And anyway, that doesn't solve the problem of Amanda's essays. No, it's something else. We shall just have to keep on watching her.

"That brings us rather nicely on to a plan of action! Of course, we must see the boys tomorrow—bother you, Hazel! But we can also follow more interesting leads. I'd like to get back into Donald's rooms, to investigate that decanter. I know what mistletoe berries look like, after all. I'd also like to question Amanda. What does she do all day, and what does she think of Chummy and Donald?"

"And we should find out more about Chummy and Donald's birthday," I said. "We need to know what Donald stands to inherit, and what exactly happens when he turns twenty-one."

"Yes!" agreed Daisy. "Well, I think that's a good list.

Write it up, won't you, Hazel? And then we ought to get some sleep. Tomorrow is a very important day for the Detective Society!"

PLAN OF ACTION

1. Meet the Junior Pinkertons

2. Question Amanda Price

3. Investigate the clue of the decanter

4. Investigate Chummy and Donald, and their birthday preparations

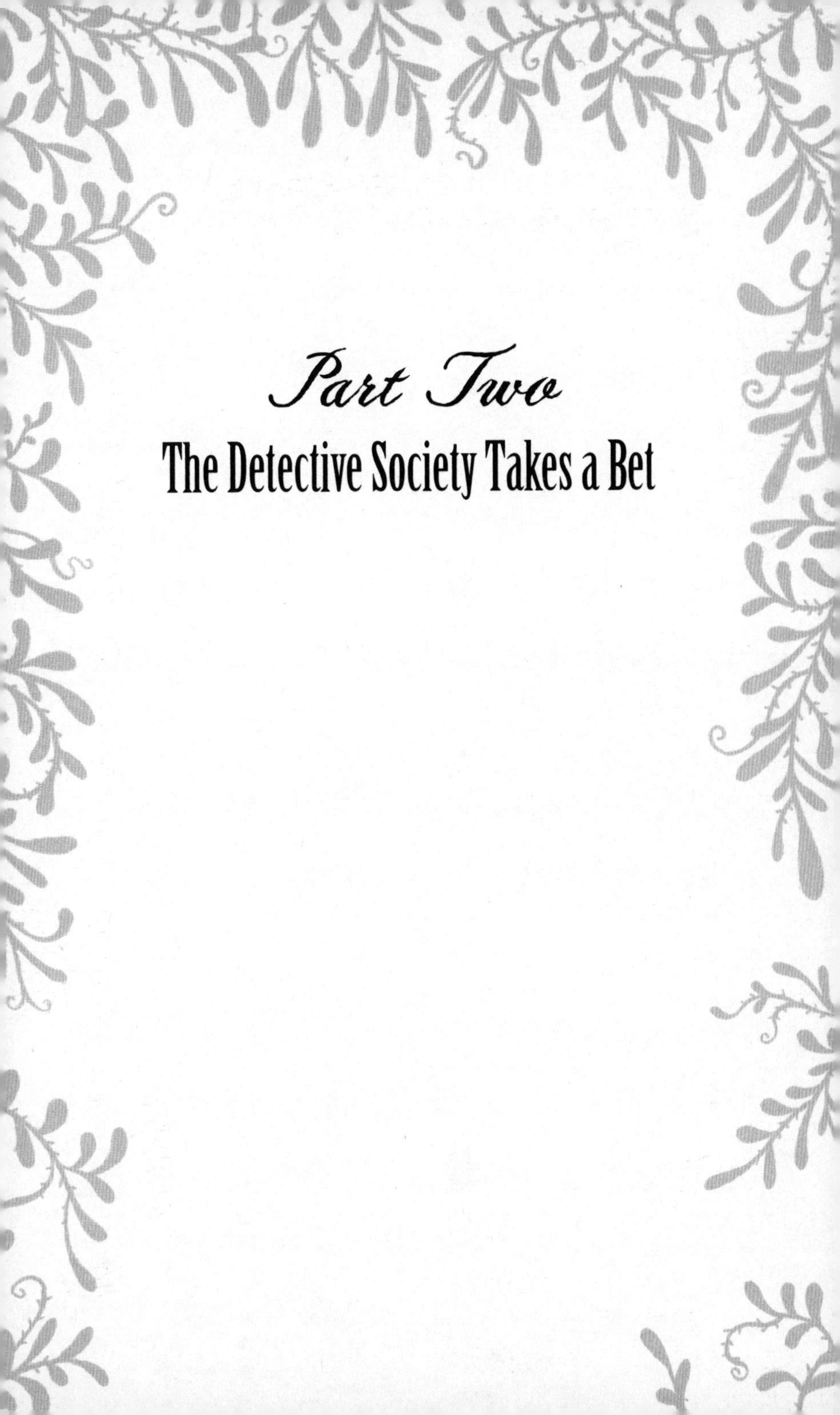

Part Two

The Detective Society Takes a Bet

We had breakfast on Monday morning in the rather stark St. Lucy's refectory. I was reminded of Deepdean's dorm dining room, only done larger, the toast rather burned and the eggs rather raw. Amanda looked more tired than ever, and after breakfast she hurried us out of St. Lucy's and across the bridge into Cambridge. "Be good," she said shortly, turning away and swinging up onto the Horse. "I'm going into town to get some work done. I'll see you back here at four."

And, just like that, Daisy and I were left alone and unchaperoned in Cambridge, free to wander wherever we liked.

In the sharp winter morning light Cambridge seemed to be quite full up with people. We were buffeted by shoppers, their arms full of parcels and their faces frantic, and the *ting* of bicycle bells was almost constant. Daisy became quite practiced at stepping aside for each one to whizz past, but I was startled every time.

Cambridge itself was made up of strange, twisting little passages, tiny streets with brightly lit shops crammed in on each side. Holly was hanging up everywhere, and the windows were clustered with toys and sweets. It was the most perfect place to do our Christmas shopping before we met the Junior Pinkertons.

For Daisy I already had a magnificent gold compact, with a great big dusty brush that sent white powder all over me when I opened it. With some adhesive tape, which I had bought from the chemist's in Deepdean, it made the most marvellous fingerprint kit.

Today, I bought a big wrapped box of chocolates for Aunt Eustacia, a handsome notebook for Alexander, a box of toffees for George and Harold, and (more reluctantly) a red scarf for Amanda. In Heffers bookshop I bought my father a wonderful book full of photographic plates of Cambridge buildings, and Daisy bought Bertie a book about George III.

"He ought to be learning about him anyway," she said severely, when I raised my eyebrows.

But of course, Daisy was not content to simply buy gifts and enjoy the festivity—not when we were on a case. Wherever we went, Daisy somehow found a way to bring up the Melling twins.

From the lady in the sweet shop we heard about the preparations for their party at Christmas: "Mr. Charles Melling has ordered the best of everything, of course.

Fine chocolates, a five-tier cake—half the students in Cambridge have been invited! No expense spared. Donald Melling will become one of the richest men in Britain on Christmas Day this year—as I understand, the only question is whether he'll be the one spending the money!"

From the bookseller at Heffers we heard about the Melling family tree, and the entail. "I hear the sums run into the hundreds of thousands. It's been held in trust until the older son turns twenty-one—that's Mr. Donald, of course—and it all goes to him. It's a pity, really—not a rule designed to be fair, is it? Everyone agrees that the heir ought to be Mr. Charles."

And from the girl in the scarf shop we heard more about what Donald intended to do with the money. "If only it was Chummy who was getting the cash! He's fun, is Chummy—took me to the races once. He's tried to make that silly brother of his give him some of the money, but he's being a stick in the mud. He wants to make sure that Chummy doesn't get any. Says he's going to blow it straightaway, on some mine or other in Africa—or is it South America? Such a waste. It isn't fair at all! I'm going to the party, though—at least that'll be a laugh!"

As we came out of the scarf shop, we almost ran into Michael Butler again. He whipped by us on his bicycle, and we both had to duck back into the doorway not to be seen. We did it instinctively—although we were investigating the Mellings, not Michael, we had agreed that it was best if no one at Maudlin had any idea what we were up to.

After he had cycled away down the street, Daisy nudged me. "It's ten to twelve," she said. "Time to go to Fitzbillies."

"Do you want to?" I asked cautiously. I had been avoiding the question.

"I know *you* do!" said Daisy. "And anyway, aren't you hungry after that dreadful breakfast?"

I was. The thought of those Fitzbillies buns made my mouth water, and my cold fingers tingle inside my gloves.

We rushed through the Cambridge streets and arrived at Fitzbillies to find it bursting with people—and there were Alexander and George, sitting at one half of a square table. Daisy called out, and Alexander looked up at the sound of her voice. I saw a burst of recognition and happiness flash across it. Alexander never can hide his emotions—he really is the most dreadful undercover detective. And suddenly I was not sure that this meeting was a good idea after all.

Then Daisy and George caught sight of each other, and I was amazed all over again by the connection that had already formed between them. Daisy is very good at people. She understands what makes them tick, just like a mechanic with a car, but I have rarely seen her *like* someone. In the whole world, she likes me, and her father, and her uncle Felix, and Bertie, and no one else—at least, until George. I was particularly amazed because boys, to her, are usually simply less interesting versions of girls. She has never understood in the slightest how I feel about Alexander—and yet she seemed extraordinarily taken with George Mukherjee.

Two minutes later we were seated in the bright glow and bustle of Fitzbillies tea rooms, which were decked out with Christmas baubles and strings of bright paper rings, and the tea maid was taking our orders. It did feel strange, the four of us sitting together without a grown-up. I was suddenly not even quite sure how I ought to sit—did grown-ups sit back, or rest their elbows on the table? What did they do with their hands and feet? I was waiting for the maid to catch us at it, to point her pencil at us and tell us off for pretending to be grown up. But she only wrote down our tea order rather distractedly (hot cocoa, Chelsea buns, four different sorts of sandwiches, and lemon cake) and then rushed away.

I stared around us. Christmas parcels were piled in every corner, pushed under tables among tired shoppers' feet. Above the steam from the teapots and the waft of the fresh buns there was a sharp scent of pine from the boughs hung up in the corners of the room—it was all wonderfully festive, and I loved it.

"Now," said George. "Listen to my idea." Alexander tugged at his shirt cuffs (somehow they were still too short) and grinned at us both.

"First," said Daisy, putting on a haughty front, "I would like to say that I am not at all happy that you have stepped in on what ought to be our case. We are the best detective society ever created, after all, and—"

"One of the *two* best, I think you'll find," said George, not at all ruffled. "The Junior Pinkertons have solved plenty of cases, you know that."

"Humph!" said Daisy, her mouth narrowing again. "All *I* know are our cases. And they prove that the Junior Pinkertons are decidedly inferior to the Detective Society, and always will be."

Alexander looked rather hurt. George merely raised his eyebrows at her.

The tea arrived, and we all began to eat. I watched George pack his cheeks with cucumber sandwiches. He ate impressive amounts for someone so slender.

"I'm taking your roast beef sandwich," said Alexander to George, with his mouth full.

"Don't you like it?" I asked George. It seemed quite an inconsiderate, Daisy-ish thing for the normally kind Alexander to do, and I was surprised.

"I can't eat it," said George. "Hindu, you know. I'm vegetarian."

I swallowed a large lump of sandwich—it was either crab paste or salmon, I can never tell—in surprise. I have become so used to tucking the un-English parts of myself away, politely pretending that they do not exist. My grandparents' religion stays in Hong Kong, along with my silk dresses and my little half-sisters. But here was George, calmly mentioning not being Christian as though it was quite an ordinary thing.

"He can't even go to chapel," said Alexander. "They beat him for it at school, at first, until his father sent a letter to tell them to stop."

"*He* cried at the beatings," said George, rolling his eyes. "I ended up looking after *him*."

Alexander tugged on his cuffs again, looking rueful. "It was wrong of them," he said.

"So it was," said George. "But there wasn't any point sobbing about it. Anyway, don't you want to hear my idea? That's what we're here for, after all."

"What is it?" I asked.

"It's quite simple," said George. "We all want to work on the case, and find out what is behind Donald's accidents. But Daisy doesn't want to work with the Pinkertons. So what about a bet?" He looked around the table, his eyes glowing. "Junior Pinkertons versus the Detective Society.

You say you're better detectives than we are, and we say that's not so. Let's prove it, one way or the other."

I felt a burst of excitement go through me. It really was a most excellent idea. For once, after all, no one had been murdered. We could play a game without worrying. In the festive warmth of the tea room, the holiday seemed very bright. "Yes!" I said.

"Hmm," said Daisy, frowning and nibbling at her slice of cake. I knew she was only pretending. And sure enough—"Oh, all right! But only because I know that we *are* better than you, and we *will* get to the truth first."

Alexander beamed. There was a dimple in his left cheek. "I agree with Daisy and Hazel," he said. "This will be excellent fun!"

"All right!" said George. "Now that's agreed, we must think of the technical side of the bet. What are we looking to prove?"

"That *someone* is really and truly after Donald," said Daisy at once. "The attacks against him are not merely pranks, or accidents; they are intended—and they are growing in severity. I believe something truly terrible will happen before Christmas Day, Donald's birthday."

"Yes," said George. "We do too. And we think we know who that *someone* is. So far we are in agreement. So we need—let's see—irrefutable evidence of *his* intention to seriously hurt Donald. It must be something that will stand up if we take it to the Master, or the police."

"Yes," said Daisy, nodding.

"And no cheating on the way to getting that information."

"Ladies never cheat!" gasped Daisy. "No guessing, no fudging answers, and no forcing confessions. Proper interviews with witnesses and rigorous examination of clues. Agreed?"

"Agreed," said George, nodding. "Now, the prize. How about this: the losing society must publicly admit to being wrong. They must tell everyone they were bettered by a rival society—that they were not good enough to win. What about that?"

It was a truly serious bet. More people know about our society than we would strictly like, especially Daisy, but we are still *secret*. To reveal ourselves to the world would ruin what the Detective Society stood for. It might even prevent us solving any more cases, for if grown-ups knew what we were doing, they would want to stop us. Could Daisy agree to the possibility of such a loss of face?

But she was already putting out her hand, very fair against George's dark one. They shook resolutely, and they both glowed at each other with the sort of excitement that Daisy always gets at the beginning of a case.

"And finally, the window for the bet to be won begins now, Monday the twenty-third of December 1935, and ends . . . on Christmas Day, at the party for Chummy and Donald's birthday?"

I liked that. It gave things a nice symmetry. I nodded, and so did Alexander. Even Daisy looked satisfied.

"Let's all shake on it," said George. We all four shook, and clinked willow-patterned teacups, and then George and Alexander turned to each other and did the most complex set of hand gestures I have ever seen.

"What on earth is that?" I asked, curious.

"The Junior Pinkertons' handshake," said Alexander. "It's terribly good, isn't it? It took us ages to get right."

"Huh!" said Daisy. "It isn't half as fine as the Detective Society handshake. Come on, Hazel, we'll show them!"

We put out *our* hands and shook. These days I can do all the moves with my eyes closed—it feels as natural as blinking. I looked over at Alexander. Was he impressed?

"Not bad," said George. "Now. The bet begins as soon as we get up from the table. Are you ready? Here is our contribution to the tea. Get set—Alex, GO!"

And quick as anything, tossing a handful of coins onto the cloth, he leaped up from the table, Alexander behind him, and pelted out of Fitzbillies.

Daisy's face was alight.

"Hazel, we must act quickly! Finish off that bun, and let us consider our next actions, so that we can go forward fortified with both knowledge and bun-break. The boys may have a head start, but you'll see—we shan't be beaten. We must go to Maudlin at once."

"Are you sure we'll be let in?" I asked. I was suddenly rather worried. We had been allowed into Maudlin the night before because we were Bertie's guests—but how were we to run about on our own in a men's college and collect information without attracting comment? We had been at home at Deepdean, and Daisy was at home in Fallingford, but at Maudlin we were both outsiders.

"Of course we shall," said Daisy. "We can get by any obstacle. We have solved *four* murder cases, Hazel, how many times must I remind you? Now, once we are past Mr. Perkins in the lodge, where shall we go?"

"Donald's rooms," I said.

"Yes," said Daisy. "The decanter will still be there—and that was where the bucket incident happened as well. But we must observe the whole staircase, not just one room. And we need to be quick! We only have two days until Christmas, and the end of the bet. Ah, good, there's the tea maid. Quick, put down your money! We must be away."

We galloped down the street to Maudlin. We went in through the lodge door—and my fears came true.

"Hey!" called Mr. Perkins. "Girls! Now, what are you doing here?"

"We've come to see Bertie!" said Daisy. "Can we go in, please?"

"I'm afraid Bertie's out," said Mr. Perkins, tugging at his moustache. "Those two boys, Alexander and George, just stopped by with a message from him. He says he particularly doesn't want you to come in—I think there are *presents* for you in his rooms." He mouthed *presents*, as though the very word was a secret. "So you're to wait here until he comes to find you. It should only be twenty minutes or so."

I heard Daisy hiss next to me. The Pinkertons were throwing tricks in our way already. How would we get out of this one?

But Daisy was equal to the situation. She approached Mr. Perkins and leaned her elbows up on the desk at which he sat.

"Oh, but that's why we wanted to creep in while he was

out!" she said angelically. "We've got some baubles that we want to hang up on his door as a surprise for him. Can't we go by? We won't go into his room—and we'll be back out here before he arrives, I promise!" She fluttered her eyelashes at him again like the most foolish debutante—Daisy, who has climbed to the very top of our boarding house in utter darkness and outwitted murderers and read the whole of *War and Peace* in two weeks.

Mr. Perkins melted most satisfactorily. "Oh!" he said. "Well . . . I'll turn a blind eye. But be quick, mind!"

"Thank you," said Daisy. "And I forgot to mention—on our way here we saw George's brother Harold. He's looking for George and Alexander. I'm not sure what about, but it seemed urgent. If you see them, do tell them that he wants them, will you?"

"Of course," said Mr. Perkins. "Go on, then!"

He winked at us conspiratorially as we went out and into the quad. Along the path we went, all the way to the doorway that led to staircase nine. The door to Michael's room was ajar, and through it we could hear three people talking. Michael must be back from town—and Alexander and George were talking to him.

"Interviewing witnesses already!" said Daisy. "They think they're beating us—but they'll see!"

She went boldly up to the door and rapped on it with her knuckles. It opened, and Michael looked out.

"Miss Wells?" he asked. "Miss Wong? You shouldn't be here on your own!"

"Oh, we're here to leave something for Bertie. And we've got a message for George and Alexander," said Daisy. "Harold's looking for them—I think it's urgent. They're to go to him at John's at once."

Michael stepped aside, and I could see George and Alexander behind him. Alexander looked at us rather ruefully, as though we had betrayed him (I had a pang of guilt), but George smiled at us.

"What a surprise," he said. "We'll have to go and see what he wants, I suppose. Come on, Alex." He pulled Alexander out of the door into the Quad, but as he passed Daisy and me he turned his head to us and whispered, "Not bad. But we'll be back!"

Daisy waved them away. "We're off to Bertie's rooms!" she said to Michael, and she dragged me up the stairs.

As we climbed, I looked around. We had been here before, last night, but then I had not been able to think of anything but Alexander. An elephant might have stepped in front of me, and I would have pushed it aside and kept climbing. This afternoon, though, all my senses were alive, and I was seeing and thinking clearly again. Our shoes clattered on the stone steps and echoed around the walls. The staircase was narrow and dark—the only windows were small ones on each landing out onto the quad behind us.

Up we went to the first landing, which was empty apart from a coin-box telephone. The door on the left, the lodge side, read Freddie Savage ("He must be away for the holidays," whispered Daisy), and on the garden side, the right, was Bertie's door.

On the landing above Bertie's rooms were two doors. On the lodge side was a room that read Alfred Cheng. This door was firmly closed, but as we went past it swung open, and Alfred poked his face out rather crossly.

"What are you doing here?" he asked us.

"Bertie asked us to leave Chummy a note," said Daisy, ready as always with a plausible excuse.

"Huh!" said Alfred, unimpressed, and he swung his door shut again.

On this landing, the door on the garden side said James Monmouth. It was slightly open, and I could see that inside it was empty. The room had clearly just been redecorated. All the furniture was covered with sheets, and the walls were freshly painted and papered. I took a few steps inside, and saw that it was laid out just like Donald's had been the night before, only the other way about. The fireplace was set in the middle of the wall opposite the door, with the sofa in front of it and a desk on its right. But while Donald's rooms had only one window, facing onto the quad, this room had an extra window between his bedroom door and the fireplace that looked out onto the garden. It was much lighter and more pleasant than Donald's lodge-side room had been.

Up we went again, to the third landing that still seemed as dizzyingly high as it had last night. This time the rooms on the garden side read CHARLES MELLING, and the one to its left DONALD MELLING. Between them was a small door to what looked like a box room. I wondered whose it was. I also wondered that Chummy had taken the garden room, though he was the younger brother—it was yet more proof of how much he controlled Donald.

Donald's door was tantalizingly open, and Daisy and I both moved toward it as quickly as we could. I could see a white dent on the stone floor, just inside the open door. I had not noticed it last night—I had been too nervous—but of course that must have been where the bucket had fallen. And there in the dimness was the table where the drinks had been set out the evening before. Glasses and decanters were still ranged across it.

"All right, Watson!" hissed Daisy. "Time to detect!"

We moved forward, into the room.

The air inside Donald's rooms smelled stale, of many breaths let out and curtains kept closed. Daisy wrinkled up her nose, and I pinched my lips together. I remembered Moss, the bedder who tidied the students' rooms, and thought that he must not be very good at his job. It was lucky for us. The table was still scattered with port glasses, there were wine stains on the cloth, and I could even see an abandoned bow tie. There was the decanter itself, too, its crystal dulled by the dark liquid still inside it. Daisy pounced at it at once, unstoppering it and taking a deep sniff.

"Daisy!" I said. "Careful!"

"Oh, it's quite all right, Hazel," said Daisy. "Mistletoe isn't poisonous enough for a sniff to do any harm."

I still thought that I would not take the risk. "*Is* it mistletoe, though?" I asked.

Daisy paused, breathing in even more deeply. Then she

nodded. "Oh yes, I should say so," she said. "And"—she held the bottle up in front of her, peering into its depths—"yes, look! You can see there's something rolling about in the residue, something round. Here, give me your handkerchief, and that empty glass."

"Why?" I asked.

"I'm going to make a filter with it," said Daisy.

I stepped backward.

"Oh, come now! You've got plenty more handkerchiefs, I've seen them."

I was going to point out to Daisy that *she* had plenty more as well—but we were somewhere we ought not to be, doing something that we certainly ought not to do, and I thought that it was best to get Daisy's plan over with as quickly as possible. So I passed her my handkerchief, and one of the clean glasses at the back of the table. Daisy held the handkerchief over the glass. "All right," she said. "Pour."

I took the poisoned decanter and poured. Red went everywhere—down the sides of the glass, over my handkerchief and even some on Daisy's hands. "Hazel!" she said. "Really! Pour like a lady!"

But at the end of the exercise we were left with a handkerchief covered with flecks of the nasty bits that always collect at the bottom of wine bottles—and seven rather squashed berries.

"There!" cried Daisy. "See? And if you look about, at

the greenery hanging up—that bunch of mistletoe is missing almost half its berries! Pick it, Hazel—no, wait, I will, you're too short."

She brought the mistletoe back to me triumphantly, and added it to the handkerchief's contents, tying it all up in a rather sticky bundle with the bit of string she always keeps in her pocket.

"We have our first pieces of evidence, Watson! *Someone* has doctored this decanter of port with mistletoe. This proves that what happened to Donald last night was not an accident, or even a harmless prank. It had malicious intent."

"What shall we do now?" I asked.

"Look about the room!" said Daisy. "Documents, pictures—anything that might help us prove that this is part of a pattern! I'll take the bedroom, you do in here."

I looked around the room, and then stepped toward the desk. It was messy, covered with papers. I saw lecture notes and essays, all scrambled together—but on top of the pile was a much more interesting document.

"Look, Daisy!" I called. "It's a deed—I think it's to a diamond mine! That's the thing Donald wants to buy, isn't it?" Then I saw the price he was paying for it, and felt rather dizzy.

"Has he signed it yet?" asked Daisy, popping up next to me. "No, look—because he can't, of course! It's forward-dated to Christmas Day, but he can't sign until his birthday. That's important, isn't it? Clear proof again of what will happen if Donald comes into his inheritance on his birthday. He'll spend the money—he'll get out from under Chummy's thumb at last!"

"Chummy really must be furious!" I said. I had a creeping feeling along the back of my neck. This, combined with the mistletoe in the decanter, and the fact that Chummy had hardly drunk any of it last night, seemed to add up to something rather chilling. Chummy had means, motive, and opportunity to have poisoned the port, and pushed Donald into the pond. Could we prove that he had set up the bucket and loosened the stone as well?

"Hazel, I have noticed something else rather interesting about this desk," said Daisy. "Look at the top of it—what do you see?"

"Family pictures," I said. "Those people must be Donald's parents."

"Yes, of course, Hazel—but who *isn't* there?"

I saw at once. "Chummy!" I said. "There aren't any pictures of him at all!"

"Exactly," said Daisy. "More evidence that the two of them don't get on. This is very good, Hazel! Excellent! Now, I've been in Donald's bedroom. There are some interesting objects at the bottom of his wardrobe: a pair of tennis shoes and a dark coat, all bundled up with bits of rope and wire. I think it's his climbing material! Really, people are bad at hiding things properly."

"Let's go to Chummy's rooms!" I said. "Quick, before Bertie comes back!"

"Excellent idea," said Daisy. "Here, put the handkerchief in your pocket."

"I won't!" I said. "Daisy, that's disgusting. It's all wet!"

Daisy rolled her eyes. "You really are the worst spy in the world," she said. "All right, I shall wrap it in my scarf."

I knew she was not really cross with me, though, and as we slipped out of Donald's rooms together and crept across the corridor to Chummy's door we beamed at each other. There really is nothing in the world like being on a case with Daisy Wells.

Chummy's rooms, thankfully, were just as empty as Donald's. His curtains had been pulled open, and I could see down into the garden below. It was surrounded by a high brick wall with a closed door on the side nearest to the library building. It looked very secret and quite lovely, even though all its green was wilted by the winter.

Chummy's sitting room was chaotic. There were shirts and ties draped everywhere—"What a dandy!" whispered Daisy. "I can see why Bertie's friends with him; he can never resist good clothes"—books were leaning together on his half-empty shelf, and papers were scattered across his desk. I peered at them. It was funny: although the twins were so different in character, their handwriting was exactly the same.

"Look here!" said Daisy. "This is interesting!" She was peering at something on the sofa next to the fireplace.

I turned and looked. It was a jacket, a tweed one.

"The laundry mark says DONALD MELLING," said Daisy. "So what is it doing in Chummy's rooms?"

"He might have left it?" I suggested.

"Perhaps—but I don't think that's it. Try to put it on—go on, try."

Feeling rather confused and awkward, I picked up the jacket and slid my arm into its sleeve. I got halfway down—and then my hand was stopped. "Oh!" I said.

"Ah, I *am* right!" said Daisy happily. "He's sewn it shut. I guessed: there's a needle and thread on the occasional table, but I can't see anything that needs mending. And remember what Bertie said about the pranks Chummy likes to play? We've caught him in the middle of one! It's not particularly deadly, but it *is* clear evidence that he's out to get Donald!"

I hesitated. This prank was so far from the mistletoe poisoning, far even from the bucket landing on Donald's head. It was so *silly*. I said so to Daisy.

"True," she said with a frown. "Nothing we can take to the Master, is it? No, we need to discover evidence that Chummy's planning a truly dangerous trick, and find it *here*. Look around, Hazel!"

We turned out the contents of drawers, and looked under the sofa cushions—but despite our best efforts neither of us found anything that looked damning. Daisy ducked into Chummy's bedroom, and came out two minutes later looking deflated. "Nothing," she said shortly. "He's got the same climbing things: rope, wire, tennis shoes. All we can accuse Chummy of is being a climber—and that isn't what we're trying to do!"

It was time to go. We had spent too long investigating already. We moved toward the door, pushed it open—and stopped short. There, standing in front of us, was Chummy himself.

He stared at us. He was wearing another bright cravat, and his chestnut hair was slicked back. "What are you doing here?" he asked, startled.

"We're lost!" said Daisy in her sweetest voice, fluttering her eyelashes. "We were looking for the—you know—the *ladies*."

Chummy, unsurprisingly, did not seem convinced. It was not one of Daisy's better excuses. "You're Bertie's kid sister. You ought to be in his rooms, if you're anywhere. What are you doing anyway, running wild on the staircase with *her*?" He glared at me, and I stepped back, alarmed. He was looking at me as poisonously as he had Alfred yesterday.

"Hey! Butler!" Chummy bellowed suddenly. "Come here at once! I've caught kids in my room!"

He hauled us both out of the doorway and onto the landing. I felt myself shaking. We were truly in a bad situation now.

"What's going on?" called Michael Butler from downstairs. I looked down and saw him climbing toward us. Alexander and George were with him. As he passed the landing below us, Alfred Cheng popped his head out of his door again. "What is it?" I heard him ask.

"Oh, do go away," shouted Chummy. "Why are you always poking your nose in where you don't belong?"

"Butler!" said Alfred, glaring upward. "He's at it again!" I could hear the strain in his voice.

"Cheng," said Michael shortly, "enough. Haven't I told you to stop complaining about nothing? This is England, and we don't accuse people of things without reason."

"Yes, this is England, where only the English count," said Alfred. "You've seen the way Melling's been treating me, and you've done nothing."

"Leave it, man, for goodness' sake. I've got more important things to deal with."

"You'll regret that," said Alfred. "*He'll* regret that. Just you wait." He stepped backward out of my sight and slammed the door. I stared at Chummy, who was grinning triumphantly, and suddenly realized, with a shock, that university students were really only like bigger Big Girls. They were not much older, or wiser—and last term had proved to me how cruel and stupid Big Girls could be. I suddenly wondered whether growing up only meant you were older, not more wise.

Michael climbed the final flight of stairs, shaking his head.

"What's up, Melling?" he asked.

"These girls were in my room," said Chummy crossly. "Send them away! I want them out of the staircase."

"You can't do that!" said Daisy.

"I certainly can," said Michael. "And in fact, that was exactly what I was on my way to do. The boys have just come back, and they've told me that you lied to them—Harold didn't have a message at all. And you aren't decorating Bertie's door, either. You can't simply wander about on this staircase without a reason—you're girls!"

"So?" asked Daisy.

"This is a men's college," said Michael. "You are not a man, Miss Wells. Now, I don't want to see you or your friend here again—not unless you have a proper invitation. This may be the holidays, but we are still in Cambridge. There are standards. Go back to St. Lucy's, where you belong."

Behind him, Alexander and George both made apologetic faces. They were only playing by the rules that Daisy had set, I thought—but it did not make what they had done sting any less.

I knew that there was no hope of Michael reconsidering. Although he was no taller than Chummy, and hardly taller than Daisy herself, he really felt like a grown-up.

He led us down the staircase, and as we walked my

cheeks burned with shame and outrage. I did not want to turn and look up at George and Alexander, although I knew they must be watching us leave. I had been right to worry about detecting at Maudlin. I had hoped to be treated like a grown-up at Cambridge. But I had forgotten that although we were older, we were still girls. We did not have the same freedoms as Alexander and George. We would be stopped, and curbed, and told where to go. From now on we would have to use all our ingenuity to discover the simplest things.

As we reached the bottom of the stairs, Daisy made one final valiant attempt to win the bet. "Is Chummy all right?" she asked.

"What do you mean?" asked Michael.

"Oh, nothing," said Daisy innocently. "Only—he seemed *so* upset that we were in his room. It must be awful, having a brother who's going to be rich, when you don't get any of the money. If that happened to me, I'd be furious. I'd—I'd want to *kill* Bertie. Chummy doesn't want to hurt Donald, does he?"

Michael laughed. "They may not like each other," he said, "but I don't think there's anything to worry about. Not even at Christmas."

"Why would Christmas be a time to worry? Because it's their birthday?" Daisy asked.

"Because they're brothers!" said Michael. "Christmas is the worst time for family. Makes me glad it's only me and my mother—no one else to argue with. At least it'll all be over on the twenty-fifth."

And that, it seemed, was that. Michael was sure that Donald and Chummy's arguments did not matter—I could tell that nothing we said would change his mind. He led us all the way to the porter's lodge, and outside. Mr. Perkins watched us go, and I knew we would not be able to get past him again so easily.

We walked despondently down the road toward St. Lucy's—and I was startled when someone shouted behind us. I turned to see Amanda cycling toward us on the Horse. Her hair under its beret was windblown and her face was set in a scowl. When she saw us she swung quickly down and said, "There you are!"

I looked at my wristwatch. Of course—it was just past four, the time we had agreed to meet Amanda. The day had flown by without my noticing.

"We've just been banned from Maudlin," said Daisy indignantly. "Imagine! I suppose you know what that's like, don't you?" she added quickly. I knew what she was thinking—it was the perfect opportunity to question Amanda.

"I wasn't banned," said Amanda. "I— Now, never you mind. It's time for you to come back to St. Lucy's, anyway. Hurry up!"

I thought she would not say anything more about being banned, but as we reached the bridge over the Cam, she paused. The sun was setting in front of us, and the roofs and walls of Cambridge had turned all rosy in the dying light. The reflection of the sunset was somehow almost lovelier than the thing itself.

"Oh!" I said, and squeezed Daisy's arm.

"There's Clare College, across the river," said Amanda. "And King's Chapel too. And look, there!"

She pointed, and her eyes made me see little things in the skyline that I had missed before—the gargoyles and towers and stone kings in their niches, the college crests and beautiful peaked windows. For a moment, everything was peaceful. Then Amanda spoke again.

"Listen," she said. "Don't worry about Maudlin. Best not to get yourself mixed up with them. Bertie means well, but—"

"But?" asked Daisy eagerly. Were we about to hear what had happened to Amanda?

"Cambridge isn't the place to be a woman," finished Amanda. "That's all there is to it." She sighed and pushed another clump of hair off her face. I noticed all over again how tired she looked. "Better get back!" she said. "Another essay to do before dinner."

"But it's the holidays!" I said.

"I've got to get ahead," said Amanda. "Because of what I said. Being a woman at Cambridge, you have to work ten times as hard as any man, just to get by. That's all."

But I was suddenly sure that was *not* all.

"But you're far cleverer than any of the Maudlin students," said Daisy, sounding sympathetic. "Bertie, obviously—but Chummy and Donald too. I can tell!"

"Hah!" said Amanda sharply. She jerked her head, and when she turned back to us her face was set. "I keep telling Bertie he oughtn't to be friends with Chummy. Chummy's bad news. He's got Donald and Bertie dangling after him, and they're going to regret it if they get caught up in his nonsense. It's best that you don't go back to Maudlin, do you hear me?"

I felt trapped. So many people were telling us that Chummy was bad—that he did not study, and he was unpleasant—but no one seemed to think that he was truly up to anything actually *dangerous*. What if he should do something else to Donald, while we were not at Maudlin to stop it? I could not help worrying.

I wrote all of that up on Monday before dinner. We made several attempts to get back out of St. Lucy's, and to Maudlin, but the St. Lucy's staff seemed to have been asked by Daisy's great-aunt to look out for us. We kept on coming across kind dons and maids in corridors who thought we must be lost, and sent us back to our rooms.

We had dinner in the refectory, all peeling white walls and tinned food, and then went back up to King Henry's rooms, where we sat in her squashy chairs and stared at each other. The red-stained napkin, with its mistletoe and berries, sat on the table between us.

"I've half a mind to just climb out of the window and go and investigate!" said Daisy.

"We can't!" I said, shuddering and thinking of the drainpipe at Deepdean. I had been up and down it several times last term, and felt firmly that if I never climbed again, I would be quite happy. "We'd be stopped by Mr. Perkins!"

"I know, I know," said Daisy restlessly. "Ugh!"

Daisy fretfully read more of *Gaudy Night* ("I know who did it," she said to me. "It's perfectly obvious!"), and then we lay in bed for ages, talking, before finally falling asleep.

When the knocking began it seemed that I had barely closed my eyes.

I sat up with a jolt, shocked. The knocking continued.

"Who is it?" called Daisy, getting out of bed and putting on her dressing gown.

"It's me!" said Amanda from out in the corridor. "Get up, do! Something's happened at Maudlin!"

Part Three

Mince Pies and Murder

I

It was only when we had stumbled down the stairs, pulling on our coats and hats and (in my case) blearily wiping the sleep from our eyes, that I realized that the sky above us was still dark and peppered with cold stars. I peered at my wristwatch, and saw that it was just past six o'clock on Tuesday morning. I yawned, and my eyes watered. I felt bewildered, but I was also jangling with nerves.

"What is it?" asked Daisy. The St. Lucy's porter's lodge was empty, and Amanda had to reach for a key from a high ledge and wrestle the little door-within-a-door open to let us out. This was most confusing—I knew we were not allowed out at night. What had happened, that Amanda should be breaking the rules?

"Shush," said Amanda briefly. The dark circles under her eyes were worse than ever, and her cheeks were pale—although that might have been from the cold. "Just come along."

Donald! I thought, all of a sudden. Had something finally happened to him, something truly serious?

Our boots clicked and echoed on the deserted streets, which were misty and chill. Cambridge at this time of night looked like something from a ghost story. It felt like I was stepping through the pages of a book. I almost wondered if it was all real, or if I was still dreaming. But I felt the cobbles under my feet, and the cold air on my cheeks.

When we reached the Maudlin porter's lodge, it too was closed, the door locked. Amanda hammered against it, calling out. At last Mr. Perkins pulled open the small door. He looked shocked. "Miss Price?" he asked. "What are you doing here? How did you hear?"

Hear what? I wondered. I clutched Daisy's arm, and we stared at each other.

"I was telephoned," said Amanda briefly. "The caller said that something had happened at Maudlin, on staircase nine. Let us in." She was standing up straight, jaw clenched and looking quite resolute, although still very pale.

"Not the girls. They've been banned," said Mr. Perkins, pointing at us.

"Oh, that isn't important now!" cried Amanda. "Let us in, do!"

Mr. Perkins stared. Then he sighed. "I'll let you in—but you'll only be sent away again," he said. "You shouldn't be here. The doctor's only just arrived."

"Doctor?" said Daisy, but neither Mr. Perkins nor Amanda would answer her.

We were waved through the lodge, and turned left to hurry along the row of archways, just as we had done before. There were no lights on in the windows above us—the college was asleep. Except, at the archway at the end, lights were blazing and the door of staircase nine was open. Our steps speeding up, we arrived in its glow.

"Hello?" called Amanda, peering upstairs. "Bertie? Where is everyone?"

A head came popping over the banisters a few floors up. It was Michael Butler.

"Price," he said—and was it my imagination, or was there a shake in his voice?—"*what* are you doing here?"

"I was telephoned," said Amanda. "What's happened?"

"Come upstairs," said Michael. "You'll see. But don't—don't step in it, will you?"

My heart beat fast.

We raced up the stairs together—one flight, and then another. We were on Alfred Cheng's landing, below Donald and Chummy's—and as we came up the last few steps, I saw it.

Spreading out at the base of the stairs and glinting in the light was a great pool of something reddish. I have been at enough crime scenes now—which is a strange thing to write, but it is true—to know what it was.

Blood.

II

Don't step in it!" Michael repeated.

He was standing at the doorway to James Monmouth's empty room, leaning against the frame as though it was the only thing keeping him up.

"Where's Bertie?" asked Daisy. Her fists were clenched against her sides.

"He's in there," said Michael, pointing behind him. "Speaking to the doctor. Price, what are you *doing*? Why have you brought the girls here?"

I felt Daisy relax. *Bertie* was all right, at least. But what had happened?

"I couldn't leave them!" said Amanda, as though that explained anything. "I told you, I was telephoned. What's *happened*?"

"I'm keeping watch on the situation," said Michael. "Someone has to. And as to what happened—well. You'll see."

His voice was calm as anything, but I could hear a tremor behind it. I could barely look at him, though, because I was staring at that pool of blood. Was Donald seriously hurt? Was he *dead*?

"Mr. Butler!" cried a voice. "Let me clean it away, please!"

We all looked up. There was a man in the Maudlin College livery standing at the top of the stairs. He was old, gray-haired, and burly, his face clean-shaven and rather round.

"Moss, stay calm," said Michael Butler.

"I can't!" cried the man, and I realized that this must be Moss the bedder. I remembered the little door I had seen between Chummy and Donald's bedrooms—of course, he must live on the staircase as well. "Please! That blood—it's too awful!"

"Moss, leave it," said Michael sharply. "Good God, man, this is not the time."

At that moment, Bertie came out of the empty room. His shoulders were slumped, and he was pale. I saw, with a nasty shock, that there was blood on his hands, and on his slippers—the very same slippers I remember him having at Fallingford.

"There's nothing the doctor can do," he said, and his hands were shaking. "He's gone."

Then he saw us, and Amanda. His face turned, if possible, even whiter. "Amanda—what are you doing here?

Why are Daisy and Hazel—? What are you *doing* here?"

"I was telephoned," said Amanda again. "Someone called me. I thought it was you. Wasn't it? What's happened, Bertie?"

Then someone came out of the door behind Bertie. He was short, with brown hair and pinstriped pajamas. At first glance, I thought it was Chummy. I was sure it must be Chummy. But then I looked up at his face—and got the shock of my life. The person standing in front of me was not Chummy at all. It was Donald.

"Where's Chummy?" I asked, before I could stop myself. "Why—why isn't—"

"Where's Chummy?" Bertie repeated. "He fell down the stairs. Chummy's *dead*."

I reeled. All along, we had been sure that Donald was the one in danger. He was the older brother, the heir. It was he who had been the victim of all the attacks. So why on earth had *Chummy* died? It was like that painting of a lady at her mirror which, when you stare at it, becomes not a lady at all, but a grinning skull.

"He didn't *fall*!" said Donald sharply. I looked at him. He seemed shaken, pale—but there was something else about the way he was holding himself, something tense, almost excited. "He was caught by his own latest prank—a bit of fishing wire that he'd set up across the top of the stairs. He came out of his rooms and tripped straight down the staircase."

With a jolt, I remembered the wire that Daisy had found in Chummy's rooms. In Chummy's rooms—*and* in Donald's.

"Is that true?" Daisy asked Bertie.

Bertie nodded, looking ill. "Happened just after two this

morning, but we couldn't rouse a doctor until just now. We've left everything where it was—the police'll have to come and look at it."

Bertie has good reason to know about police. He had been as much a part of what happened at Fallingford as we were, and although he does his best to be cheerful and carefree about it, I know it shadows him just as it does us. Fallingford really was one of our worst cases. It is the one that I still wake up at night thinking about, and the one that Daisy and I barely ever discuss, even nine months later.

"Did you see the fall?" Daisy asked. She was going into detective mode, I could tell.

"I didn't see anything," Bertie said quickly. "I was in my rooms the whole time. Squashy, what *are* you doing here? Amanda, why did you bring them?"

Something about the way he had given his alibi worried me. It did not seem quite right—it was so vague. A worm of worry threaded its way through me, and from the way Daisy looked, I could tell she was having the same concern.

"I told you, I was telephoned," said Amanda. "Someone phoned our staircase in St. Lucy's to say that something had happened, and I took the call. I thought it was a prank at first, but I lay awake thinking about it, and then I decided I had to come and see. I had to bring the girls, too—I couldn't leave them on their own. I thought it might have been you, calling."

Bertie was looking bewildered. "I didn't call!" he said. "Butler called the doctor, and then I called the police, but that's all. Are you sure the person was from Maudlin?"

"Of course I'm not sure!" said Amanda. "Those lines are always so bad, you know how it is. But whoever it was said they were here, calling from the coinbox phone on staircase nine, and that something dreadful had happened."

I got a little chill. A phantom caller—it almost sounded like a ghost story.

"I'm surprised you came at all," said Donald. "Chummy said— I mean, aren't you avoiding us?"

Amanda flushed and stepped away from him. "I've been busy," she said.

"Lots of essays still to do?" asked Donald.

They stared at each other, and my skin prickled. Essays, again! What *was* going on?

"Wells is right," said Michael Butler. "I only telephoned the doctor. Moss, did *you* telephone Miss Price?" Moss shook his head wordlessly. "So it must have been Cheng. Here, Cheng! Come out of your rooms!"

I suddenly realized that the whole staircase was here, except one person—Alfred Cheng. His rooms were directly across from where Chummy had landed. Why was he not part of the group?

Then Alfred's door opened and he appeared, wearing a pair of gorgeous silk pajamas and an annoyed expression.

"What is it?" he asked.

"Did you telephone Miss Price?" asked Michael.

"*Tonight?* Why would I do that? Have you all lost your minds?" He scowled around at us.

"I can't believe you went back to bed," said Michael. "You really are a cool customer."

"We all have to sleep some time," said Alfred. "And what can I do? He'd already fallen."

"Cheng, Chummy is *dead*!"

"And you've never seen a dead man before?"

"*I* have," said Bertie. "That's why I care."

"My uncle was shot last year," said Alfred. "Shot in the street. Death happens all the time. Why should I bother about one more?"

It was a horridly cold thing to say, and it made me shudder. But then I remembered the argument we had seen between him and Chummy, how cruel Chummy had been, and I thought that perhaps I could understand why Alfred had gone back to his rooms, and why he was not sorry Chummy was dead.

The door to the room where Chummy had been taken opened again, and someone else came out, a doctor with glasses and close-cropped silver hair.

"Gone," he said briefly to Michael. "Nothing I could do. Too much blood lost. Even if I could have got here sooner—you said he fell just after two this morning—there would have been nothing to be done. A very unfortunate accident. You've called the police, yes? I do hate to distress you further, but they will need to look into the chain of events before I can allow the body to be moved, or sign the certificate."

"They've been called," said Michael. "The Master's asked if you'll go and speak to him, now that you're done—he's in his lodgings, just past the dons' gardens and the library. I can take you there, if you'd like. Donald, you'd best come as well, as next of kin. Wells, will you look after everything while I'm gone?"

Bertie nodded, and Michael led the doctor and Donald away down the stairs. Alfred withdrew back into his rooms, and Bertie, Daisy, Amanda, and I were left alone, staring at one another. There was so much I wanted to ask—so much I needed to know—but I could not see how to begin.

Then I caught sight of something. Moss the bedder had gone back up toward the top landing, and now he was kneeling down at the very top of the stairs, fiddling with something. It had to be the wire, I realized, the fishing wire that Chummy had tripped over.

"Daisy!" I said urgently. "Bertie!"

Bertie spun round jumpily and then gave a shout. "Moss! Don't touch that!" he cried.

"The wire can't be left!" said Moss. "What if someone else should trip over it?"

I was horrified, and from the intake of breath Daisy gave, she was too. Evidence was being destroyed before our very eyes! I imagined the fingerprints that might have been there before Moss had gone to work.

"They won't!" said Bertie, rushing up a few steps. "Do leave it, man, the police will need to see it to understand the accident. It'll only be a few more hours. Leave it, I say!"

"I only want to clear things away!" said Moss, rather sullenly.

I was suddenly very curious. I remembered Chummy's and Donald's rooms. They had both been ill-kept. Why should tidiness matter so much to Moss now?

"If I'd seen it before I went to bed last night, I'd have taken it down," he went on.

"What time *did* you go to bed?" asked Daisy quickly.

Moss blinked. "Half past twelve or thereabouts," he said. "All right! I'm leaving it." He stepped away, and I looked up and saw clearly what he had been working on. A thin, taut piece of wire was stretched across the top of the stairs. It was tied off against the upper banister on one side, and on the other was attached to a nail that had been driven into the skirting board. I moved a few steps up to stand by Bertie. From there, I could see that the nail looked new. I filed that away in my brain as something to consider.

"Bertie," Daisy whispered, coming up beside us. "That fishing wire. Have you seen something like it before?"

Bertie stared at her. "I . . . well. Promise you won't say this to anyone?"

We nodded.

"All right. It looks like a throw-line. Must be Chummy's. We've all got some just like it. Climbers use it to help chuck ropes up where they're needed."

"You're sure it's Chummy's?"

"Of course!" said Bertie. "Chummy set the prank, Squashy. He would have used his own line!"

But Daisy and I looked at each other. Chummy had certainly had fishing line, we had seen that—but so had Donald. We had been wrong about who would be the victim. What else might we have been wrong about?

I shall try the police station again," said Bertie. "Manda, you keep watch."

He clattered away downstairs, and we heard him telephone from the box outside his rooms. His voice rang up to us through the gap in the stairs.

"Someone's on their way? You're sure? Yes, I know what day it is—but my friend is *dead*. Come on, man!"

Poor Bertie! I thought. He was the sort of person who covered up his upset with anger.

It all seemed so unreal. So much activity, in the dead of night. Could it still really be Christmas Eve today?

But then the holiday part of me gave way to the detective. Someone was dead, right under our noses, and we were on the spot. This changed the case—it changed everything—but it was up to us to keep investigating it.

As always, I am very glad to have Daisy as my partner in crime. In an instant she had rounded on Amanda.

"What really happened? *Tell* me!"

Amanda started. "What do you mean?" she asked.

"I want to know why you woke us up!" said Daisy. "What are we doing here? What are *you* doing here?"

It was a very fair point.

"I couldn't leave you!" said Amanda, folding her arms and glaring.

"But we were asleep," I said slowly. "We would have been all right until later in the morning. And I didn't hear you answer the telephone. The St. Lucy's phone is set up just like this one, right in the middle of the staircase, but I didn't hear it ring, and I didn't hear you talking to anyone. I didn't hear anything at all until you knocked on the door and called to us."

Amanda looked flustered. "Of course you didn't!" she said. "*Our* telephone has a very quiet ring. I wouldn't have heard it either, except that my rooms are just next to it. I spoke quietly too."

"Hum," said Daisy. "So—you woke up, and answered the telephone. At what time?"

"At about half past two," said Amanda steadily.

"All right, so then you went back to bed, got up again at six, woke us up too, and brought us over here because you suddenly decided that the telephone call you received from a mysterious caller wasn't a prank after all?"

"Yes," said Amanda. "That's what happened. Do leave

me alone. It's— I'm tired. There's such a lot to do, and now Chummy's *dead*—" She broke off with a gulp, and I saw that tears were streaming down her face. Why was she suddenly so upset?

Bertie came clattering up the stairs again. "Manda!" he cried, when he saw Amanda's tears. "Squashy, stop upsetting people! The police should be here any minute. And then you all ought to *go*. You can't hang about. It's nothing to do with you!"

"It is!" said Amanda and Daisy together. They both stopped and stared at each other.

"I'm your sister," said Daisy.

"I'm your friend," said Amanda. "You can't be left on your own!"

"Of course I can!" cried Bertie. "I'm older than you, Squashy. I don't want you mixed up in this. *I* don't want to be mixed up in this. Why do you all have to be so meddling?"

Daisy and Amanda both looked very hurt.

Then there was a shout from down below. "Mr. Butler?" called Mr. Perkins. "Hello? The policeman is here!"

By now I thought I knew what a police investigation was: men in heavy greatcoats and hats, full of authority. But the policeman who climbed the staircase up to where we were waiting made me realize that I only really knew investigations led by Inspector Priestley, our policeman from Deepdean. This policeman was not an inspector at all, only a blue-coated bobby. He was bald and blue-eyed like a baby, his stomach straining out of his police jacket and his face flushed from the climb. He stared at us all and cleared his throat.

"PC Cross," he said. "Good morning. I hear there's been an accident. Who is in charge here?"

"Mr. Butler's gone to speak to the Master," said Bertie. "He'll be back soon. I'm Bertie Wells."

"Mr. Wells, good morning. And—what are you three doing here?" asked PC Cross, staring at Amanda, Daisy, and me doubtfully.

"The girls are all from St. Lucy's," said Bertie. "That's my sister, Daisy Wells, her friend Hazel Wong, and my friend Amanda Price."

"I was telephoned," said Amanda, as though that explained things.

"And it was a—Mr. Melling who fell down the stairs?" asked PC Cross. He sounded as though he was ticking off items in a list in his head. He did not seem very sure of himself.

"Yes," said Bertie shortly.

"Then I am here to investigate Mr. Melling's death," said PC Cross. "Tell me how it happened, if you could."

"It was an accident," said Bertie. "A stupid accident! He set up a bit of fishing line across the top of the stairs as a prank, and then fell over it himself."

"Was he in the habit of doing such things?" asked PC Cross.

"Yes," said Bertie. "He loved playing tricks on people—especially his brother, Donald. See here, can the girls go? They've nothing to do with this."

"In a moment," said PC Cross, holding up his hands. "I want to speak to everyone first—I want the fullest possible picture of what happened. Miss Price, explain to me about the telephone." He turned to Amanda and stared at her.

"Someone on this staircase telephoned me to say that there had been an accident," said Amanda. "That's why the three of us are here."

"Who was it?"

"I don't know, but they said they did it from the coinbox phone, downstairs," said Amanda. "I don't see why this is important!"

"Well—" PC Cross began, but at that moment there were voices from the archway downstairs. I could hear Michael Butler, and Donald, and another man. But I could also hear—

"Good grief!" said Bertie. "Whatever is Aunt E doing here?"

Feet came storming up the stairs, and then we were face to face with Aunt Eustacia. She was in a rage.

"There you are!" she cried, her chin jutting and her eyes looking as though they might bore holes straight through us all. "Price! I told you to look after them. And you have led them to the scene of a *death*!"

Behind her appeared a tall, rather bony-looking old man in a cap and gown. We had seen him at dinner on Sunday night, I realized—this was the Master of Maudlin. "Eustacia," he said, "I am so sorry. I had no idea there were *women* in the college."

"Apologies accepted, Master," said Aunt Eustacia. "Price, explain yourself immediately."

"I was telephoned," said Amanda doggedly. It seemed to be her answer to everything—and every time she said it, I thought even more what an odd story it was. "I decided it was best to keep them with me."

"Did you indeed!" cried Aunt Eustacia. "A most foolish decision, Price. Really, I expected better from you. I hope you feel quite ashamed of yourself."

"I'm sorry, Miss Mountfitchet," said Amanda, looking as though she wanted to cry again. "But I *was* called. I thought it might have been Bertie who was hurt, so I brought the two girls."

"We're quite all right, Aunt Eustacia," said Daisy. "Really we are! Don't worry about us."

Aunt Eustacia fixed her with a piercing gaze. "It is my job to worry about you, Daisy Wells," she said. "And it is your job to make sure that I have no cause for it. Now, I must ask you and Miss Wong to accompany me and Miss Price back to St. Lucy's at *once*."

"Aunt Eustacia!" cried Daisy. "Wait. I can't leave Bertie!"

"You most certainly *can*," said Aunt Eustacia.

"Miss Wells," said the Master. "You ought not to be here at all. This is a Maudlin matter. It is a Maudlin student who has died in the most terrible circumstances, and it is up to us to deal with the situation. I have been reliably informed, also, that Mr. Butler requested that you remove yourself from Maudlin College yesterday, and you have not yet been formally readmitted. Please leave at once. Officer, thank you for attending so quickly. I hope your investigation will not take long?"

"You are most welcome, Master," said PC Cross politely.

"It does seem straightforward, but there are certain things I want to understand. If I could just ask Miss Price—"

"I'm afraid Miss Price is coming back with me," said Aunt Eustacia. "She can have had nothing to do with the death. I wish you all the best in your search for the truth. Master, I bid you good morning."

She put one thin but firm hand on my shoulder and the other on Daisy's, got us both behind Amanda, and rushed all three of us down the staircase like a wave breaking. We were powerless to stop her, and so was PC Cross, although I saw his face as we left, and knew that he was still curious about Amanda. I could tell that he was very methodical, and I had the uncomfortable feeling that we would not be rid of him easily.

"Aunt Eustacia!" said Daisy. "Must we go back to St. Lucy's?"

"Most certainly!" said Aunt Eustacia. "Where else were you expecting to go, Daisy?"

Daisy was silent.

"Anyway, it is almost breakfast time," said Aunt Eustacia. "Change out of your night things, and then I expect to see you in the refectory, good as gold. Is that clear?"

"Yes, Aunt Eustacia," said Daisy politely. "Absolutely, Aunt Eustacia."

But as we crossed the bridge again she turned and winked at me, and I knew that Daisy's plans involved much more than breakfast.

What are you doing?" asked Amanda. We were in the refectory so early that water for tea was still being boiled and the toast was pale from being heated on a barely lit range.

"Making my final Christmas list, of course," said Daisy. "D'you want to see?"

As Daisy would say, people are beautifully predictable—give them the chance to see anything, and they lose interest in it at once.

"No fear," said Amanda. "You really want to go Christmas shopping again today?"

"It'll take our minds off things," said Daisy. "I'm sure Aunt Eustacia will approve. And it's the perfect cover for you to go and do some more on your essays."

"Done," said Amanda at once.

"Anyway," said Daisy. "The list. Do you mind?"

Amanda moved back to the other side of the refectory to

bury herself in the book she was reading, and Daisy immediately whispered in my ear, "As you may have realized, the list is only a cover! We must go out into Cambridge to see if we can find any more clues. But first we must have a detective meeting to discuss the important developments in the case. A *murder* has been committed. And it's not even the right victim!"

"I know!" I whispered back. "How could it be Chummy who died? It should have been Donald—he's the heir, and he was the one who was hurt in the other attempts. Unless—do you think it's true, what Bertie said? That Chummy set up the fishing line, and then tripped over it himself by mistake?"

"Well," said Daisy, "it is the most obvious explanation."

"And you think it's true?" I asked.

"No!" said Daisy. "Not for one moment. Who trips over their own trap? That would be idiotic, and Chummy did not seem like an utter idiot. But there's another, better reason why I don't think Chummy set up the fishing line."

"What is it?" I asked.

"We searched Chummy's rooms yesterday afternoon, and we went through his things. We saw that he had fishing line, just like the one used in the trap, but we also saw something else: that jacket of Donald's that he was sewing up. And that tells me something. Chummy *was* planning a prank yesterday—but one that was nothing to do with fishing line. The line itself was left quite carelessly at the bottom of his wardrobe, as though he was not planning to use it. The jacket was a joke designed to irritate Donald, but not designed to murder him—unlike the fishing line, which most certainly *was*. And here's something else: why would Chummy spend time sewing up the jacket if he had been planning on killing Donald that very evening? It's not logical." Daisy shook her head. "No, Hazel, I believe we can rule out the idea that Chummy set that trap—and *that* makes for a very interesting theory that has just occurred to me. We assumed, didn't we, that Chummy was behind both the silly pranks against Donald *and* the more serious attacks?"

I nodded.

"Well, what if Chummy *was* playing the silly pranks, but was *not* the attacker? What if someone was using his pranks as cover for their more dangerous attempts—the ice bucket, the poisoned port, the pond, and finally the fishing-line trap? If so, there are two possibilities. Either Donald was behind those attacks but allowed himself to be caught in his *own* traps to throw everyone off the scent until his final attack on Chummy last night—this is unlikely, but not impossible. Or else there is a third party, someone else on the staircase, who is both cunning and ruthless, and who was determined to get Chummy, no matter who else was hurt accidentally along the way. Witness what happened to Donald."

"You think that *Chummy* could have been the target all

along?" I asked. "Even though Donald was the one who fell foul of all the pranks up to now? Even though Donald is the rich one?"

"Well, he isn't rich yet," said Daisy. "And even so, no one else apart from Chummy would stand to get any money if he died. Chummy, on the other hand—well, you've seen it. Chummy might have been popular throughout Cambridge, but most of staircase nine hated him. His own brother most of all."

"We did find fishing line in Donald's rooms as well as Chummy's!" I said. "He could have set the trap. But . . . what if it *was* one of the others?"

"D'you know, it's interesting," said Daisy. "Think of all those previous attempts—not the pranks, I mean. Apart from the door incident, Donald wasn't alone for any of them, was he? Bertie, Chummy, Alfred, and Donald were climbing together when the rock fell, and we were all at the party where they drank the mistletoe. Lots of people were in the quad when Donald fell in the pond, as well. We thought it was most likely that the attempts were made by Chummy against Donald, but now Chummy is dead, I think we have to realize that we were looking at the case wrong all along. Yes, Hazel—I think we must accept that Chummy was always the target. And the attacker finally got the correct victim last night!"

I thought about what she'd said: how several people had been present for so many of the attacks. "It could be anyone in the college then!" I said. "Anyone in Cambridge!"

"That's not true," said Daisy. "Some of the other attempts, yes. But because they've carried on into the holidays, we know that it must be someone at Maudlin, now, this Christmas. And last night narrows things down very tightly indeed. We know from our run-ins with Perkins that he guards the entrance to Maudlin carefully, and locks up the main gate at eleven at night, and we also know that's when Michael Butler locks the door to staircase nine. We heard the doctor mention that Chummy fell just after two o'clock. Let's say five minutes after two. If Moss is telling the truth about when he went to bed, we know that the trap was set after twelve thirty, which means that the only people who could have set it between twelve thirty and two were the people who live on staircase nine. So—Donald, Alfred, Michael, Moss—and, I suppose, Perkins, because he has the keys to the college."

"And Bertie," I said.

"Hazel!"

"I know he wouldn't do it!" I said. "Of course he wouldn't. But we still have to rule him out."

Daisy glared at me. "Really, Hazel," she said. "How could you even think it?"

But I heard from the tone of her voice that she was concerned as well. It was not a long list to put Bertie on—and he had acted oddly when we'd asked where he had been last night. Why?

"To go on to the *better* suspects," said Daisy, glaring at me, "Donald is of course a very strong one. He hated Chummy and, more importantly, he was quite controlled by him. You heard their conversations about the party. Donald was afraid that Chummy would bully him into giving over his money—we know that he *wanted* to buy the mine, but who knows whether he would have been able to go through with it with Chummy still alive? We saw that he had fishing line in his rooms, and he has been present for all the pranks. As we've already said, it could be that becoming the victim of them was just a cover, to make it seem as though he could have nothing to do with them. After all, he did survive them!"

I thought about Donald struggling in the pond, and was not sure. It did seem a terrible gamble.

"Alfred hated Chummy too," I said. "Chummy was horrid to him because he's not English, and Alfred might have wanted to punish him for it because Michael Butler wouldn't. He's a climber, so he's probably got fishing line as well, and he's been there for all the pranks."

"Yes. And Alfred behaved suspiciously after Chummy's fall. Michael had to call him back out of his rooms. Why should he step away from the scene like that, unless he had something to hide?"

"What about Moss?" I asked. I felt the detective side of my brain ticking. "His room's on the top floor, next to Donald and Chummy's. He was on the spot!"

"His motive is less obvious at first examination, but we did see him act suspiciously. He was trying to destroy evidence!" Daisy said. "Yes, Moss jumped into my head at once. And Michael Butler, too—no motive yet, but he was there. And although he's not a climber, he has access to everyone's rooms. He might have been able to borrow some fishing line from someone without them noticing. We can't rule him out! Do we have anything else to mention?"

"Perkins," I said. "He doesn't seem likely, but he would have had keys—we need to rule him out at least. And we know that Amanda can't have done the murder. She wasn't on staircase nine last night. But . . . wasn't it strange, the story she told? It doesn't fit. I didn't hear a call, did you? And no one here's admitting to calling her."

I glanced over at Amanda to make sure she was not

listening. But she was safely lost in her book. I had been worrying about the story of the call since Amanda first mentioned it. So many things were *wrong* about it. Amanda was clever. Why would she not question the caller and ask who it was, or call the operator back to discover whether the call really had come from Maudlin?

"Oh, absolutely, Hazel!" said Daisy. "I smell a rat as well! Why would anyone on staircase nine apart from Bertie want Amanda on the scene, anyway? Or—"

"Or was she just lying?" I finished for her.

Daisy nodded. "Or *was* she just lying? After all, we didn't hear her answer a call! Hazel, I think you need to add her to the suspect list. Something's going on with her that we must uncover. And why was she suddenly upset Chummy was dead? She never liked him beforehand." She smiled grimly. "I do believe we're nearly done. We have our list of suspicious persons. Now all we need to decide is how we go about detecting. There are some leads we can follow in Cambridge itself—the fishing line, for example—but what we really need to do is get back inside Maudlin. But how? We've only just been warned away, by the Master no less."

"I think I've got an idea," I said slowly. "I'll write up our suspect list . . . but then we need to go and see the Junior Pinkertons."

SUSPECT LIST

1. Bertie Wells. MOTIVE: Unknown. OPPORTUNITY: He lives on staircase nine, and he was there at the time the prank must have been set. ALIBI: Says he was in his rooms. Is this true? NOTES: He is a Maudlin student and a climber, and had opportunity to commit all the previous pranks.

2. Donald Melling. MOTIVE: He is Chummy's older brother, but was very controlled by him. Now that Chummy is dead, he will still inherit the money on his birthday, but be able to dispose of it however he likes. OPPORTUNITY: He lives on staircase nine, and he was there at the time the prank must have been set. We found fishing line in his rooms. ALIBI: None yet. NOTES: He is a Maudlin student and a climber, and had opportunity to commit all the previous pranks-although he seemed to be the victim of them. Was this just a clever ruse?

3. Alfred Cheng. MOTIVE: He hated Chummy, and was overheard saying he wanted to punish him. OPPORTUNITY: He was on staircase nine on the night of the murder. ALIBI: None yet. NOTES: He is a

Maudlin student and a climber and had opportunity to commit all the previous pranks. Suspicious behavior observed. He went back into his rooms after Chummy's fall. Why?

4. Michael Butler. MOTIVE: None yet. OPPORTUNITY: He lives on staircase nine, and was there on the night of the murder. ALIBI: None yet. NOTES: He is part of Maudlin. He could possibly have staged the door, the mistletoe, and the pond, though not the climbing accident. Not a climber, though he could have taken the fishing line from someone else's rooms.

5. Moss. MOTIVE: None yet. OPPORTUNITY: Was on staircase nine on the night of the murder. ALIBI: He says he went to bed at 12:30, when the trap was not yet set. Is this true? NOTES: Not a climber, though he could have taken the fishing line from someone else's rooms. Was seen trying to destroy evidence.

6. Mr. Perkins. MOTIVE: None yet. OPPORTUNITY: Lives in Maudlin, though not on staircase nine–he has keys, though. ALIBI: None yet. NOTES: Could he really have set all the previous traps? Seems very unlikely. We must rule him out.

7. Amanda Price. Was not on staircase nine on the night of the murder, but says she was telephoned in the middle of the night. Is this true-and if not, why would she lie?

Part Four
Cocoa and Criminology

I

There were carolers singing beside King's College Chapel as we passed, their breath smoking with the song. Christmas was everywhere—in the bright shop windows, in the parcels done up with string, the Christmas trees and boughs of holly, the sides of ham and poor drooping geese being carried home on shoulders and bicycles by bright-cheeked passers-by. I felt full of secrets and nerves as we pushed through the crowds. It all seemed so bright and exciting, but something dreadful and mysterious had happened only a few streets away. Would we be able to solve the case?

Amanda had come out of St. Lucy's with us, pretending that she was chaperoning us before peeling away to go . . . wherever it was she went, to write her essays. We were left to our own devices.

A man and a woman bickered over a long list, and a little girl dragged on her mother's hand. "Elsie, if you carry on like this, Father Christmas won't give you any presents!" cried the woman crossly. "Really! It's Christmas Eve! You shouldn't be so naughty!"

"I don't know why people behave as though Christmas is happy," said Daisy to me as we passed them. "Really, it's the most dreadful time of the year for families." I glanced at her, wondering whether this was her way of telling me that she was still worried about Bertie being a suspect. But she looked away at the carolers, and would not meet my eye.

Perhaps it was only that she was still unsure about working with the Junior Pinkertons. Daisy had been very reluctant to agree to my plan. "But we're so far ahead!" she said. "We can't work *together*, Hazel, not after we've been there at the scene of the crime, and discovered so many important pieces of evidence! If we carry on, we'll be able to prove that we really are the best society! Have you forgotten that we have a bet?"

"We *had* a bet, but now Chummy's dead, everything's changed. The case is more important. We're investigating a murder and we *need* them, Daisy. We can't get back into Maudlin, at least not immediately. But the boys will be less conspicuous. They can creep in and look around while we're following leads outside the college."

"I am a perfect spy. I *always* blend in," muttered Daisy, but I could tell that she did see my point. "I could get in, I know it! Oh, bother it, all *right*. But I insist on still being in charge of the investigation!"

"Of course," I said. Privately, I was not at all sure that George would agree to that, but I decided that we would deal with the problem later. The first order of business was to get Daisy to St. John's College.

It was just past ten in the morning when we stood outside St. John's porter's lodge. We looked at each other, and then Daisy knocked. A porter opened the door—not moustachioed Mr. Perkins, but a skinny old man with a large beard, wearing a bowler hat.

"May I help you?" he asked.

"We'd like to see Mr. Mukherjee and Mr. Arcady," said Daisy. "Mr. Mukherjee the younger, I mean."

"What do you want with them?" asked the porter suspiciously.

"We'd like to wish them Merry Christmas, of course," said Daisy. "We've got a Christmas card for them."

"Humph," said the porter, and he withdrew with a snap of the door.

I was not sure whether he would take our message, but five minutes later the door opened again and Alexander and George tumbled out.

They both looked as though they had dressed hastily, but while Alexander's shirt collar was askew and his hair was chaos, George was immaculate. He had something like Daisy's talent for wearing clothes—he looked so proper, I almost did not notice the color of his skin. I saw that it was a trick he had taught himself to fit in, just as I had learned to appear carefree at Deepdean. He glanced between us curiously, while next to him Alexander yawned and smiled. I thought he was smiling at me, until I saw his eyes shift to Daisy and his smile grow. I looked down at my feet.

"You've got something for us?" asked Alexander.

"Have you got new information about the case?" said George. "That porter's watching, by the way."

"Hold out your hands and look pleased," said Daisy. She took a folded card out of her pocket and put it into George's waiting hands.

We had found it in a shop along the way. On the front of the card was a picture of two cats pulling a Christmas cracker. Daisy had laughed until she cried when she saw it. "Funny!" she had finally gasped. "Because cats don't have opposable thumbs, you see!" I was not sure I quite saw the joke, but it was perfect for our purposes. We bought it, and inside it I wrote:

Chummy is dead! This is now a murder case! We need your help. (Merry Christmas.)

George opened it, read my message, and looked up in horror.

"Are you sure?" he asked.

"Perfectly," said Daisy. "We were at Maudlin this morning. We are now investigating Chummy's murder."

Wait!" said Alexander. "*Chummy* died? But—"

"I know," I said. "We thought it would be Donald as well. We didn't expect what happened, but it's true."

"Did you see the body?" asked George. "Are you sure it was murder?"

"No," said Daisy, sighing. "Only the blood. We always do have the worst luck, with bodies. They're forever disappearing on us. But yes, we think it has to be murder. Chummy wouldn't have set a trap and tripped over it, and that means someone else did—someone with murderous intent."

"I think we ought to go somewhere else to talk," said Alexander. "The porter's glaring. Come on, there's a tea room just down the road." He motioned with his arms, rather hectically. I could tell that news of the murder had upset him. As we began to walk, he came over to me. "Hazel!" he said. "It's really true?"

I nodded. "We wouldn't make it up!" I said.

"I know," said Alexander. "I do believe you. But—*golly*. It's just like the Orient Express all over again. I don't really count the Bonfire Night business, as we weren't there. But this—*another* murder! It's awful."

"At least you're on the spot this time," I said, glancing up at him. "I mean, to help us properly. Now that it's murder, the bet has to be off. We've got to work together."

Alexander nodded seriously. "You're quite right," he said. "What does Daisy think?"

"She agrees," I said, the words coming out a little more sharply than I had meant them to. "We know we can't solve the case without you. We've been banned from Maudlin now by the Master himself."

"No!" said Alexander. "Really?"

I found myself telling him the whole story of everything that had happened so far this morning. It was so easy to talk to Alexander—he laughed, or gasped, in all the right places, and I heard myself chattering away like Daisy herself. I knew I ought to wait until we had sat down, but it was so nice to speak to him properly at last.

We went into the tea room, and were led to a corner table.

"Honestly, Hazel, you were supposed to wait!" said Daisy once we had sat down. "Although I did tell George everything while you were explaining to Alexander, so I suppose we can move straight on to the important thing, which is this: Chummy Melling is dead, and so the Junior Pinkertons must help the Detective Society get to the solution."

It was a typically Daisy way of putting things.

"What Daisy means is that we need to work together!" I said to George. "We can't get into the college on our own at the moment, but *you* could, and you could report back to us. You see, all our suspects are there. The murderer *has* to be someone who was on staircase nine last night, when the trap was set!"

"I suppose the bet does have to be off," said George. "And just as things were getting interesting! But look—what'll you do while we're at Maudlin? If we agree we're working together, you've got to really do it. You can't just borrow us for the morning, find out what we've discovered, and then not share what *you've* learned with *us*."

"Of course we won't!" said Daisy, as though that was not what she had been trying to persuade me to do only an hour before. "If you go to Maudlin for us, and help us get in too, we'll tell you everything we already know. We saw the scene of the crime this morning, and yesterday afternoon we found several crucial clues which help prove that Chummy did not set last night's trap . . . and that he was the intended victim all along."

George considered. "Shake on it?" he asked.

We all four shook. It felt very solemn, but at the same time very exciting. There had been two of us—now there were four. I thought at that moment, looking around at George's serious face, and Alexander's eager one, and determined Daisy, that the murderer hardly stood a chance.

"So, what's your evidence?" asked Alexander, after we had given the maid our orders: cake and cocoa all round, for such a cold morning. "What makes you so sure we were all wrong about Chummy and Donald?"

"We went into Chummy's rooms yesterday and saw that he was getting ready to play a silly sewn-up-jacket prank on Donald—nothing serious. We think that Chummy was behind all the harmless pranks, but not the dangerous ones. Those must have been set by someone else, either Donald, who had fishing line in his rooms, and who could have been trying to make it look as though he was a target, or another person on staircase nine. We think Chummy was the victim all along. The injuries to Donald were either mistakes, or just clever blinds by Donald himself. Do you see?"

"I think I do," said George, narrowing his eyes thoughtfully. "Lots of people hated Chummy. Donald, of course, but also Alfred—and Moss."

"Moss?" I asked.

"Moss used to work for Chummy and Donald's parents," said George. "We found out on Sunday—Mr. Perkins told us. Moss thought it was unfair that their parents had always preferred Chummy, even when they were very small boys. Apparently they tried to break the entail, but had no luck.

Because of that, Moss made Donald his favorite. He's always been Donald's ally, and he came to Maudlin because he knew Donald was going to be a student there along with Chummy. He's been telling all the other staff about how controlling Chummy is, and how he wished that Donald could get out from his shadow."

This was extremely interesting. I looked at Daisy.

"What did Perkins himself think of Chummy?" asked Daisy. "He did have keys to staircase nine, after all—he was another person who could have set that trap!"

"Didn't like him," said Alexander. "Thought he was arrogant. It's funny. Everyone who works at Maudlin feels the same way. Butler thought Chummy was a pill too." Alexander sounded very American for a moment. "He was bored of being dragged into arguments between Alfred and Chummy. And Chummy would set up parties, and hold them in Donald's rooms—they'd go on for hours, and then everyone would try to sneak away down the drainpipe, after Michael'd locked up the staircase. It drove him mad."

"What about Bertie?" I asked. I saw Daisy's face, but I had to go on. "We need to rule him out, at least! I know they were friends so it isn't very likely at all."

Alexander and George looked at each other awkwardly.

"What?" asked Daisy. "What is it?"

"What did Bertie tell you about where he was last night?" asked George.

"He told us he was in his rooms the whole time," said Daisy. "Why? What do you know?"

George and Alexander glanced at each other again. Then George took a deep breath.

"All right," he said. "Bertie wasn't telling the truth."

"What do you mean?" asked Daisy.

Her composure had slipped. She looked quite frantic. I suddenly felt the true force of her worry about Bertie, and I wished she had been able to tell me. But, as I know quite well by now, that is not the way Daisy works.

"Promise you won't be upset?" asked Alexander, looking at us both nervously.

"I shall be upset if you don't *tell* me!" said Daisy.

"I promise," I said. Daisy narrowed her eyes at me.

"Okay," said Alexander. "What time did Moss say he went to bed?"

"At twelve thirty," said Daisy. "The trap can't have been set before then, unless he did it and is lying. And Chummy fell down the stairs at about five after two."

"If Moss did it, then Bertie's innocent anyway," said Alexander. "And if he's telling the truth—why, Bertie's innocent for sure. See, Bertie was with us from twelve fifteen until two fifteen last night."

"*What?*" said Daisy. She put her cup of cocoa down very hard on its saucer. I swallowed my bite of seed cake the wrong way, and coughed.

"He told us not to tell you," said Alexander. "I'm sorry—I shouldn't have said anything, really. But if it's a case of proving he didn't do a murder . . ."

"But how could you be with him?" asked Daisy. "The porter locks the gates at eleven o'clock, and Perkins would have noticed if Bertie had come back to college later than that. And he was on the staircase at six this morning, when we arrived!"

"We all went climbing," explained George. "Harold had promised to take the two of us, and he invited Bertie along as well over dinner last night. So Bertie went back to Maudlin before the eleven o'clock curfew, and then he slipped out of his rooms, down the drainpipe, and over the dons' garden wall—that's how all the climbers get in and out. We met him by John's gates at twelve fifteen. We climbed Senate House—it's an easy route, and they led us up. We climbed down at two fifteen. That's when Bertie left us to go back to Maudlin, and that's when we went back to our rooms."

"That's why we're both so tired this morning," explained Alexander.

Daisy was gasping. "But what about *us?*" she cried. "Why weren't we invited?"

"I'm sorry Bertie didn't invite you two. I was hoping you'd turn up with him last night," said Alexander.

I felt myself smiling at him. He sounded so sincere. "At least we've ruled out a suspect!" I said, trying to keep thinking like a detective. "Come on, Daisy, it isn't so bad."

"Isn't so bad! Just because you don't want to climb! Bother Bertie! I shall have *words* with him next time I see him. How dare he! And how dare he frighten me like that! But you're right, Hazel. This rules him out for good. That leaves us with five real suspects: the four other people who were on staircase nine last night—Donald, Alfred, Michael, and Moss—and Mr. Perkins as well."

George nodded. "Correct. Those are our five too. So we'll go to Maudlin and begin the interviews. What about you?"

"We'll follow the lead of the fishing line," said Daisy. "If it's from a shop in Cambridge, the shopkeeper may remember which of our suspects bought line like it."

"But what if they all bought some?" asked George. "We already know there was some in Chummy's rooms as well as Donald's."

"Then we shall have to think again," said Daisy severely.

They were bouncing off each other in a way that I had never seen Daisy do with anyone but me. Last term Daisy had hated the fact that I was writing to Alexander, that I had another close friend, other than her. Now here she was with a new friend of her own. It was so odd to see. I always thought she was unchangeable, but here she was changing in front of my eyes.

"We ought to write down the things we need to find," I said. "Where the fishing line came from, for example. *And* what really happened with Amanda and the telephone call. We know she can't be a suspect, but we think she might have something to do with what happened."

"Yes," said George, nodding, as Daisy shot me a cross glare. I knew she felt that giving away our lead about Amanda was rather traitorous. "We should add Amanda Price to our list to investigate. You two can question her while we go to Maudlin." He paused thoughtfully. "We also need to make a map of the crime scene so we can recreate the crime."

"And find some more clues and alibis," said Daisy, cheering up again. "This sounds almost like a treasure hunt, doesn't it? Funny! Hazel, write all those down—you might as well call it 'treasure hunt,' so if we're caught with it we can say that we were just playing a game. Alexander, you as well—then we all have copies."

"This isn't a game, Daisy!" I protested. "It's a *murder*."

"There are games all the way through this case," said Daisy. "It began with a prank, and even the murder has been disguised as a joke gone wrong. I think that a game is perfectly in keeping with the situation. Don't be po-faced, Hazel. Anyway, to the adults we are still nothing but children, too young and silly to properly understand what has happened."

I took out this casebook, and Alexander took out his, and we tore out two pages. On each of them we wrote the same list.

We all put down money on the table for the tea maid. "Ready?" asked Daisy. "Three . . . two . . . one . . . detective societies, GO!"

And the game was afoot.

TREASURE HUNT

- Follow the clue of the fishing line
- Uncover the truth behind Amanda's phone call
- Make a map of the crime scene
- Recreate the crime
- Find more clues
- Rule out some suspects using alibis

Daisy seized my hand, and the moment we touched, all my fears disappeared. We went rushing out of the door and into the street, giddy and spinning, and there was no one and nothing else in the world.

"Where are we going?" I gasped.

"We," said Daisy, "are going shopping again!"

"But, Daisy—"

"Shopping for *fishing line*, Hazel. It's the perfect Christmas present."

I beamed at her. This was typical Daisy cleverness—twisty at first, but quite obvious as soon as you thought about it properly.

We wound through the little back streets of Cambridge, and I suddenly noticed that the clouds above us were hanging heavily in the sky. It was getting very gloomy, and there was a bite to the air, as though I might be able to snap it just by putting out my hands. I wondered if it might begin to snow soon.

We went past a butcher's and a grocer's and a chemist's, and at last we tumbled into a little fishing-tackle shop, its walls studded with brightly colored lures that almost looked like Christmas decorations themselves. The shop owner was balding, huddled in a raincoat that smelled strongly of oil, but he responded very well to Daisy's string of bright, silly questions. Yes, miss, that was their most popular line, especially among the students. Must be a craze for fishing—funny what young people got up to these days. Which students? Oh, he couldn't say. Such a lot of 'em come in. A short man with brown hair and a snub nose, wearing a loud jacket? Why, that could describe half the men he saw! But a Chinese man? Why, yes, now you come to mention it, he was in a couple of times. And old men? Oh, even more popular with them than the students! Yes, the Maudlin livery sounded familiar, but he made a point not to ask for names. Now, would you like to purchase some of that line, miss? Excellent, excellent.

We came out of the store with a roll of fishing line and an interesting piece of information. Whether or not Moss, Donald, Perkins, or Michael had bought fishing line, Alfred Cheng certainly had. We had our first clue that pointed toward one of our remaining suspects.

Daisy sighed happily. "I know I said what an annoyance it is to be a girl, but at the same time it's delightful to be underestimated sometimes," she said. "It is so *easy* to get things out of old men!"

Down the road we walked—and that was when something happened that felt rather like a Christmas miracle. I was looking into shop windows as we passed, enjoying the light and bustle of them, the tinsel and baubles hanging in the windows. I peered into a little tea-shop window, its glass half smoked over with the warmth from the tea and buns.

But I could still just see in, and there, sitting with her back to the window, was someone with fluffy, fly-away hair that I knew very well.

"Daisy!" I cried, just as Daisy nudged me and said, "Look!"

She was not pointing into the tea shop, but instead at a rusty, green-painted bicycle propped up outside the shop door. "It's the Horse!" said Daisy.

"And Amanda's inside!" I said. "That's what I was going to tell you! Should we go in?"

"Of course!" said Daisy. "Is that a question at all, Watson? We've agreed that there is something suspicious about Amanda's behavior, and we know that we need to uncover the truth about that phone call. If we go and confront her without warning, she may give away crucial information that she has hidden until now. Are you ready?"

"Ready," I said, nodding at her, and together we burst into the tea rooms.

As we stood in the doorway, I had a moment where time came unstuck. It was last year, and it was Miss Tennyson looking up at us in horror from her table in the Willow. But then I blinked, and we were back in Cambridge. The case that faced us this time was quite different—and so was our suspect. Amanda did not even look round, so intent was she on what she was writing. We had the chance to go all the way up to her and stand one on either side of her chair, her outdoor coat draped across it, to peer down at the paper in front of her.

It was a History essay, boldly handwritten. *George III*, I saw, and *rebels, led by*. But the thing that shocked me was not the words at all, but the hand they were written in. I had seen this writing before, I realized, twice: in Chummy's rooms, and then in Donald's. I had noticed the similarity before, but I had simply thought that their handwriting was so similar because they were twins. But if this was *Amanda's* handwriting . . . we had the answer to the question of why she was so busy with essays. She was not just writing them for herself.

"You're writing their essays!" exclaimed Daisy, and Amanda jumped, splashing black ink across her page. She cursed, and blotted.

"What are you doing here?" she cried. "Why aren't you—? Go away, can't you? I'm writing!"

"We won't go away until you tell us what you're doing," said Daisy. "I don't think it looks very legal at all. Bertie said you were giving him lecture notes, but he didn't say you were writing Chummy's and Donald's essays for them as well!"

Amanda glared. "They pay," she said. "I need the money. And I can do it all—I've managed so far, haven't I?"

"Have you?" I asked. I looked at her, and thought that she did not look as though she was managing in the slightest.

"I'm the cleverest in my year," said Amanda. "Not that the dons acknowledge it. D'you know that the last essay I did for Chummy got ten points more than mine? I wrote both of them, but he's a man, so his must be better."

"You didn't write any essays for Bertie, did you?" Daisy asked.

Amanda turned red. "Not for money," she said. "He's my friend."

I suddenly understood at least part of the exchange we had seen between Bertie and Chummy—they were both in on the essay-writing trick. I also saw what I ought to have realized all along: that Amanda's feelings for Bertie were not just a pash. She lit up for him in a way that I recognized.

"Oh, bother Bertie!" cried Daisy. "Getting himself mixed up in something else illegal! He really has acted dreadfully this term. I can't think what's got into him! But, listen, you mustn't write any more essays. Not for him, not for anyone. You'll be sent down for it, and so will they!"

"I may be sent down anyway," said Amanda. "Bertie told me at the beginning of the holidays that someone at Maudlin's worked out that the boys have been buying essays and notes from me. Chummy went into his rooms after dinner one night and there were papers and books missing—lots of the things I'd done for him. He was sure that someone had found out what was going on, but he didn't know who. That's why I've been steering clear of the college recently. Bertie thought it was for the best, until Chummy had dealt with it. Anyway, I know I ought to stop, but I've got to keep going now I've started. Bertie needs me to!"

I was terribly worried. I wanted to help Amanda, but I did not know how to. She was so angry, and so in pain. It made me hurt just to be near her.

Then Daisy nudged me. She was looking at Amanda's

coat. I stared at it, confused. It did not look very extraordinary. I could see rust and bits of paint from the Horse, ink stains on the cuffs and pockets—she really had been working hard on her essays—mud on the hem, and specks of red dust on the front.

"Can't you go away?" asked Amanda. "Really, it's too much! And if you dare tell anyone what you know, I'll tell Miss Mountfitchet that you've been going around Cambridge on your own, all right?" She glared at us.

"All right!" said Daisy. "We'll leave you alone. But, look—I'm going to have it out with Bertie. This can't go on. I don't care what you say: you've got to stop. He's got to learn to stand on his own two feet. Come on, Hazel! Let's go."

"What did you notice?" I asked, as soon as we were out of the tea room.

"The mud and the dust," said Daisy, leading me back down the street in a rush. "The mud was very fresh, barely flaking, and it was only on the hem. And the dust—I'm sure it was brick dust."

"So?" I said. "There are brick buildings all over Cambridge. St. Lucy's is made of brick. Amanda might have leaned against it anywhere."

"Yes, but, Hazel, you know as well as I do (or you would, if you paid attention) that *new* brick doesn't flake like that. No, it must have been from an *old* brick building. And, more importantly—"

But she never finished her sentence. We came down a passageway to a wide-open market space, full of stalls. Some were billowing with the most lovely food smells, while others were piled high with jewel-like jams and hats and balls of yarn. There was a great heap of Christmas trees in one corner of the square, and standing in front of them, a rather puzzled look on his face, was Bertie.

Daisy let out a hiss of rage, and went storming toward him. I followed behind her as quickly as I could.

"I say," Bertie was asking the stallholder as we arrived, "do you have a sort of—small-room-sized one? These are all awfully large. And do you sell baubles and tinsel? You know—things to, er, dress it? My sister, she needs—" He broke off as he saw us, and his cheeks went rather red. "Squashy!" he said. "Hazel! What are you doing here? You've spoiled the surprise! I was looking for a Christmas tree. Funny, you never think about where they come from, do you? Chapman always organized it. But I thought that as it was just, well, us this year . . . we ought to have a tree."

"I can cut this one down to the right size," said the stallholder, his breath misting out white, "but you'll have to buy baubles elsewhere. They sell 'em in Woolworths, sir, quite cheaply."

"Oh!" said Bertie.

"Bertie," snapped Daisy. "I want *words* with you."

"Goodness me, be careful, sir!" laughed the Christmas-tree seller—and then he faltered and stopped as he took in Daisy's face properly.

"Come over here," said Bertie, and he guided us away to the center of the square. "What's up?"

"*You lied to us!*" hissed Daisy. "You didn't tell us that you were out of your rooms last night climbing buildings with Harold and George and Alexander! You didn't take us with you!"

"Of course I couldn't take you with me! Girls don't climb!" snapped Bertie. I backed away as quietly as I could. This was one conversation that I did not want to be part of.

"I am not a *girl*!" cried Daisy. "I am your *sister*! And you are an idiot. How long have you been getting all your lecture notes from Amanda? Did she write essays for you, too?"

Bertie went white. "I'll have you know that Manda offered to do it," he said.

"But you knew it was wrong of her! You must have! Bertie, what's *happened* to you this term? You're . . . not doing credit to Fallingford. You've got to start looking after yourself properly!"

"Don't talk to me about Fallingford!" cried Bertie. "What happened there—well, everything changed. It's just the two of us now, and I'm trying to make a proper Christmas for you. And now my friend's died. I think we're cursed. I think *I'm* cursed, Squashy." His face crumpled. "I came back some time after two this morning. I thought I'd been caught: all the lights were on, and there were people running up and down the staircase. I came out of my rooms, hands up—and found that Chummy was *dead*. I don't think anyone even noticed I'd been gone."

"Oh, Squinty, you fool," said Daisy. "Here, come on—" And she reached up and pulled him into a hug. It made me see how much they cared for each other, despite everything. Their family had shrunk, and shrunk again, and these days, I knew, it really was just the two of them. I realized too how achingly glad I was that Bertie had nothing to do with the murder. Daisy's family have rather become mine, in England, and what matters to her now matters to me, as though we are two halves of the same person.

"We'll still have Christmas, you ass," said Daisy to Bertie, muffled in his coat. "Come on, pay for that tree of yours, and we'll take it to Maudlin and help set it up."

"Hazel, this is perfect!" she whispered to me, as Bertie made his way back to the Christmas-tree stall. "Bother the Master's ban. We have a way back into Maudlin after all!"

Part Five

Deck the Halls

I

The stallholder helped Bertie strap the Christmas tree to his bicycle, and together we wheeled it through the streets of Cambridge, stopping at Woolworths for tinsel and baubles. The sky was gloomier than ever, and as we passed King's College Chapel something tickled my nose. I looked up to see that little dark specks were falling from the clouds, turning feathery and white as they drifted past the tops of the buildings.

"It's snowing!" I said in delight. Real, proper snow is still so alien to me. The first time I saw it I felt that I really had stepped into a storybook, and I never can quite get rid of that burst of wonder in my chest.

"What a bother!" said Bertie, panting rather, the bicycle wobbling dangerously as it turned a corner. "Golly, isn't this tree spiky? I never knew."

As we approached Maudlin, I felt butterflies in my stomach. Would we really be allowed back in? What if the Master stopped us? But Bertie strode up to the porter's lodge door and pushed it open, shouting, "Hoy! Any fellows about to give a hand?"

"Us!" cried someone I knew very well, and out of the lodge doors came George and Alexander.

"Hello!" said Alexander in delight. "Daisy! Hazel! We've got—" He paused and stared at Bertie.

"—things to say later," said George, coming up behind him and winking at us.

They picked up one end of the tree, and with Bertie went staggering through the door into the Maudlin porter's lodge like a six-legged beetle. Daisy and I followed along. Bertie and George both had very definite ideas about how best to carry the tree, and they both shouted orders at Alexander, who laughed good-naturedly and did most of the lifting.

As we all passed the porter's cubby, Mr. Perkins said, "Hey! You shouldn't be here!"

"Let them, Perkins!" cried Bertie. "*Please*. I know what the Master said, but it's Christmas Eve!"

He looked so tragic that Perkins tutted, and his moustache trembled. "Oh, very well," he said. "But mind, don't let them out of your sight!" We were allowed past his post. My heart was beating hard in my chest.

Left we went, along the length of the quad. Snowflakes settled on the dark green spikes of the tree, and on the shoulders and heads of the boys. They were not shouting anymore. The subdued atmosphere of Maudlin had settled on us all along with the snow. This was a place where a murder had taken place, and I felt it.

"Staircase nine!" gasped Bertie. "Come on, up the stairs!"

As we passed Michael Butler's door at the bottom of the staircase, I tensed. I knew that if he came out, he would stop us. Then the door opened and Daisy and I ducked behind the tree.

"Excellent idea, Wells," said Michael's voice. "Managing?"

"The boys are helping," said Bertie.

"Let me know if you need anything," said Michael, and then he retreated back into his rooms, and the door closed. I breathed out. The Pinkertons had done what we asked—with Bertie's help, they had got us into Maudlin.

The boys panted upstairs, sprays of pine needles bouncing down to scatter against my coat and burrow their way down past my scarf to the neck of my jumper.

Daisy rushed ahead and pushed open the door, and we all surged in. The boys leaned the tree against the far right-hand wall, and Bertie clicked on the electric light. I looked around his sitting room. It was just like Chummy's: a fireplace in front of me, a desk to its right, a window that looked out onto the quad we had just come from, and another to the left of the fireplace that looked out over the dons' garden. A sofa and a chair were arranged around the fireplace, with a table under the window, and far to the left was another door, slightly ajar—I could see a bed and a basin, and clothes draped across the floor. The whole place was untidy: there were scarves and socks and cravats scattered everywhere, just like Chummy's rooms.

"You're untidier than ever!" exclaimed Daisy. "Bertie!"

"Oh, quiet!" said Bertie. "All right, now what do we do about the tree? Why is it leaning like that?"

"I expect it needs a pot," said Daisy, rolling her eyes.

"So it does! We need to get a pot. A big one, I suppose?"

Bertie stared at us all doubtfully, and I got the distinct sense that he was feeling the way I had in the tea shop—as though he was playing at being a grown-up, and was about to be found out.

"Go and ask Moss for one," said Daisy. "We'll be quite all right here."

"All right," said Bertie. "But don't get yourself in trouble, Squashy!"

And he left the room.

II

He had scarcely closed the door when Daisy whirled on the boys. "Quick!" she cried. "What have you discovered so far? We know which shop the fishing line came from, and that a Chinese man went in and bought some. We *also* met Amanda, and discovered that she has been writing essays for Chummy, Donald, and Bertie, as well as lecture notes—and that someone at Maudlin knew. That's why Amanda hasn't come into the college. Bertie told her to stay away until Chummy had discovered who it was!"

"Who do *you* think it was?" asked Alexander. "One of our suspects?"

"It can't be Donald, obviously, or Bertie," said Daisy. "If it *is* one of our suspects, it could have been Moss, Michael, Perkins, or Alfred—and whichever of them it was, it would strengthen their motive against Chummy."

"Wait, it can't have been Perkins!" said George. "We've ruled him out!"

"We've been listening in to interviews," agreed Alexander. "Just like we did on the Orient Express. We followed PC Cross about, and got everyone's alibis for yesterday evening. I've written them down, here." He took out his notebook, and I peered at it. Alexander is the one who taught me shorthand, earlier this year, and so I can read it. Daisy craned over at it as well, but I knew that to her, it was just scribbles. I felt a moment's pride at that—here was something that only Alexander and I shared.

"Perkins knows that the staircase nine lot are trouble-makers—he was quite rude about them, though he clearly has a soft spot for Bertie—and he said that no one apart from Maudlin dons and students came into the college last night," George went on. "He's quite sure of that. Then he said the important thing. He went to bed just after twelve—he lives above the lodge with his wife. But his wife stayed up. There's an ill second-year student, Walter Cookridge, from staircase four, and Perkins's wife is looking after him: she's got him set up on a little bed down in their living room. There isn't any way that Perkins could have crept out without disturbing them both—so, you see, he's ruled out! And he gave some other useful information. Because of the ill student, it took Perkins an age to drift off. He looked at the clock at quarter to one, and he remembers hearing something outside his window then. He thinks someone was climbing on the lodge tower."

"Bertie?" asked Daisy sharply.

"It can't be!" said Alexander. "He was already with us by then. And anyway, he went out down the drainpipe into the dons' garden, and over that wall. He wasn't anywhere near the lodge tower. So it was someone else. Everyone from staircase nine says they were in their rooms, but *someone* wasn't telling the truth."

He sounded affronted. Alexander dislikes lying more than anyone else I know.

"Michael locked up the staircase at eleven, and then he says he was in his rooms, working," said George. "Chummy and Donald were messing about on the top landing just after half past twelve, shouting at each other and bothering Moss, so Michael went upstairs to tell them off. After that he went back to his rooms and went straight to sleep. He wasn't woken by anything until the crash.

"Donald mentioned the same incident. He argued with Chummy—I think it was over that jacket, the one you saw. He says he shouted at him, Michael came up to shut them up, they went back to their rooms, and that was it. He went to bed, and stayed there until Chummy fell."

"Didn't he mention Moss?" I asked.

"Exactly," said George. "That's missing—and that's not the only thing. But go on, Alex. Tell them about Alfred."

"According to what Alfred told PC Cross, he was in his rooms the whole evening. Reading until he went to sleep, and he was woken by the fall."

"Dull," said Daisy. "And possibly untrue. Alfred is becoming an excellent suspect. What about Moss? And what did Perkins tell you?"

"Moss was behaving oddly," said Alexander. "He's definitely hiding something. At first he said that he finished his tasks on the staircase just before twelve thirty and went to bed. His rooms are up next to Chummy's and Donald's. Cross asked about Chummy and Donald's argument, and Moss hesitated—said he'd forgotten, that it wasn't anything, that he only went out and saw it for a moment before he went back to his rooms."

"He says he was woken up by the fall," said George. "Same story."

"Any clues, apart from all of that?" asked Daisy. "Did you manage to get into anyone's rooms?"

Alexander shook his head. "We did try!" he said. "Only everyone was in them, waiting to be questioned by PC Cross."

"But now that you're here—" said George.

Bertie came back in, hauling the most enormous terracotta pot, piled high with Christmas decorations.

"Moss found it for me!" said Bertie triumphantly. "Isn't it fine? And he threw in all these as well. He says we can decorate the staircase."

The four of us flashed one another a look. This was the perfect opportunity to look at the staircase, and perhaps investigate some of the rooms.

"Excellent!" said Daisy. "Oh, come on, then, put the tree up so we can decorate it first!"

The next hour or so was a whirl of Christmas. The boys put the tree in the pot, realized they had nothing to hold it up, and ended up piling in Bertie's wellingtons and several textbooks that he swore he did not need until next term. We pulled the baubles out of their bags—they were lovely and bright red and green and gold—and strung them up over ropes of crackling tinsel. Then we fixed candles onto the end of each branch (they listed rather dangerously, I thought, and I was worried about what would happen when they were lit) and stood back to admire the effect. It was haphazard, but lovely, and I felt proud. I had never actually decorated a tree before—it was always something the servants had done—and I could see from Bertie's and Daisy's faces that it was the same for them.

"Not bad!" said Bertie triumphantly. "There, d'you see, Squashy, we don't need any help!"

"Of course we don't," said Daisy. "Just us. And Hazel."

"And us!" said George, winking at her. "What say we move on to the staircase?"

"Excellent," said Daisy. "Bertie, you stay here."

Outside we went, strung with tinsel and baubles. I stared up through the dizzying gap in the stairs all the way to the far-off roof. It really was a tall, thin place, all angles and stone.

Daisy lowered her voice. "We must have a thorough understanding of the space if we want to uncover who committed the crime," she told us. "Hazel and I have investigated the staircase before, but now we must create a full and clear map of the area."

"Exactly as I said," said George, grinning.

"Of course you did," said Daisy, rolling her eyes at him. "But *I'm* saying it now, which makes it more official. Hazel, you may draw it."

I understood what that really meant: that Daisy would be directing me, and criticizing what I did. There was a time when I would not have seen that at once, and a time after that when I would have resented it—but these days I have made my peace with it. Daisy is Daisy, and she makes demands with the pure clarity of someone who does not consider anyone else. She knows what she wants, and she will get it, no matter the cost. And I rather admire her for that.

"All right," I said, slipping this casebook out of my pocket under a covering of tinsel and labelling a fresh page STAIRCASE NINE, MAUDLIN COLLEGE.

"Now," said Daisy, "let's see . . . tinsel there, and, let's see, a cluster of baubles there. This place really does need a woman's touch."

George raised his eyebrows at her, and she winked at him. "Now," she whispered. "The layout. Hazel, pay attention. We know that the entrance on the ground floor has a door which gets locked, and it was locked on the night of the murder at eleven o'clock, long before the trap was set. On the left we have the bathrooms, with Michael Butler's rooms on the garden side. Mark that up, Hazel."

I drew boxes on the left to be the bathrooms and a little box on the bottom right labelled MICHAEL'S ROOMS. Next to it I noted down the notice board, and the first flight of stairs. Then I looked about at the landing we were on.

On the left was the door that read FREDDIE SAVAGE, and on the right was the door we had come through, Bertie's. He stuck his head out for a moment and rolled his eyes at us all before going back inside.

I added both rooms to the map and, between them, the coinbox telephone. It was out in the open, for anyone on the staircase to use.

"Convenient!" said Daisy, wreathing it with tinsel.

"Noisy!" said George, and I knew what he meant. I saw

again how difficult it would be for anyone on staircase nine to make a call without anyone else hearing them.

"Most interesting," agreed Daisy. "Very interesting indeed. Do you know, I think there is a very obvious solution to the problem of Amanda's call."

"That *there was no call*," said George.

"Yes," said Daisy. "Hazel and I suggested that long ago. But if so, if no one did call Amanda, we cannot simply dismiss her story. There is one very important question to answer. *How did she know that something was wrong?*"

I caught Alexander's eye. He looked as bewildered as I felt. A chill went down my spine.

We climbed the stairs again, and came out onto the next landing. The horrid sight Daisy and I had seen last night, blood pooled on the stone, had been wiped away, but I could still see the shadow of where it had been. This was where Chummy had landed, and I saw the bit of broken stone that his head had hit against. It was most unlucky, for each flight of stairs only had twenty narrow steps—but it had happened. I shuddered, and marked my map with a cross.

To our left was Alfred Cheng's rooms, and on the right, the garden side, was the room marked JAMES MONMOUTH. This was the room that was being refurbished while its owner was away for the holidays—the room into which Chummy had been carried just a few hours ago.

He was still there!

I saw that Daisy had had the same thought. She looked at George, and—"We must get in," he said at once.

"No!" I said. "We can't!"

"Of course we can," said Daisy. "For once, we have an opportunity to observe the body itself!"

"Alexander!" I said pleadingly.

"Daisy's right," said Alexander uncertainly.

I was shocked. I knew he did not really think so. How could he pretend to agree with Daisy, just because he thought her pretty? But his agreement had outweighed my opinion. The other three wanted to go in.

"Decorate around me, while I pick the lock," ordered Daisy. She pulled a pin out of her hair and moved toward the door. Alexander stepped behind her, to tuck a strand of tinsel above the lintel, and I hung a bauble on the handle itself.

"What are you doing?" asked a voice behind us. It was Alfred, peering out of his rooms again with a look of annoyance.

"Decorating," said George. "Christmas."

"Do it more quietly, can't you? I need my sleep," said Alfred, before closing the door again.

Something occurred to me then. Every time we climbed the stairs, we seemed to attract attention. Our footsteps rang on the stone steps, and our voices echoed off the walls. How had the murderer climbed quietly, without anyone hearing them in the middle of the night? No one had mentioned hearing someone moving on the staircase after the argument between Chummy and Donald at half past twelve.

But at that moment, the door to James Monmouth's room opened with a click, and I could not think of anything else but that. I was imagining what would be inside. I remembered the dreadful door at Fallingford, the only thing between us and Mr. Curtis, the guest who had been killed. Detecting is all very well when it is about the puzzle, but when it truly becomes about a body, I like it far less.

Daisy clicked on the electric light, and all four of us slipped inside. There, on the sofa, was a shape, covered in a dust sheet.

"We shouldn't be doing this!" I said one more time.

"I don't know why you're so squeamish," said Daisy. "It's all part of being a detective!"

I glared at the other three, summoning all the bravery I have gathered over the past year. I was going to stop them.

And then I noticed the shoes.

They were poking out of the bottom of the sheet. They were black, and rough on the bottom, with canvas tops. Once I had seen them, I could not look away.

"Look," I said quietly. "He's wearing tennis shoes."

"That's what Harold gave us to wear last night!" said Alexander. "Everyone wears them to climb, he told us so."

Eyes wide, Daisy took a step forward and twitched at the sheet.

The legs she had revealed were clad in baggy, dark-brown trousers, not night things.

"Look," she whispered. "He's wearing bags and a coat, not pajamas. He is dressed to go outside!"

I remembered that Mr. Perkins said he had heard someone clambering about on the tower as he was falling asleep. We had thought it must have been one of our suspects . . . but what if it was the victim? What if *Chummy* had been climbing last night? He could have gone out of his rooms through the window by the drainpipe, and back down the same way. He must not have had time to change out of his climbing clothes and into his pajamas before he died. Perhaps that was why he had gone rushing at the stairs without looking where he was going—because he was tired, and not thinking straight.

But Daisy was moving up the body again, and I thought with a flush of horror that if I had to look at Chummy's poor broken head I really would scream. "Stop, Daisy!" I said. "Leave him alone. Don't look any more!"

"All right, all right. Why, you look quite green!"

"It isn't nice," I said faintly. "I think I prefer it when there is no body."

"Me too," admitted Alexander. He did not look very well. "I think we should go."

"You," said Daisy petulantly, "have no imagination. But I do admit we have made a useful discovery. We ought to move on from this room now, though, before someone notices we've stopped decorating the staircase!"

Out we went onto the landing, and began to go up the steps toward the top floor, where Chummy and Donald's rooms were.

"More baubles there, I think!" cried Daisy, then dropped her voice to a whisper. "Look! There! That's where the fishing line was tied!"

It had gone, but there was the nail, still shining. PC Cross had not yet taken it away. Daisy rushed to the top step and crouched down.

"Here, d'you want a magnifying glass?" asked George, taking one out of his pocket.

"Oh, no thank you. A lady always carries her own," said Daisy, pulling out her own tiny one.

Together they examined the nail in the skirting board. I got out the length of fishing line we had bought, and held it up. It would have been easy to set up the trap.

"The nail is knocked in deep," said George. "Interesting!"

"Yes!" Daisy agreed. "The noise of hammering would have bothered the whole staircase if it had been done last night. No one mentioned it any more than they did someone climbing, so—"

"—it must have been done earlier, to let the killer set the trap quietly whenever they needed to!" George finished. They beamed at each other.

"While the decorators were working on the room below, perhaps?" asked Alexander. He stared at Daisy hopefully, but she did not turn her head. After a moment, he looked at me. I blinked, and pretended I had been looking at this casebook.

"Hey!" cried a voice suddenly. "Hey! What are you four doing?"

We all looked up in shock.

Moss the bedder had come out of his little box room and was standing over us. He looked haggard and very distressed, and his livery was crumpled. It seemed as though he had still not slept at all.

"Good morning, Moss," said Daisy cheerfully. "We're decorating the staircase for Christmas."

"I'm—I'm sorry I startled you," Moss said. "It's only that I don't like seeing you there. It doesn't seem safe, after what happened. Mr. Charles's fall—it was my fault."

"*Your* fault?" asked Daisy sharply. The four of us bunched together. Was this a confession?

"He was in my charge," said Moss. "I shall be removed from my post! It was because of me!"

Suddenly our situation felt quite menacing. We were alone, at the top of the stairs, with a man who was one of our suspects.

"What do you mean?" Daisy pressed.

"I always told Mr. Charles not to play pranks on Mr. Donald—that it wasn't fair, that Mr. Donald couldn't take it. But I couldn't stop him—I never could. He laughed it off, and his parents let him. That was why I took the job here, to look after Mr. Donald when no one else would. I knew he needed it. And now—this! I tell you, it's my fault."

His lips were trembling. Was he confessing? Had he tried to stop Chummy, and taken things too far?

"But you told the policeman you were in your room," I said.

"I—" Moss began. "I was. Yes. And it's my fault!"

"Why do you keep saying that?" asked Daisy. "How could it be, if you were in your room?"

And that was when the door to Donald's rooms slammed open, and Donald himself burst out of it.

I say!" Donald cried. "What are you all doing out here? Are you having a party without me?"

I looked at him, and felt astonished. He was still in his pajamas, but he had put on a paper hat, of the sort you get in Christmas crackers, and draped a length of tinsel round his neck like a scarf. He was clutching a glass in his hand, half-full of some dark liquid, and on his face was a smile, a bold tilt to his features that suddenly reminded me very much of Chummy.

"Come in!" said Donald—and it sounded like an order. An order from Donald, who yesterday had bent to Chummy's will and crept about in his shadow. I was amazed.

We stepped into his living room, and found it even mustier than it had been last time. Bits of half-eaten toast were now strewn about, on plates and off them, and a toasting fork lay across the grate, half in the dead ashes of a fire.

"Mr. Donald!" cried Moss. "How are you?"

"Chummy's dead," said Donald, and he sounded quite gleeful. "He's not here anymore. I'm marvellous!"

"It was an accident," said Moss hopefully. "It was his own prank, wasn't it, Mr. Donald? It was my fault for not stopping it."

As he said that, I had a sudden feeling that Moss was *not* guilty. He was merely afraid that *Donald* was. It was only a suspicion, though I thought I was right. But how could I prove it?

"I don't care what it was!" said Donald. "It means that he's not here to bother me anymore. I can do what I like! I already feel better. It's like a weight's been lifted off me."

"But, Mr. Donald, you must agree that it was an *accident*!" said Moss again. I felt Daisy tense beside me, and I knew she had understood what I had. How could we make the truth come out?

"Imagine!" said Donald. "The party tomorrow night will be all mine now. I'm changing the guest list! I shall hire the jazz band I want! Things are looking up. I shall most certainly be buying that mine, too."

"Mr. Donald!" said Moss, rather desperately.

"Why, we should all be happy! Chummy's not about to play pranks on any of us."

"Oh yes," said Daisy quickly. "He did play some awful ones, didn't he? That one with the jacket . . . and what he did to poor Moss as well! Poor Moss, you must be quite shaken up."

I did not know what she meant, but I saw that, for some reason, her shot had hit home.

"How did you know that?" gasped Moss.

"He was a toad!" cried Donald. "That jacket was my best, and he sewed up the sleeves. I found it and we rowed in the corridor. Butler came up to tell us off, and Chummy pretended to listen to him. As soon as he was gone Moss came out, but Chummy pinched Moss's keys from his belt and locked him in his rooms. I tried to grab them off him, only he went out of the window in his rooms, up the drainpipe, and onto the roofs."

"Chummy locked Moss in his rooms?" asked George sharply.

"Did it all the time," said Donald. "The keys're easy enough to grab from the ring on his belt. He'd make Moss go back into his rooms and lock him in from the outside. I had to let him out again, after Chummy'd fallen. He still had the keys on him. I had to get them back out of his pocket when he was lying there!"

I felt electrified. I saw why Moss had said that it was his fault: he thought that allowing himself to be locked in by Chummy meant that Donald was free to set the trap. And one other thing was clear: if Moss had been stuck in his rooms from the moment Chummy locked him in until after he had fallen, then he simply could not have got out to set the trap. We could rule him out. I had been correct: Moss was innocent.

"You think I should be upset, don't you?" asked Donald. "Well, you're idiots. You don't know what it's like, having a brother who's better than you. Everything was Chummy, Chummy, Chummy. *Chummy ought to be older! Chummy ought to have the money!* That's what everyone said. No one cared about me. But that's changed now it's just me. I can be myself at last!"

I suddenly wanted to leave the room very much. I turned and stared at Daisy. Of course, she understood.

"We're going to go down to Bertie's rooms," she said to Donald. "Come on, you lot."

We went out onto the landing again, and the door closed behind us. I shuddered. "Let's go downstairs," I said.

"One moment," said Daisy. "Something has just occurred to me. Cover for me—talk while I'm gone!"

And quick as a flash, she darted to her right, through the door into Chummy's rooms. Alexander glanced at me and George, and then he launched into one of the cheerful, friendly conversations he is so good at. He talked about snow and about presents, and he was just getting onto the subject of Christmas dinner (apparently Americans do not really go in for Christmas dinner. Instead, they have something called Thanksgiving that happens a month before and seems to be Christmas without the presents) when Daisy came darting back out of Chummy's rooms. Her hands were empty, but her eyes were glowing.

"That was very productive!" she breathed. "I looked in Chummy's wardrobe, and the fishing line Hazel and I saw yesterday *is still there*, untouched since we last saw it! That's conclusive: Chummy did not set the trap! There *is* a murderer at large, and we are narrowing down our suspects!"

I stood at the window of Bertie's rooms and stared out at the dark afternoon through its little diamond panes. For a while we had to behave as though we were not detectives, but only ordinary schoolchildren, getting ready to celebrate Christmas. I twisted the catch, and pushed the two halves open so that I could peer out at the drainpipe to my left, and the winter garden below. Above me were Chummy's rooms, and I was horrified to think about swinging out of Chummy's window onto the drainpipe. Up here seemed high enough.

I pulled the window closed and turned back to the room. The gramophone was on, and a man's voice flowed out, a rich and laughing jazz song.

Bertie knelt at the grate and prodded the fire, while George and Alexander watched. The flame leaped up, and the room was warm and bright. The tinsel on the walls shone, and it did feel like Christmas Eve.

Daisy came to lean against me, and we watched together as Bertie pulled out a tin of mince pies from a little trunk under his desk. He laid the pies on the hearth rug, and it looked almost like a midnight feast in the middle of the day.

My stomach rumbled. I realized that it was past lunch time, and I had not eaten anything for hours. My nerves had been singing with detective excitement and seed cake, but now I felt myself coming back to earth with a thump.

I bit into my first mince pie and my mouth flooded with spices and candied fruit. For a while, everything was quiet. We all sat or leaned or lay across the sofa, or the carpet next to the fire, and demolished all the mince pies. I could sense the five of us drawing closer together.

Then there was a knock on the door, and in walked Michael Butler.

The fire cast heavy shadows across the room—the sky outside really was darkening, although the snow seemed to have stopped.

"PC Cross is coming up," said Michael shortly. "Wants to talk to us all again. I've called in Cheng as well . . . ah, here he is."

The door opened again, and in came Alfred. He had the sort of expression on his face of someone who knew he was not welcome, and had decided to come in anyway.

"Cheng," said Michael coolly. "The policeman is on his

way. Will you help the investigation this time, or simply slip away again?"

"Of course," said Alfred, though he flinched as he said it. "I see no reason not to help simply because I disliked the man."

"Disliked him? You hated him!"

"And with good reason!" said Alfred, his voice rising. "He was foul to me, Butler, but you could never see it for what it was."

"Because it was nothing!" cried Michael. "If you were English, you'd understand."

"I don't know why you're all so proud of being English," said Alfred. "Everyone is someone else's cousin. You even look alike!"

There was a heavy tramp of feet on the stairs, and a knock on the door.

"Excuse me," said PC Cross's voice. "May I come in?"

Michael and Alfred stepped away from each other.

"Of course," said Bertie.

PC Cross opened the door, his stomach still straining against his blue jacket and his face red. Behind him, looking annoyed (and still wearing his paper crown), was Donald.

I knew that Daisy had dismissed PC Cross as a clodhopper, but that was the very thing about him that made me uneasy. The fact that he had not simply accepted the accident explanation showed me that he would keep on plodding until he arrived at the truth.

"Good afternoon," said PC Cross, removing his tall blue hat respectfully. "I'm glad you're all here: I'd like to speak to you together. There are some things about this incident that I still do not understand."

"Chummy set up the fishing line and then tripped over it," said Bertie, distressed. "Why do I have to keep on saying it?"

"But why would he do something so dangerous?" asked PC Cross. "Did he not understand that someone could be seriously hurt?"

"Chummy loved to play tricks," said Bertie. "It went wrong. That's all."

"But if it was an accident, who telephoned Miss Price? Why was Mr. Melling wearing outdoor shoes, and why did he trip over his own trap? I know I'm not the quickest fellow, and that means that I need to understand. If I don't, my supervisor certainly won't, and I shall be in hot water. It's odd—I have been a policeman for fifteen years, but I have never before investigated a death. I never seem to be in the right place at the right time. It's become a station joke. So I mean to get to the bottom of this, now, and prove that I *can* do it. My superior officers are all on their Christmas holidays, it being the afternoon of the twenty-fourth of December. I want to have it cleared up by the time they return. So, if you please—who telephoned Miss Price?"

The room went silent. And then . . . "*I* called Amanda," said Donald. "I crept downstairs just after it happened and telephoned her. I wanted her to come and see Chummy. I wanted to, er, upset her. I—I should have said so earlier. I apologize."

I gasped. Was it possible we had been wrong?

"I made the call, that's all!" Donald repeated. "So that's cleared up. Now will you leave us in peace?"

"Soon," said PC Cross. "I have asked for the body to be moved. Someone will come for it this afternoon. But before I come to any conclusions, my questions must be answered."

"This is idiotic," said Donald.

"I am sorry that you think so," said PC Cross. "But before we continue, there is one more thing. If you made the call, Mr. Melling, then I do not have any further questions for Miss Price, and that means that she and the other young ladies do not need to be mixed up in this any longer." He looked at me and Daisy.

"Oh, we're quite all right!" said Daisy. "Though very upset, of course, we are bearing up marvellously. We can stay."

"Nevertheless, I would like to ask that you and your young friends"—he looked pointedly at Alexander and George—"stay away from this staircase until my investigations are over. I believe you two girls were removed from Maudlin yesterday by the Master. Now that your involvement in the case is over, his orders should be respected."

I saw that he would not be budged, any more than he would stop digging. This was a bad thing for the murderer, and it was almost as bad for our detective societies. PC Cross would keep on halting our investigation until his own was completed.

IX

Well!" said Daisy. "If you insist. George, Hazel, Alexander, I feel a sudden and urgent need for some fresh air."

With PC Cross and the Maudlin students watching us, we filed out of Bertie's rooms. Then we clattered down the stairs at a most furious pace (pulling on our coats as we did so) and rushed out of the entranceway to the staircase. Daisy took my elbow, and led us all round to the left, through the archway to the library and the dons' garden.

"Hold up," said Alexander in alarm, the tip of his nose turning pink with the cold. "We can't go in there. We're not allowed!"

"Nonsense!" said Daisy, wrapping one arm more firmly through mine and reaching out with the other to twist the big metal ring on the garden door. "If PC Cross has removed us from the staircase, we must just take the chance to investigate the garden. After all, we know that Chummy used the drainpipe that leads to it last night, and Bertie climbed through it as well. It is part of the crime scene, and we must examine it!"

I wanted to disagree with her—the great metal ring of the door in front of us seemed to be the very symbol of how closed-off Cambridge was turning out to be—but then I thought about it. We might never get another such chance, especially as the snow was beginning to fall again.

"All right!" I said. "But some of us need to keep watch."

"Excellent idea, Watson," said Daisy. "Thank you for volunteering. And who from the Pinkertons?"

"George will," said Alexander quickly. George looked at him and rolled his eyes.

"Of course I will," he said drily, "*Alex.*" I got the uncomfortable feeling then that he had reached exactly the same conclusion about Alexander's feelings that I had.

"*George*," said Alexander, cheeks turning redder. "Come on, Daisy, let's go detect!"

Daisy seemed not to see his expression. She was already grappling eagerly with the door. "Hurry up!" she hissed at Alexander. A moment later, they had both disappeared into the dons' garden.

George and I were left on our own. I smiled shyly at him. He was so different from the George I had had in my head for so many months, and yet he was the same. Clever, confident, always pushing his way into conversations, he was the other half of the kind, open Alexander, just as I was Daisy's. There were so many things I wanted to ask him that I hardly knew where to begin.

"Were you sent from India?" I asked at last. "To go to school, I mean?"

George quirked his lips. "I came all the way from London," he said. "I was born here, and so was Harold. It's only my father who's from India—but, of course, that's the only part of me anyone can see. I'm really more British than Alexander."

"Oh!" I said. "Do you ever—I mean, not that I do—does it ever make you upset?"

"Every day, of course," said George. "The trick is never to let it show, and always to dress the part."

I wondered what he had thought of me before he met me, and what he thought of me now.

"I always liked you, from the first letter you sent to Alex," said George, just as though I had asked him. "And Alex likes you too. Although as I said before, Alex isn't *always* the best judge of people. I don't know why he's wasting his time over Daisy."

"She's my best friend!" I said.

"She's brilliant," said George. "She's the sort of person you don't forget. But I don't think she's the sort of person who falls in love."

He must have seen my horrified expression, because he

said, "So. We're down to three suspects. Alfred, Donald, and Michael."

"We are," I agreed, trying to tear my mind away and settle back on the case. "Moss is innocent, and he thinks Donald did it."

"He does!" George agreed. "I saw that as well. Not that it proves anything, but it's interesting."

"I worked out something else too, when we were drawing the map," I said.

"Oh?" asked George, rubbing his gloved hands together. Snow was beginning to drift down again, settling on his shoulders and turning his dark hair white.

"Every time we went up the stairs, we disturbed someone. You saw: Alfred and Moss. Every sound we made echoed like anything. Even if the nail was already in place before the night of the murder, it would have been hard for the murderer to set the trap without making a noise and alerting someone to what he was doing. And I realized: imagine Michael trying to get all the way up the stairs and into Chummy's rooms without someone hearing him! If Moss had been listening out, and had heard him coming all the way up the staircase, he'd never have mistaken him for Donald, who would only have had to creep across the landing!"

George nodded. "I know," he said. "I've been thinking that too. Alfred might just have managed it—he'd only have had to go up one flight of stairs—but Donald wouldn't have had to climb any stairs at all."

"Yes!" I said. "He's got a motive, and he knew that Chummy was out of his rooms and Moss was locked away, so it was safe to set the trap. If it was him . . . it fits."

"*If*," said George. "This is all good guesswork, but we don't know for certain. We need more evidence."

Behind us, the gate creaked open.

It was Alexander and Daisy. Alexander was filthy at the elbows and knees. He even had some mud in his hair. Daisy, however, had only one small spot of dirt at the end of her nose. She was smiling, and she had one hand held behind her back.

"Hullo," she said to us.

"We found something," said Alexander, behind her.

"Would you like to find out what it is?" Daisy asked teasingly. "I know we're working together. But all the same, I want you to play a game for it."

"Oh?" said George. I saw a spark come into his eyes.

"A guessing game," said Daisy. "You two have three guesses as to what is behind my back. If you guess right, I shall show it to you. But if you get it wrong, I will punish you."

"Daisy!" I said.

"All you have to do is get it right!" said Daisy. "It's quite easy, really."

"All right," said George. "I promise, we'll win."

"First guess," said Daisy. "Ready?"

"Of course. The thing behind your back is . . . a glove."

Daisy's smile widened. "It isn't a glove," she said. "Not even close. Second guess. Hazel, your turn."

"The thing behind your back is . . ." I paused. I stared at Alexander, and it was funny how my detective senses showed me exactly the blue of his eyes and the three freckles on his nose and the way the mud clumped in his hair. It was terribly embarrassing, and I looked down. "The thing behind your back is a roof tile," I said, and I knew as I said it that it was wrong.

"Wrong again," said Daisy, and she nudged Alexander triumphantly. The dimple in his cheek appeared again, and I felt myself go hot all over. "We did find some of those, freshly broken and scattered on the ground, supporting our theory that Chummy was climbing about on the roof last night, but it isn't that. Last go."

"Mine again," said George. "Let's see. This is difficult. But—well—the thing behind your back. Could it possibly be . . . a bit of wood?"

Alexander's face fell. "How did you know?" he asked. He looked at Daisy, and I had another twinge. Why *should* he look at her like that all the time?

"It is a garden," said George. "You were *holding* the clue, so it couldn't be footprints. It wasn't tiles, you said so. It might have been clothing—but you were so sure it wasn't a glove that I decided that couldn't be it either. A bit of wood seemed the only thing left. So, show it!"

Daisy brought her hand round, and there in her palm was a length of branch.

I could see at once why they had picked it up. It had been broken at both ends, quite deliberately—it looked like it had come from one of the trees in the garden—and the breaks were still fresh and yellow. Both ends looked squashed as well, as though they had been pressed hard against something, and there was a dent in the middle of it that ran across its width, as though something had knocked into it. It was most interesting, and almost certainly a clue.

"There," said Daisy. "Look at that! Now, that wasn't the only thing we found. There were plenty of footprints, as well, all the way from the bottom of the drainpipe to the garden wall."

"One set?" asked George.

"No," said Daisy. "More than that. Two distinct sets, and there may have been more. We could hardly see beneath the snow. Alexander had to brush a good deal of it away."

"So, what now?" asked George. "We've got the wood, but how does it fit in? Who does it point to?"

And that was when the snow began to fall in earnest.

Part Six
The Plot Thickens and the Snow Falls

It was like a feather duvet bursting in the sky. I gasped. Alexander spread his fingers wide and laughed with delight, and George stuck out his tongue as though he wanted to eat it. Daisy simply tipped her head up to the sky and let the flakes fall across her face. When she looked down again, there were perfect white feathers on her eyelashes and eyebrows. She looked rather like the Snow Queen. Alexander and I both put out our hands to brush the snow away, and then paused.

"We won't be able to hang around here for much longer!" said George. "What say you to a detective meeting, while we can?"

"Yes indeed!" said Daisy. "I do believe we are on the way to the truth, but we are not there yet. Come on, under the archway. Hazel, get out your casebook. It's time for a meeting."

We huddled together under the arch between the Library Quad and the East Quad, breathing out white air as the snow fell around us. I gripped a pencil in my gloved hand as tightly as I could, and began to write.

"Now!" said Daisy. "We have had plenty of updates on the case. What do we know?"

"We've ruled out one of our suspects," I said at once. "Moss. He was locked in his rooms by Chummy just after twelve thirty, and stayed there until Donald let him out, after Chummy fell. He couldn't have put up the fishing line."

"Very true," said Daisy. "It is a pity, though. He seemed like such a lovely suspect at first."

"He thinks Donald did it," I said. "George and I both agree."

"Interesting!" said George.

"What is?" asked Daisy.

"Seeing how another society detects. Alex did tell me, but it's different in person."

"Oh? And how do *you* do it?" asked Daisy, rather spikily. She hates being told that the Detective Society is anything less than perfect.

"We go through clues first!" said Alexander. "George's idea."

"*So?*" said Daisy, still dangerous.

"Well, there was the stick—branch—whatever it was. And the nail, and the fishing line, and those essays of Amanda's. And Amanda's coat, if you're counting that?"

"Things are all very well," said Daisy severely, "but they don't make any sense without people."

I took a deep breath. "Can't we compromise?" I asked. "We could go chronologically, as we discovered the evidence."

George and Daisy looked at each other, and then they both nodded.

"Bertie's out," said George. "We can give him an alibi from twelve fifteen until two fifteen."

"When Chummy had already fallen," said Daisy, nodding again. "Now, Chummy and Donald had an argument about that jacket at half past twelve. Michael came up to tell them off, went back down to his rooms again, Chummy locked Moss in *his* rooms at the top of the stairs when he came out, and then went out of the window of his sitting room, up the drainpipe, and onto the Maudlin roofs at about quarter to one. That's when he was heard by Perkins. Chummy was still wearing his outside clothes when he died, so he must have only just returned when he fell. That gives the murderer a window of—let's say twelve forty to two—to set the trap. All those timings are agreed on, aren't they?"

We all nodded.

"Hazel and I were talking about how the trap was set while you two were in the garden," said George.

Daisy shot me a rather shocked glance.

"We're telling you now!" I protested. "It's not really a clue, it's something we both noticed. Every time we've gone up and down the stairs—when we were decorating the stairs earlier, for example—someone has come out to see what we're doing. Everything echoes. I don't think you can get up the staircase without someone hearing you. It would be very difficult for anyone at the bottom of the stairs to get all the way to the top without being noticed."

"Exactly," said George, nodding. "We should test it in stockinged feet, just to make sure, but it does *seem* impossible. And another thing: we know that Moss is suspicious of Donald, which tells us that *he can have heard no footsteps coming up the stairs*. Otherwise he'd have just as much reason to suspect one of the others, whose rooms are farther down the staircase. Now, Alfred would have only had to come up one flight, but Michael would have had to climb three, his steps echoing all the way. You've heard how sounds carry upward! Alfred didn't mention footsteps past his door either, which could mean one of two things. First, that *he's* guilty, or second, that Michael didn't come past his door."

"I think there's another point against Michael," said Alexander. "His character doesn't seem to fit with the attacks, does it? They were all so random and risky, but Michael seems quite a careful person. When the port was poisoned with mistletoe, lots of people were ill at the party, including Michael. And if Chummy was the target all along, why would Michael run the risk of pushing the wrong brother into the pond? It just wouldn't be his way."

"Very true," said Daisy, frowning. "Michael really is not the most brilliant of suspects, although he did not like Chummy. If it was Alfred, though, I can imagine him lashing out and not minding who he hurt, as long as he got to Chummy eventually. He's the sort of person who gets what he wants, and doesn't mind who else is upset along the way. And if it was *Donald*—why, he could drink enough port to be ill but not seriously hurt, and then jump into the pond and pretend to be drowning. He could cover his tracks."

"*Moss* thinks it's Donald, after all!" said Alexander. "Donald does have a motive, and he's been behaving so oddly since Chummy died. He's happy about him being dead!"

"This is all perfectly true, but we're getting ahead of ourselves!" said Daisy severely. "We ought to go on to Amanda next. I know she can't be a suspect, but she's more and more suspicious. We found odd things on the front of her coat—brick dust and mud—and, as Hazel and I also discovered, she has a connection to Chummy. She's been writing his essays for pay, as well as Donald's and Bertie's, and we know that someone at Maudlin discovered this."

"So?" asked George. "Amanda can't have been on the staircase on the night of the murder."

"But then how did she know about the fall?" I asked. "Did you believe what Donald said to the policeman just now? That he called her?"

"No," said Daisy decisively. "He was just saying that so PC Cross wouldn't ask any more awkward questions and go away—and that in itself makes him more suspicious!"

"Wait up," said Alexander. "I've just had another thought. The dons' garden wall is brick. I noticed it again just now. And that garden's full of mud. What if—tell me if I'm being idiotic. What if that other set of footprints we found in the garden belonged to *Amanda*? After all, who leans against a wall *forward*? That dust would only make sense if she was *climbing* the wall. Then imagine she went up the drainpipe and onto the staircase through one of the garden side rooms. She could have been there at the right time yesterday night. She could even have set the trap. If Donald *didn't* make that call, she could still have known about the fall, without being told, if she was there!"

My heart raced. It might fit. It certainly sounded more likely than Donald calling her. "*That* would explain why she woke us up, too!" I said. "She would have needed to tell someone that there had been a telephone call, so we could confirm her story later. But . . . wait. Amanda doesn't climb! Or at least, she hasn't told us she does."

"Girls can climb just as well as boys, Hazel!" said Daisy. "And climbing seems to keep coming into this case. As far as we know, it's only the male students who are in the secret climbing society, but why shouldn't a St. Lucy's student climb as well? Remember, Bertie told us that even as a society member, you don't always know who the other climbers are outside your own chapter—it's that secretive."

I had a sudden, dizzying memory of climbing up the side of House during our last case at Deepdean. It is true that some girls (like Daisy) are excellent climbers, and also true that I am not one of them.

"Could you ask her?" said Alexander.

"You can't just *ask* about someone's secrets," said Daisy. "You have to pry them out, like oysters. But . . . oh, bother it, you might be right. If Amanda went through the garden, she might have picked up that wood there and pushed it into a window, to keep it open."

"Do the marks fit?" I asked. We all peered at its flattened ends, and the bump in the middle.

"Hmm," said Daisy. "It's almost as though it was jammed *against* something, isn't it? Something that bumped back out against it."

"But if it was Amanda, how could she have set the other traps?" I asked. That was puzzling me. "Amanda might have been able to drop the mistletoe into the decanter by creeping in up the drainpipe while everyone was out one day, but how could she have pushed Donald into the pond? She wasn't at Maudlin for that dinner. She was waiting for us on Mill Lane when we went outside afterward."

"We can't be certain of that, Hazel. She might have slipped in over the wall again and been hiding in the dark, somewhere close to the pond!" said Daisy. "It might explain why the wrong brother was pushed in. She was in a rush, and trying to get away again before she was seen. All the other pranks work as well, if we believe she has access to the college through the dons' garden. She could have slipped up the drainpipe and set up the bucket trick, and she could have been climbing near the men, and worked the bit of stone loose. And if she wasn't exactly on the spot, then she couldn't make sure the right person was hurt, which explains the odd randomness of the attacks better than any other theory!"

We stared at each other, and I felt an electric fizz in my stomach. I almost forgot how cold I was. Had we suddenly uncovered the murderer?

SUSPECT LIST

1. ~~Bertie Wells. MOTIVE: Unknown. OPPORTUNITY: He lives on staircase nine, and he was there at the time the prank must have been set. ALIBI: Says he was in his rooms. Is this true? NOTES: He is a Maudlin student and a climber, and had opportunity to commit all the previous pranks.~~ RULED OUT! He was climbing

with George Mukherjee, Harold Mukherjee, and Alexander Arcady from 12:15 to 2:15—he could not have set up the fishing line.

2. Donald Melling. MOTIVE: He is Chummy's older brother, but was very controlled by him. Now that Chummy is dead, he will still inherit the money on his birthday, but be able to dispose of it however he likes. OPPORTUNITY: He lives on staircase nine, and he was there at the time the prank must have been set. We found fishing line in his rooms. ALIBI: None yet. NOTES: He is a Maudlin student and a climber, and had opportunity to commit all the previous pranks—although he seemed to be the victim of them. Was this just a clever ruse? He argued with Chummy at 12:30, and then had the best opportunity to set the trap as soon as Chummy climbed out onto the Maudlin roofs. He seems very glad that Chummy is dead. He also told PC Cross that he phoned Amanda about Chummy's death, but we believe this is a lie—making him even more suspicious.

3. Alfred Cheng. MOTIVE: He hated Chummy, and was overheard saying he wanted to punish him. OPPORTUNITY: He was on staircase nine on the night of the murder. ALIBI: None yet. NOTES: He is a Maudlin student and a climber and had opportunity to

commit all the previous pranks. Suspicious behavior observed. He went back into his rooms after Chummy's fall. Why? He seems truly to hate Chummy, the reason why he went back into his rooms after Chummy fell—is this enough motive to have killed him? Is he the person who found out about Chummy paying Amanda to write his essays?

4. Michael Butler. MOTIVE: ~~None yet~~. He disliked Chummy intensely. OPPORTUNITY: He lives on staircase nine, and was there on the night of the murder. ALIBI: None yet. NOTES: He is part of Maudlin. He could possibly have staged the door, the mistletoe, and the pond, though not the climbing accident. Not a climber, though he could have taken the fishing line from someone else's rooms. It would have been extremely difficult for him to get all the way up the stairs without being heard. Is he the person who found out about Chummy paying Amanda to write his essays?

5. ~~Moss. MOTIVE: None yet. OPPORTUNITY: Was on staircase nine on the night of the murder. ALIBI: He says he went to bed at 12:30, when the trap was not yet set. Is this true? NOTES: Not a climber, though he could have taken the fishing line from someone else's rooms. Was seen trying to destroy evidence.~~

RULED OUT! Although we know he has good reason to dislike Chummy, having worked for the Melling family and believing Donald to have been unfairly treated by his parents and brother, we know that he was locked in his rooms by Chummy from 12:30 until just after the fall, when he was let out by Donald. He could not have escaped to set up the fishing line. He is innocent—but he clearly believes that Donald is guilty. Is this true?

6. ~~Mr. Perkins. MOTIVE: None yet. OPPORTUNITY: Lives in Maudlin, though not on staircase nine—he has keys, though. ALIBI: None yet. NOTES: Could he really have set all the previous traps? Seems very unlikely. We must rule him out.~~ RULED OUT! His wife and the ill student, Walter Cookridge, give him his alibi. He did hear something important, though: Chummy climbing about on the Maudlin roofs at about 12:45.

7. Amanda Price. Was not on staircase nine on the night of the murder, but says she was telephoned in the middle of the night. Is this true—and if not, why would she lie? We believe she was lying, and that she was in fact on staircase nine at the time of the murder. NOTES: From the evidence of mud and dirt on her coat, she may have climbed over the dons' garden wall and up the drainpipe to staircase nine. This

would give her means and opportunity to set the trap, and she has a motive–Chummy was buying essays from her, which she hated, and she recently discovered that someone else on staircase nine knew about the cheating. She has been behaving suspiciously, and if she is a climber she could have set all the traps–we must consider her one of our best suspects.

Excellent," said Daisy. "Now. Plan of action, if you please. We need to investigate Amanda immediately!"

I nodded. "Ought we to recreate the crime as well?" I asked. "Creep about on stockinged feet, I mean, just to see whether Michael could have managed it."

"Yes—only we have to make sure not to run into PC Cross as we do it!" said Daisy. "Bother him, what a clodhopper he is! I wish that we had the tools the police do. I'm sure we have twice the brains!" I thought of the fingerprint kit waiting for her, wrapped, in our rooms in St. Lucy's, and smiled to myself.

"But isn't that the best thing about us?" asked George. "We *aren't* the police, so we don't have to behave just like them. We detect differently."

"True," said Daisy. "Grown-ups don't notice us, which is a wonder."

"They don't notice you *now*," said George. "But they will one day. We are growing up, after all."

"Well, *some* of us are," said Daisy, looking at me. I thought of Alexander and was glad my cheeks were already pink with the cold.

Then there was a furious shout behind us. I turned, and saw Aunt Eustacia. Her face was bright red, and she was wrapped in a magnificent purple coat. Behind her hurried Mr. Perkins, looking distressed.

Alexander very quickly slid the bit of wood up his sleeve. He had to tilt his wrist to hold it in, and it did look odd—but only if you were searching for it.

"Daisy!" cried Aunt Eustacia. "Hazel! Goodness me, it's like having charge of a pair of monkeys. Whatever are you doing standing in the snow like little matchgirls? Anyone would think you had nowhere to go. Price came back to college half an hour ago and simply said you were at Maudlin—this is the end for her. I cannot trust her anymore. I can't think what's got into her this holidays!"

We all shot a look at one another. Did we know?

"Now, enough of this gallivanting!" said Aunt Eustacia. "Men cannot be trusted, you ought to learn that. Come away back to St. Lucy's at once, if you please. The Master will be furious when he hears of this. Boys, you must move along immediately. Really! Aren't you old enough to know better?"

Half an hour ago, we might have resented her—but now that Amanda was a suspect, I suddenly saw that it was an excellent idea to go back to St. Lucy's, so that we could watch her properly.

"Goodbye," I said to George and Alexander.

"Goodbye," said Alexander, staring at Daisy.

"Goodbye," said George, with a smile.

Daisy nodded her head and turned away.

"You shall have high tea in my study," said Aunt Eustacia, "once you have taken off those wet things, of course. I believe there is even a Christmas cake for dessert—not, luckily enough, from our own kitchens. I prevailed on the cook to purchase one from Fitzbillies, so we are quite safe. Oh, look at you both! It'll be a wonder if you don't catch a chill. Hurry up now!"

I felt my stomach rumble. We had been eating little bits of things, cake and mince pies, all day, but although they were delicious I was longing for butter and toast, or potatoes with a thick stew. I wanted the certainty of a proper meal, proof that ordinary life was carrying on outside our strange little bubble.

We stepped out of the lodge (Daisy turned to wave at Mr. Perkins, who was huddled once more in his cubbyhole, clutching a fresh mug of tea), and down the cobbles of Mill Lane. We were suddenly buffeted face and body by the weather. There was so much snow riding in the wind now that it was like a blanket. It was not a soft powdering, or a lovely carpet. It felt like a wild thing, fighting against us, like Cambridge itself.

III

We were sent away to change out of our wet things, and when we came down to Aunt Eustacia's study I at last discovered that there was one part of St. Lucy's that I truly liked. The study might be faded, but it was still one of the most beautiful rooms I had ever been in. The red velvet curtains might be rather frayed and old, and the chairs mismatched, but a log fire crackled in the grate, and the white walls were all but hidden by shelves and shelves of books. They went up almost to the ceiling, and the books looked worn with use and love. My heart swelled.

Tea had been set out on the table, ready for our arrival. It was simple but delicious: muffins, ham, boiled eggs, and toast and butter, with Christmas cake for dessert. Aunt Eustacia had taken off her wet coat and hat and was sitting in a large armchair, warming herself by the fire. As we came in she nodded briskly at us both.

"Good afternoon, girls! Do sit down. Have some toast. After what I have just seen at Maudlin, I would like to talk about your futures."

This was a rather daunting way to begin. I looked at Daisy for encouragement. She was piling food onto her plate, so I followed suit. I took a fortifying, pillowy bite of muffin, and tried to look sensible and eager and not at all like a detective.

"Now," said Aunt Eustacia. "You seem content to spend your time fooling about with Men and Mysteries, so I should like to remind you that there is more to life. You both want to go to university, yes?"

"Oh no," said Daisy, in her best and most foolish voice. "I shall be presented at Court and marry a lord, and go and live in the country, and make jam."

"Don't be silly, Daisy," said Aunt Eustacia. "I know you better than that. What about you, Hazel?"

"I—" I said. I had always thought I should like to go to university. But now that I had seen Amanda, so frustrated at being clever and still passed over, I wondered if I would really be content. Why should I go to Cambridge when I could not even take a degree at the end of it, like the men? "I suppose."

"Well, that's a start," said Aunt Eustacia. "What would you study? What do you like?"

"I—I like books."

"Oh? What sort?"

"Er," I said, and of course the only image that came into my head was my pile of casebooks, slowly stacking up in my tuck box at Deepdean. "Mystery books."

"Haven't you had enough of mysteries?" said Aunt Eustacia.

"She likes other books as well," said Daisy. "She's always reading."

"Well then! What about History, or Classics? Or even English? It's rather new, but I hear excellent things. And you, Daisy—why not Mathematics? Or Archaeology perhaps? It is a more respectable way of digging things up."

"Certainly not!" cried Daisy. I knew she was thinking of her plans to set up the world's greatest detective agency (President: the Honorable Daisy Wells).

"All I ask is that you consider it," said Aunt Eustacia. "I don't like to see girls wasting their talents. You are both clever, that I can see. And if you have brains, you ought to use them. It isn't good for women to be ignored and sidelined. Things may go along all right, for a while, but in the end there is always an explosion. Take Price, for example. I gave you into her charge because I've seen the way those Maudlin boys treat her. Even your brother, Daisy, takes her for granted. I think she's got rather a pash on him, but of course that's quite the wrong avenue to pursue. I can see that, but Price, it seems, cannot. She's cleverer than the lot of them, stronger too. We had games to celebrate our thirtieth anniversary last month, and she won every medal there was. Shouldn't wonder if she climbs, too."

"Climbs?" said Daisy sharply. Aunt Eustacia could not mean—

"Oh, I'm sure Bertie will have told you about that secret society of theirs?" asked Aunt Eustacia. "The youth all think the dons don't know! As though we weren't young once, and students ourselves. Who do they think were the climbers before they arrived? Well, the women students have a society of their own. More daring than the men's, though of course the men have never heard of it. If you want secrets kept, trust women to keep them."

My mind was whirling. Here was confirmation of the very thing we had been suspecting—and from an unexpected source! I remembered how quickly Amanda had regained her breath after leaping off the Horse, the first time we met her. She was stocky, and strong, of *course* she was an athlete! Aunt Eustacia really was related to Daisy. She was just as sharp and noticing.

Daisy was sitting up very straight. "How fascinating!" she said.

"Indeed," said Aunt Eustacia. "I do wish Price hadn't got you all mixed up in the Maudlin accident. Stupid boys, playing pranks! Why did you go back there?" She peered down her nose at us.

"Er," said Daisy. "Bertie, of course. We were worried about him."

"And so you should be!" said Aunt Eustacia. "I've been worried about him, mixed up with those foolish Mellings. More money than sense—or Donald will have on Christmas Day. An odd family, that. Daisy, you ought to be glad we don't have an entail. Sends all the relatives wild, imagining what would have to happen to leave them in control of the money. Now, Hazel, have you any siblings?"

"I have two sisters," I said politely, skating over the exact truth that they are only my half-sisters, and that both our mothers are still alive and living in our father's house. "Younger ones."

"Girls really are the best option," said Aunt Eustacia. "I'm sure your father must have been upset not to have a boy, but really, they are more trouble than they're worth. Look at my brother! *He* was wild. And *his* son—well! Speaking of Felix, Daisy, I got a telegram from him last week. He might be coming for Christmas dinner this year. Did he tell you so? Hope he doesn't bring that actress he was carrying on with last year. She was most unsuitable. He needs a clever wife, otherwise he'll get bored. I don't know why some men think that they want to be married to idiots. Imagine the conversation around the dinner table! Dreadful."

"What? When will he be arriving?" asked Daisy, rather breathlessly. "Tonight?" Her eyes were shining.

"Oh, he didn't say," said Aunt Eustacia. "He never does. Now, who will have a piece of Christmas cake?"

She held out the plate, and Daisy took one gladly. After a pause, I did the same. I have never been quite sure about Christmas cake. The little buzz of almond to its icing always makes me think, quite foolishly, of cyanide. Daisy has taught me quite a lot about poisons since our second case, and I know that a taste of almonds means cyanide. Daisy knows it too, and relishes marzipan as a result. But as we ate, sitting next to the crackling fire, it only smelled of Christmas.

It was the twenty-fourth, I remembered, Christmas Eve—only a few hours until Donald's birthday. How would we be able to solve the case by Christmas Day?

We went back to King Henry's rooms, and I wrote all the latest up in my casebook. Daisy sat at the window and watched the snow fall.

I nudged her, just as I had on the train. Could that only have been two days ago?

"I'm all right, Hazel!" said Daisy. "I'm only thinking about the case. We now know that Amanda really is what we suspected her to be: a climber! We must watch her this evening, in case she should try something else. She is absolutely our best suspect, after Donald. Really, it's just like Bertie to be friends with both Chummy and Amanda. What an idiot! How he managed to get himself mixed up with more death—"

"But we've been mixed up with *five* murders now," I pointed out.

"Yes, but we're *professionals*," said Daisy, sounding for a moment as though she was the grown-up, and Bertie the child.

"Are you going to dress for dinner?" I asked.

"Oh, what is the point?" asked Daisy. "It's not like Maudlin here. Imagine, this college is what we are supposed to want! Aunt E's study may be nice, but you must admit that St. Lucy's as a whole is decidedly second-rate in comparison to Maudlin. And *this* might be our whole lives, if we let it. No thank you! I have decided that I do not need to go to university to become a consulting detective."

"Do you mean you don't want to marry a lord, after all?" I asked, smiling at her.

"Don't joke, Hazel," said Daisy. "I'm not marrying anyone. I keep trying to explain to you—men do not interest me. I'm not like *you*."

I looked away. "I can't help it!" I said. "I wish I could."

"People are odd," said Daisy. "Why can't you just be friends with Alexander, like I am with George? That isn't complicated at all."

"You're not like other people, Daisy," I said. "I don't think George is, either."

"That's why I'm interested in him!" said Daisy. "We are very similar, and that is rare. I think he is the cleverest boy I have ever met. But I don't want to *marry* him."

"I don't want to marry Alexander!" I said, and blushed.

"Hazel, I don't know why you insist on lying to me," said Daisy. "You're quite mad about him. You gape at him like a fish. It's exactly the way *he* looks at *me*." Then she blinked.

"Oh," she said. "I'm sorry. I shouldn't have said that, should I?"

I shook my head, ears ringing.

"You see? I have learned something from what happened last term!" Daisy cried. "I didn't mean it, you know that. You are still my best friend in all the world, and the best detective I know who is not me."

I could not help laughing, although what she had said still stung. She really did not mean anything by it. I hugged her.

"Apology accepted!" said Daisy, beaming. "D'you know, I feel I do want to dress for dinner. It is Christmas Eve, after all!"

Dinner that night was, as Daisy had suspected, very different from the elegant one we had at Maudlin. It was in the refectory, which still looked rather grim, although a tree had been set up in one corner, surrounded by a scattering of Bluestockings who were staying for Christmas and for Donald's party. There was no glitter of silver and crystal here, or gold-liveried servants—instead there was a definite air of tins and bottles, and only one harried maid slamming plates down in front of us and splashing the sauce. The first course was sardines, so small that they were nearly lost under a soup of tomato sauce, and then pigeon, which was exciting until I found a ball of shot still in mine. I bit down and almost broke a tooth, and never quite recovered from the shock.

"I do promise better fare for Christmas itself," said Aunt Eustacia, chewing her pigeon with a rather sour look on her face. We were sitting up on High Table with her, as a special treat. "Really, the kitchens are outdoing even themselves tonight! I shall have to go speak to them. Oh, and Daisy, I've just heard that that uncle of yours *will* be joining us for Christmas Day. He called me an hour ago. He's motoring up from London this evening, and he ought to be with us by tomorrow morning at the latest. And he'll have his fiancée with him."

"Fiancée?" cried Daisy.

"Indeed," said Aunt Eustacia, pursing her lips. "It's quite typical of him to spring something like this on us. I thought there was something wrong with the line, when he said it at first. He intends to marry someone called Miss . . . Lovedon in London, on New Year's Day. Do you know her?"

"Miss *Livedon*!" Daisy said, gaping.

But I was not surprised. It seemed meant to be. I imagined Miss Livedon and Uncle Felix running about the world hand in hand, catching spies and criminals and saving Britain. It was terribly romantic.

"Ah, that's it," said Aunt Eustacia. "He wants us all to be there, which I do appreciate. But such short notice! Now, this fiancée. Is she a good sort? Do you approve?"

"Oh yes!" I said.

"She's quite awful," said Daisy. "I think she's exactly what he needs. And of course we shall be at the wedding."

"Of course you shall," said Aunt Eustacia, and Daisy nudged me gleefully. We were both so excited that we had to make an effort to keep on watching Amanda.

She was sitting down in the main part of the hall, and she was only picking at her food. She stared off into the distance, and jumped at small noises. The bags under her eyes were worse than ever, and she seemed utterly distracted. Was this her guilty conscience? I wondered.

She came up to us after the pudding plates (plum cake and custard from a tin) had been cleared away. There was another girl with her, thin and serious, with straight dark hair and large glasses.

"I did what you asked," the girl said to Aunt Eustacia. "I made Amanda sit with me and play Snap and Beggar-my-neighbour all afternoon."

"Excellent work, Harriet," said Aunt Eustacia, nodding. "Amanda, I hope you are feeling better for it?"

"I'm perfectly all right. I think I shall go to bed early," said Amanda crossly. I was rather concerned. She did look so peaky.

"After the carols, I hope?" said Aunt Eustacia.

I could tell that Amanda wanted to say no, but she sighed and said, "Of course, Miss Mountfitchet." She tugged restlessly at her hair as she walked away, though, and I was quite worried that she might pull some of it out. I was also sure that she was up to something. We had to watch her closely.

I was glad that Amanda stayed for the carols. It meant that we could too, and still keep watching her all evening. After the meal was done, all the students and dons gathered in a circle around the tree's green branches and flickering candles and sang.

Daisy and I joined in (we had one hymn sheet to share, and Daisy took it), and the harmonies echoed around us in the cool dimness. It was so lovely that I got a shiver down my spine. Snow was falling outside again, in gentle little flurries, and the air itself felt silver with anticipation.

"Goodnight, Aunt E," Daisy called cheerily, with a theatrical yawn, as she put down her hymn sheet after the final chorus of "Hark! The Herald Angels" had died away. "See you on Christmas morning!"

Daisy and I walked back to King Henry's rooms together, and although the corridors of St. Lucy's were cold and bare, and echoed as we went down them, I could not shake the

Christmas feeling. I looked out of our sitting-room window and saw that the storm had died down, leaving behind a thick expanse of snow. It glowed with a ghostly radiance in the darkness, and I turned away from it, toward our bedroom.

"Hazel," said Daisy, "whatever are you doing?"

"Getting changed," I said.

"Sometimes," said Daisy, "I think you have improved, and other times I think you are exactly the same trusting Hazel you always were. Surely you have realized that going to bed was merely a blind? Amanda is up to something, and we must follow her to discover what it is. But, of course, she must not know what we are up to. That is why we have pretended to go to bed like good little girls. Really, we are neither good nor little."

"I know!" I said. "I was only going to put on my warm things, Daisy. I wasn't getting ready for bed! Of course we're following Amanda tonight."

"Oh!" said Daisy. "In that case, remember to put on your coat, and another jumper for good measure. There's no knowing where we may have to go!"

After we had changed, we waited, our noses pressed to the door leading out of King Henry's rooms onto the staircase landing, for what seemed like an age. Amanda's door was above ours, so if she was to leave her rooms, she ought to come past ours. Except—

The door to our bedroom was open a little way, and through it I heard a noise. It was a pinging, a gentle clang. I sat up, because I knew that sound. It was the noise a drainpipe made, when you were clambering hand over hand down it.

Daisy sat up and waved her hand at me. Then she began crawling forward, on her hands and knees, toward the bedroom. I scuffled after her, holding my breath. Daisy went to the bedroom window, the one that looks out over the river and Cambridge, and very carefully, without opening the catch, she raised her head up, so she was peering out.

She gasped.

"What is it?" I breathed. My stockings caught on a stray bit of wood, and I winced. I wanted to see what Daisy was seeing.

"Come and look!" hissed Daisy. "Hazel, we were right!"

I untangled my stocking (the wool ripped, and I cursed my clumsiness) and crawled up next to her to look. I raised my head cautiously at first, but Daisy was nudging me so hard that I realized I had nothing to fear. Outside, the world was white and blue. Everything was shadow and snow, mixed up together in the most confusing way, so at first I did not understand what I was looking at. There was a black blot at the edge of the unbroken white beneath the window—a tree? A statue? But then it moved.

"It's Amanda!" said Daisy. "She's climbed down out of

her window. She really *is* a climber, just as Aunt E thought! She *was* at Maudlin last night, and now she's going back to do something else dastardly!"

I watched as the figure in its coat and hat stood up and began to track carefully away from St. Lucy's, toward the bridge and Maudlin. It left behind heavy dark pockets where each foot had trodden, and I noticed something.

"Daisy!" I said. "It can't be Amanda. That person's wearing trousers!"

"Of course she is," said Daisy dismissively. "Who'd go climbing in a skirt if they could put on bags? She must have a climbing uniform. It's her all right. Look, she's doing that trick with her hair."

I looked, and sure enough, the person reached up and tucked away a flyaway bit of hair under its hat. It really was Amanda, after all. I was embarrassed. If a woman could be a climber, why was it such a stretch to believe that she might wear trousers to do it in?

"What do we do?" I asked—though I knew how Daisy would reply. And sure enough . . .

"There is no time to waste!" she said. "We must follow her. Quick, before something else awful happens!"

I looked at my wristwatch, and saw that it was almost eleven at night. That meant that in only an hour, it would be Christmas. I tingled all over. Christmas in the snow! Christmas . . . with a murderer.

Luckily, we were already in our outside things. Daisy threw open the window (unnecessarily hard, but she does love to be dramatic), and I peered round her at the drainpipe. It looked dauntingly far away, and the night was freezing. A gust of cold air blew onto my face.

"Daisy!" I said. "We can't. It's snowing!"

"Not anymore," said Daisy. "And anyway, we've done this before. Hazel, haven't I *trained* you for this? You ought to be pleased to have an opportunity to use your detective skills."

It was quite true that I had gone down a drainpipe before, but not in the snow, the temperatures cold enough to freeze my fingers and feet. I was terrified; there was no other word for it. What if we should fall? Daisy's plans are often quite mad, but this one seemed to have more than the usual chance of one or both of us dying.

"Oh, come along, Hazel!" cried Daisy. "Don't be a coward. I know you're brave really."

"I'm sensible," I said, through gritted teeth. "I don't want us to freeze to death."

"We won't! We're only— Oh, Hazel, hurry up, otherwise we'll lose Amanda! Look, if you don't go, I shall have to do it without you. And then won't you feel dreadful? Leaving your president to investigate on her own? Haven't we agreed, after last term, that that's a terribly bad idea?"

We had, rather—or, at least, we had really seen what happened when we tried to work without each other. But there was not wanting to go it alone, and then there was agreeing to climb out into the frozen night. We were twenty feet from the ground, which does not sound like such a lot. But it looked it. It was far enough to drop, and not get back up. Chummy had died from a ten-foot fall, after all. I had a sudden vivid vision of his last seconds, pitching forward and finding nothing to catch him until he hit the stone of the landing. Daisy tells me that she dreams about flying quite often, but all my flying dreams turn into falling, and I wake in a sweat.

"Hazel, enough of this!" said Daisy. "I am going out there, and if you want to honor the Detective Society you will come out after me. It is up to you to make your decision!"

She scrambled up onto the window ledge, took one look back at me, and swung like a monkey to the left, grabbing hold of the drainpipe.

In all my years with Daisy, this was the greatest test she had ever set me. Could I bear to follow her?

Of course I could.

The drainpipe was so cold that it burned. My palms ached, and I was trembling with cold and fear. In that moment, as I kicked with my feet and clawed with my hands and levered myself downward, I cursed Daisy Wells, the Detective Society, and the last year of my life. I did not want to die on Christmas Eve. I did not want to die at all. I wanted to be safe in my bed, waiting to do all the ordinary things that an English girl at Christmas would. I wanted most desperately to be boring.

The drainpipe clanked and creaked under me and the breath caught in my throat. It was not very far down, but my hands were swollen with cold, more like paws than fingers, and I could barely make my legs move.

"Come on, Hazel!" whispered Daisy—but suddenly, I simply could not move anymore. It was not at all a case of trying. I could not shift an inch. I clung, trembling, and I knew in that moment that I was about to die. It was the stupidest thing I had ever done in my life, and it would be the last. I hung, agonizingly, dangling in mid-air, and then I plummeted down.

Strong hands caught me about the waist. They broke my fall, and I dropped into a bank of snow, burning cold.

"What on *earth* are you doing?" hissed a voice above me. I looked up, my insides crawling with dread.

It was Amanda.

I stumbled upright, shaking.

"I should ask you exactly the same question," said Daisy, as crisply as though she were in a drawing room, instead of outside a Cambridge college in the middle of the night, with a murder suspect. "Why are you out of St. Lucy's?"

"That's none of your business," said Amanda angrily. "What do you mean, following me like this?"

"What do you mean, climbing out of your rooms? And why didn't you tell us you were a climber? Does Bertie know?"

"He— No," said Amanda. "It's a secret. Women aren't supposed to be climbers. Yet another thing we can't do. I was going to tell him last night, but I never got the chance. It's a good thing, really, considering what happened." She sounded very bitter.

"So you *were* at Maudlin last night," said Daisy. "That's

why you knew about Chummy. There never was a phone call, was there? Donald didn't ring you at all. You made it all up!"

For the thousandth time, I wished that Daisy were not so brave. We were facing up to someone who, although she had caught me to stop my fall, really might be the murderer. I moved to stand next to Daisy and wondered how on earth we could slip out of this bind.

Amanda opened her mouth.

"Don't deny it!" said Daisy. "We saw the dirt and brick dust on your coat. And we found the bit of wood that you used to prop open the window. It was dropped in the dons' garden!"

"No, Donald didn't call me. I was there yesterday evening. But I didn't use any wood!" said Amanda. "When I got to Bertie's rooms, the window was already open. I left it like that when I went out again. I never dropped anything in the garden!"

"Hah!" said Daisy. "So you admit you were there? We've got you now!"

She was right. As she always says, there is nothing people enjoy so much as correcting you. But . . . I had an empty, worried feeling. What Amanda had said about the wood was not what we had been expecting. If Amanda had not dropped it, who had? Was it evidence, after all, or only a coincidence? And if Donald had not called Amanda, then why *had* he lied? Was it because he was the murderer? I opened my mouth to ask her, but Amanda suddenly began to talk.

"I—" she said. "I—oh, you infuriating things! Yes, I was in Maudlin last night. I climbed over the wall into the dons' garden, and then up the pipe to Bertie's rooms. I wanted to show him that I'm a climber as well."

I knew then that what I had seen in her face before was true. Amanda really was in love with Bertie.

"I got there at about one in the morning," she continued. "All the lights on the staircase were on, so I thought Bertie *must* be in his rooms. I thought I'd knock on his window and surprise him, but when I got closer I saw that his window was already open. I realized that he must have gone out climbing, so I climbed in. The room was empty, and I sat down to wait. I didn't know what else to do. It was warm by the fire, even though it was banked, and I didn't know how long he'd be. I kept on thinking I heard him, but he never came through the window.

"I closed my eyes. I thought it was only for a moment, but I was woken up by a clattering noise, the most dreadful yell, and then a horrid crash above. When I looked at my watch, it was just after two. I heard doors opening, and Alfred and Michael shouting at each other, and then Donald yelling too. I went to the door, and listened. I heard them shouting Chummy's name, so I knew he was the one who had fallen. Then they said—Michael said, I think, "Take him in here—Monmouth's away for the holidays." I heard the door above me open and close, and I knew that I had to leave at once. I got outside as quick as I could, and I managed to get over the wall and into the road without being seen."

My heart was thumping. There were things in Amanda's story that were new. I imagined how she must have stood in the cold garden, looking up at the rooms of staircase nine. All the lights on—*all* the lights. Was that important? My brain was clouded by cold. And the clattering she had heard . . . what was that? Could it be the murderer, running down the stairs? But—no, it was not quite right. Where had I heard *clattering* recently? I could not think.

"And then you came back here and got us up," said Daisy.

"I really wasn't thinking clearly," said Amanda, rather bitterly. "The lie about the telephone call was stupid. I ought to have waited for the next morning, but I lay there stewing for hours. I wanted to get back into Maudlin, to find out what had happened, and I wanted Bertie to have his family there too. He told me about what happened at Easter and I knew another death would hit him hard. He really was friends with Chummy, you know. Why, what are you looking at me like that for? What's wrong? Here, you don't think I did it, do you?"

Daisy and I had moved closer together.

"*Did* you do it?" asked Daisy in a low voice. "If you did, you might as well confess now. There are more of us than there are of you!"

Amanda gave a bark of laughter. Her face was very pale and drawn, and her fists were clenched.

What would she say? What would we do if she said yes?

"You stupid—why, you idiotic child! *Kill Chummy?* I was too busy writing his essays. Yes, I hated him, but he was paying me money. Cambridge isn't cheap, and my parents aren't wealthy like yours. I needed it. Why would I want to kill him, and make the money stop? And I didn't even have time to look after you properly. When would I have the time to *kill* anyone?"

I let out a breath with a gasp. My face felt on fire.

"But why were you going back to Maudlin now?" asked Daisy.

"I wanted to speak to Bertie," said Amanda. "Like I told you, I know about what happened at Fallingford earlier this year and I thought he might be worried. I didn't want him to be alone."

It was such a ridiculous thing to be doing that it felt real. And her mentioning Fallingford was like a secret password. I realized that Bertie truly trusted her, even if he did not love her back. He had told her what had happened last Easter. Daisy turned to me, and I saw that she had understood the same thing.

And that was when we all heard Bertie shouting.

For one odd moment I thought I must be imagining it. We had just been talking about him, after all. But no, there was his voice, calling, and as Amanda and Daisy both turned their heads toward the noise I saw his slender figure running over the bridge toward us, through the unbroken snow.

His feet were caked in white, and he was not wearing a hat. That was the thing that struck me first. He was waving his arms.

"Hoy!" he shouted. "You! There! I need— Wait. Squashy? *Manda?* What are you doing out here?"

"We're talking!" Daisy shouted. "We needed some fresh air. What's up?"

"Squashy," Bertie panted. "It's . . . it's Maudlin. I telephoned Harold, and then you, but . . . you didn't answer, so I came . . . to get you. I need you. Something's happened. *Someone else is dead.*"

Part Seven

In the Deep Midwinter

We ran back to Maudlin together. It was the middle of the night, but the little door in the gate was hanging open. When we ducked inside, Mr. Perkins's cubby was empty and abandoned, its light still burning. Something was terribly wrong.

When we reached it, the door to staircase nine was open as well, and a chaos of male voices was echoing down the stairs. Up we went, so fast I was dizzy. Where were we going? Whose rooms would it be? But we kept on going up—all the way to Donald's door.

Inside was utter confusion. Alfred was there, shouting, and so were Michael, Moss, and Mr. Perkins. Donald was slumped on his sofa, wrapped in a silk bathrobe. There was another magnificent spread in front of him: sliced chicken and chutney and bread and a Christmas cake. I thought he must have eaten so much that he fell asleep, and wondered how he could manage to sleep through such a row. And then I looked again at the scene, and my eyes did another switching trick, and saw the truth.

Donald was not asleep. He was not moving at all. His eyes were slightly open, and so was his mouth. Cake crumbs were spilling out of it, there was icing on his lips, and there was a smell that I knew very well: a bitter almond tang that made my mouth wither.

Donald was not asleep. Donald was *dead.*

Once again, the pieces of the mystery were flung up into the air, coming down in quite a different shape. Donald had been our best suspect after Amanda. We knew he had lied to the police about Amanda's call. He had means, motive, and opportunity, and he had been behaving awfully since Chummy's death. How could he be dead now?

There was a drumming of feet on the stairs behind us, and I turned to see George, Alexander, and Harold rushing toward us.

"Bertie!" cried Harold, moving to stand next to him, his eyes full of concern. "Are you all right? We came as soon as we could after you telephoned. Oh, look at him! It's true!"

"He took dinner in his rooms," said Moss. "I came to take the things away and found him like this!" He looked genuinely upset.

"Where did that cake come from?" Daisy asked, narrowing her eyes at the remains on the table.

"It was an early birthday present," Moss explained. "It arrived for Mr. Donald this afternoon."

"When?" asked Daisy. "After we'd gone? But—"

"Do be quiet, Squashy!" said Bertie, and Daisy closed her mouth—but she widened her eyes at me, and I could tell that she had plenty more to say.

"Tomorrow's birthday party will have to be cancelled," said Alfred. And suddenly, without any warning, he burst out laughing.

I felt rather sick. It was such a nasty thing to do. Two people were dead, and Alfred was going out of his way to show that he did not care. He had gone back into his rooms after Chummy's death, and now he was laughing about Donald's.

PC Cross appeared in the doorway, breathing heavily and looking bewildered. "I don't believe it," he said, to no one in particular. "All these years without a death, and then two at once." He nodded at Mr. Perkins. "Thank you for the prompt telephone call, I'm glad I could be on the scene so swiftly. Has the doctor been called?"

"It was another accident," said Bertie, ignoring PC Cross's question. But I knew that was not true.

"Smell the cake!" hissed Daisy in my ear. I stepped forward, leaning over the table, and sniffed. At first I only smelled marzipan, but then I got a tang that was too sharp to be marzipan.

Almonds.

Almonds meant cyanide.

Donald had been *poisoned.*

I looked at Daisy, and George and Alexander. We had to discuss the case—it had just taken a most frightening turn. Donald could not be the murderer, and so the real killer was still on the loose. It was up to us to work out who it was, and there were not many suspects left.

"This does look like an accident," said PC Cross. "I must make sure I am thorough, though. Please stay here, everyone, and I will interview you all in turn. Who saw Mr. Melling last?"

"I haven't seen him for hours," said Bertie. "I was at dinner with Cheng. Butler was there as well."

"You found him?" PC Cross asked Moss.

"Half an hour ago," said Moss, tears in his eyes. "I wanted to make sure he was all right. What will happen to me now?"

PC Cross did not answer. He was frowning around the room. "*Where* is the doctor?" he asked. "And—didn't I ask you children to stay away?"

"I called them!" said Bertie. "I want them here!"

I caught George's eye.

"We'll go outside!" he said at once.

All four of us slipped out into the corridor, closing the door. I had eaten a slice of Christmas cake just a few hours ago, and the memory of its almond scent, after what we had just witnessed, was making me feel ill.

"Meeting!" Daisy whispered. "Quick!"

"Why don't we go to the rooms opposite Alfred's?" asked Alexander, glancing behind him.

"But . . . Chummy's body!" I said.

"It's been taken away," said George. "Didn't you hear PC Cross say it would be? Nothing to worry about."

"Bother!" said Daisy. "I mean—excellent. To the room!"

II

We all slipped down to the second landing and into James Monmouth's rooms. Alexander pushed the door closed behind us and clicked on the light. I thought I would be all right, now that the body had gone—after all, there was nothing left but clean, papered walls—but somehow the dust sheets still thrown across furniture made my skin crawl.

"Oh, Hazel!" said Daisy, noticing me shiver, and she marched over and began whirling sheets off their chairs and sofas. I jumped every time, but it turned the room from a collection of ghosts into nothing more than a living room, newly done up.

"Thank you," I said quietly to Daisy, as she came back to stand next to me, and she winked at me.

"All right!" she said. "Detectives! Attend, please."

"Hold up," said George. "You led the meeting last time. Isn't it our turn?"

"Oh, let Daisy do it!" said Alexander.

"We're equal partners in this," said George calmly. "It's certainly our turn. Alex, get out your notebook. I call this meeting to order."

Daisy wrinkled her nose at him, but all the same I could tell she was pleased to have someone who she could argue with as an equal.

"Donald is dead," she said, and I could tell that the meeting would have two leaders after all. "He's been poisoned with cyanide in that Christmas cake! Hazel and I both smelled it. So what do we know?"

"I never thought Donald would be the next victim!" said Alexander. "I was sure he was the murderer, weren't all of you? Now it *has* to be Amanda!"

"But it isn't her!" I said. "It's true that she's a climber, but she didn't do the last murder, and she didn't do this one either."

We told the boys what we had heard—from both Amanda and the student whom Aunt Eustacia had asked to look after her, Harriet. Amanda had not left St. Lucy's all afternoon, and we had been with her ever since. And according to her, she had not been farther than Bertie's rooms the night before.

"But she might still have done it!" objected George. "You've only got her word, and her friend's!"

"Yes, but—" I thought hard. "No! This murder—the

cake—rules her out. Moss said that it was a present, left outside Donald's rooms this afternoon, didn't he? Well, it must have been put there after PC Cross came and asked all those questions after lunchtime. Amanda couldn't have done it in the early afternoon, because she was with Harriet all afternoon until dinner. After dinner we were watching her, and when we went outside we saw that the snow on the bridge between Maudlin and St. Lucy's hadn't been trodden in by anyone apart from Bertie. She didn't have the opportunity. She's out of the picture."

"She certainly is!" said Daisy. "So we're still after a murderer, and a very cunning one. To have left out poison in a present like that! Of course, if it wasn't Christmas, we could solve the mystery quite quickly. There are only a few chemist's in Cambridge with poison books—for people to note down their names when they buy poisonous things—and all we'd need to do is go into them and read the entries."

"But it is Christmas," said George. "And we can't wait!"

"I know," said Daisy, pleased. "But really, we don't need very long. If the same person killed *both* Chummy and Donald—and I can't imagine there can be more than one murderer running around Maudlin—then we've got to go back over what we know about the *first* murder to help solve the second. And we've only got *one* more good suspect for that: Alfred. All we need to do is prove that he did it."

I knew, logically, that she must be right. If we could solve

Chummy's murder, then we would solve Donald's murder too. Alfred was the most likely suspect. Except . . . something had been bothering me, something rather embarrassing. I did not *like* Alfred at all. He was rude and unkind and grabbing. But if our history together had made me become part of Daisy's family, then I was tied to Alfred by history also. I might show my most English side in England, or try to, but meeting George, and seeing the way he approached life, had reminded me that the Hong Kong part of me was just as important. Alfred was a part of my home, and that mattered to me. I would never get in the way of justice, of course not, but were we *sure* that Alfred was to blame? And until we were, was I not bound to suggest other ideas?

"I don't think it was him," I said. "I think it was . . . Michael Butler."

Hazel!" said Daisy. "We've practically ruled him out! He couldn't have gone all the way up the stairs to set the trap without either Alfred or Moss hearing him."

"Yes!" said Alexander. "George and I tried walking all the way from the bottom of the staircase in our stockinged feet after you'd gone, and PC Cross still came out and caught us halfway up. It can't be done."

"It's only a theory," I said. "But we have to consider all the options until we're sure, don't we?"

"Very true," said Daisy, pursing her lips. "*However—*"

"D'you know what we haven't had time to do, though?" asked George suddenly.

"What haven't we had time to do?" asked Daisy.

"Recreate the exact moment of the first crime," said George. "Harold came to get Alex and me before we could do it this afternoon. We know how and when the murderer set the trap, but what about Chummy's movements? We know he must have come back from his climb, gone out of his rooms, and tripped down the stairs. But *why*? Why did he leave his rooms at two in the morning? And why, when he did, was he moving so quickly that he couldn't simply put out a hand against the wall and stop himself when he caught his foot? He must have been going at almost a run to fall so hard."

"He went out to . . ." Daisy paused. "Goodness!" she said. "He can't have been on his way to bother Donald again if he was going *down* the stairs, could he? Donald's rooms are just across the landing—but *Alfred's* rooms *are* down the stairs from Chummy's. More evidence pointing to him!"

"But why at two in the morning?" asked George. "What could Chummy have needed to go and see Alfred about at that time? And why so fast? *Think* about it! We didn't find a note, did we?"

"No! But . . . something might have made him cross?" suggested Alexander.

"What, though?" asked George.

We all pondered.

"Here, let's pretend we're in Chummy's rooms, and I'll be Chummy," said George, going to the living-room window. "He comes back from his climb, swinging onto the windowsill from the drainpipe, and closes the window behind him. He leaves marks on the sill as he gets down, just like— Wait! Look at this!"

"What is it?" I asked, going to stand next to him. Daisy and Alexander crowded in behind me. I ended up quite crushed against Alexander's shoulder, almost dead from embarrassment.

"No one's using this room," said George. "And it's all newly painted. So why are there dirty marks on *this* windowsill?"

I squinted at where George was pointing. It was true: there were dark scuff marks on the freshly painted sill and the wall directly underneath it. I glanced around and saw that the rest of the room was pristine; the decorators must have only just finished their work a few days ago.

"Perhaps the students come in this way sometimes, when they've been climbing," said Daisy dismissively. "Anyway. This isn't the room we ought to be focusing on. It's the one above it! Carry on with the reconstruction."

"All right, so Chummy gets into his room, and stands there for a moment. Then he sits down and . . ." George paused. "Why didn't he take off his shoes?" he asked. "I would, if I'd just come in from the outdoors. Alex, pretend you've just got into the room. Sit down."

Alexander rather gingerly sat on the sofa in front of the fireplace. I knew he was remembering what had only recently been lying there, and did not blame him at all for feeling squeamish.

"What do you see?" asked George.

"The fireplace," said Alexander. "The wall. The window. The desk's too far away to the right, really."

"So what happened?" asked Daisy. "What made him get up and rush out of the door, before he'd even managed to take his shoes off? Did he hear something?"

I could tell she was frustrated.

"But no one's said they heard anything on the staircase before Chummy fell," I said. "Amanda"—I thought back—"Amanda said she heard a scream, and then a crash as Chummy fell."

"No, Hazel, that's *not* what she said," said Daisy. "What Amanda *said* was: *I was woken up by a clattering noise, the most dreadful yell, and then a horrid crash.* So we have to account for—" She froze. "Detectives!" she gasped. "I have just seen it! At last! How could we all have been so stupid? I know why there are marks on this windowsill, and where the wood came from. *I know why Chummy left his rooms!*"

We all stared at her expectantly. I felt a rush of excitement. The solution was almost in our hands, hovering just out of reach, but drifting closer every second.

"Climbing," said Daisy. "Listen! Climbing's gone all the way through this case. Chummy was a climber. The fishing line that was used to set his trap was a climbing line. The murderer must have climbed as well. So why didn't we think that climbing might have been used to kill him? Imagine it. After the trap is set, the murderer waits—not in their own rooms, but in *this* room, James Monmouth's rooms, which they know is empty for the holidays, just below Chummy's. They've got this window open, so they can hear the rattle of the drainpipe as Chummy goes back into his rooms. He comes from the roofs, remember, so he wouldn't go past anyone else's window. As *soon* as he's inside, and his window is closed, the murderer climbs up the drainpipe, a length of wood in their coat pocket. They jam it across his window—they would have already measured it, to make sure it's exactly the right length to fit across the windowpanes, so the window can't be opened—and then they knock.

"Chummy looks up from the sofa. Either the curtains are open, or he goes to the window and opens them. He sees the murderer, staring in at him. He tries to push open the window itself, but he can't because of the wood! I think the murderer must have taunted him—made faces, something like that. Then they pop away out of sight.

"Chummy's annoyed. He loves playing tricks, so he must not have liked being the subject of one. And of course he hates that he can't open the window to follow. So he turns and rushes out of the door, downstairs, to catch them up before they reach their rooms. And he pitches headfirst down the stairs."

"All the murderer would have to do then is knock the bit of wood away into the garden, climb back down to the empty room—explaining the scuff marks on this newly painted windowsill, from their feet when they scrambled back inside—and rush out into the staircase, moments after Chummy's fall. In the confusion, no one would notice that they came from James Monmouth's rooms, and not their own. Daisy, that's genius!" cried George. "I believe you've got it!"

Daisy beamed, and gave a small bow.

I could see it in my head, and I could see that it was right. It answered so many questions—it was so neat and perfect. My heart skipped. But if the murderer was a climber, it could only be one person.

Alfred.

Everything fitted.

"You really think *he* did it?" I asked, swallowing.

I imagined what would happen to Alfred if we accused him of murdering two Englishmen. Would he be given the opportunity to explain himself? Or would PC Cross and the rest of the police, and a jury and judge, simply look at the color of his skin and make up their minds on the spot?

"I think he's the most likely suspect," said George.

"But what if we *are* wrong?" I asked. "Once we've accused him, we won't be able to take it back!"

"That is very true," said Daisy. "PC Cross is a terrible clodhopper. So?"

"Think about it!" I said. "What if it were me? Or . . . or George? We're not British, Daisy—at least, not in the way you are, or Chummy or Donald. Would we be given a chance to defend ourselves if we were accused of a crime? Would we be listened to properly?"

"Neither of you would ever kill anyone!" said Daisy.

"But what if we were suspected?" I asked. "I don't just mean killing someone! What if we were accused of . . . of stealing? Or lying? We could argue, and try to prove that we were innocent—but they *might* not believe us. We have to be utterly sure before we say it's him!"

I knew I was speaking the truth. British people were always waiting for the moment that proved we were not like them. We could study Britishness at the best schools, like I had, or we could even be born British, like George—but we did not look right, and deep down, everyone knew that meant we could never *be* right. It made me feel quite lost, for a moment. I have grown up wishing I could be absolutely English. That was why I had come to Deepdean. But now that I am nearly fifteen I see that, sometimes, being absolutely English is not the perfect thing to be.

"That's a stupid thought, Hazel," said Daisy angrily. "Stop it at once."

"Hazel's right," said George. "We have to be sure. Nothing matters more than the truth. At the moment, even though we think Alfred is the most likely suspect, either Alfred or Michael *might* be guilty. Let's search Alfred's and Michael's rooms for clues, while we know they are upstairs with PC Cross. We have two suspects, and there are two societies. Here, let's toss a coin. The winning society is allowed to choose their suspect, and they must follow them to the conclusion. Are you in?"

"Yes," said Daisy, eyes sparkling. I knew she wanted to pick Alfred.

George put his hand in his pocket, and pulled out a bright new shilling. "Heads we take Alfred, tails you do. All right?"

"All right," said Daisy, bright with the challenge. "Do your worst!"

The coin flew up in the air, and we all watched it spin. It landed on the stone floor with a crack and a silver flash, shuddered, and lay still. We all peered down at it.

It was heads.

"We've lost," said Daisy to me heavily. "Alexander and George have the guilty suspect!"

We were sitting in one of the cubicles in the bathrooms opposite Michael Butler's rooms. Daisy was on a rickety little chair, and I had perched on the side of the bath, its tap dripping. It had clawed feet, and a sort of industrially clean smell, and cold came off it in waves.

"We haven't!" I said, pulling out this casebook. "Not yet. Let's lay out the facts before we go in there and search. We need to be methodical about what we are looking for."

"Oh, all right," Daisy said, sounding entirely unconvinced. "Go on then. Get out your casebook, and let's begin. *Case for Michael Butler being the murderer*. I'll summarize and you can note it all down.

"Well, we already know that Michael couldn't have gone up the stairs to set the trap for Chummy without being overheard—even if we're right about the murderer using

James Monmouth's rooms, he'd still have had to walk up two flights—so that's no good to us. Let's concentrate on the murder of Donald instead. The facts are these: some time after we left staircase nine, someone left a present of a poisoned Christmas cake outside Donald's rooms. I smelled almonds, and I know you did too. It all does sound ridiculous, doesn't it? Poisoned with a slice of Christmas cake. If you read it in a book you'd never believe it.

"All right, let's pretend that it was Michael. He went up to Donald's rooms before dinner, leaving the cake. But, Hazel, we've got that same old problem. Michael's all the way at the bottom of the stairs. How could he get up to Chummy and Donald's floor without being noticed? He'd be taking a terrible risk. And . . . *why* would he do it? He didn't hate *Donald*, did he?"

"Never mind that," I said, rather desperately. "What about the means? Michael could have got cyanide from a chemist."

"He could indeed," said Daisy. "I know how easy it is to buy it. There was a wasps' nest in the drawing room a few years ago, and Chapman had to pour cyanide solution on it. He bought it from the Fallingford chemist's, a whole bottle of it. He didn't do it very well, poor thing: he breathed in the fumes and Hetty had to end up helping him—otherwise he would have offed himself. All Michael—or Alfred—would have to do would be to add their names to the poison book. Of course, Alfred would be far more noticeable. If a Chinese man went into a chemist's and asked for poison, he wouldn't be forgotten in a hurry!"

I felt rather ill. We were supposed to be making the case for Michael, but Daisy could not seem to stop suspecting Alfred.

"All right," said Daisy. "What *about* Michael's motive? If he did it, it can't be simply that he didn't like Donald, or Chummy. There are very few people in the world, no matter where they are from, who would kill someone, kill *two* people, because they didn't like them very much. He has nothing to gain by their deaths, and as far as we know, he didn't even *know* them before this year! And even if he was the person who discovered the essay scam—why wouldn't he simply turn Chummy in to the Master? It doesn't make sense."

I sighed, and Daisy did too, like an echo.

I put my hand in hers, comfortingly, and she held it so tightly that my bones clicked.

"We can't give in!" I said. "Let's do as we agreed and go to Michael's rooms. We can look around while he's upstairs with PC Cross. You never know!"

"I suppose you never do," said Daisy, sighing even harder. "Watson, you really are a brick."

But as I made new notes about our suspects, I did not feel much like a brick at all.

SUSPECT LIST

1. ~~Bertie Wells. MOTIVE: Unknown. OPPORTUNITY: He lives on staircase nine, and he was there at the time the prank must have been set. ALIBI: Says he was in his rooms. Is this true? NOTES: He is a Maudlin student and a climber, and had opportunity to commit all the previous pranks.~~ RULED OUT! He was climbing with George Mukherjee, Harold Mukherjee, and Alexander Arcady from 12:15 to 2:15—he could not have set up the fishing line.

2. ~~Donald Melling. MOTIVE: He is Chummy's older brother, but was very controlled by him. Now that Chummy is dead, he will still inherit the money on his birthday, but be able to dispose of it however he likes. OPPORTUNITY: He lives on staircase nine, and he was there at the time the prank must have been set. We found fishing line in his rooms. ALIBI: None yet. NOTES: He is a Maudlin student and a climber, and had opportunity to commit all the previous pranks—although he seemed to be the victim of them. Was this just a clever ruse? He argued with Chummy at 12:30, and then had the best opportunity to set the trap as soon as Chummy climbed out onto the Maudlin roofs. He seems very glad that Chummy is dead. He also told PC Cross~~

~~that he phoned Amanda about Chummy's death, but we believe this is a lie-making him even more suspicious.~~ RULED OUT!. He has become the second victim.

3. Alfred Cheng. MOTIVE: He hated Chummy, and was overheard saying he wanted to punish him. OPPORTUNITY: He was on staircase nine on the night of the murder. ALIBI: None yet. NOTES: He is a Maudlin student and a climber and had opportunity to commit all the previous pranks. Suspicious behavior observed. He went back into his rooms after Chummy's fall. Why? He seems truly to hate Chummy, the reason why he went back into his rooms after Chummy fell-is this enough motive to have killed him? Is he the person who found out about Chummy paying Amanda to write his essays? He is now one of the two suspects in Donald's murder. He had opportunity to leave the cake outside Donald's door yesterday late afternoon, and he could have bought poison from a Cambridge chemist's.

4. Michael Butler. MOTIVE: ~~None yet.~~ He disliked Chummy. OPPORTUNITY: He lives on staircase nine, and was there on the night of the murder. ALIBI: None yet. NOTES: He is part of Maudlin. He could possibly have staged the door, the mistletoe, and the pond, though not the climbing accident. Not a climber, though

he could have taken the fishing line from someone else's rooms. It would have been extremely difficult for him to get all the way up the stairs without being heard. Is he the person who found out about Chummy paying Amanda to write his essays? Could this be enough of a motive? He is now one of the two suspects in Donald's murder. Although it would have been very difficult, he did have opportunity to leave the cake outside Donald's door yesterday late afternoon, and he could have bought poison from a Cambridge chemist's.

5. ~~Moss. MOTIVE: None yet. OPPORTUNITY: Was on staircase nine on the night of the murder. ALIBI: He says he went to bed at 12:30, when the trap was not yet set. Is this true? NOTES: Not a climber, though he could have taken the fishing line from someone else's rooms. Was seen trying to destroy evidence.~~ RULED OUT! Although we know he has good reason to dislike Chummy, having worked for the Melling family and believing Donald to have been unfairly treated by his parents and brother, we know that he was locked in his rooms by Chummy from 12:30 until just after the fall, when he was let out by Donald. He could not have escaped to set up the fishing line. ~~He is innocent-but he clearly believes that Donald is guilty. Is this true?~~

6. ~~Mr. Perkins. MOTIVE: None yet. OPPORTUNITY: Lives in Maudlin, though not on staircase nine—he has keys, though. ALIBI: None yet. NOTES: Could he really have set all the previous traps? Seems very unlikely. We must rule him out.~~ RULED OUT! His wife and the ill student, Walter Cookridge, give him his alibi. He did hear something important, though: Chummy climbing about on the Maudlin roofs at about 12:45.

7. ~~Amanda Price. Was not on staircase nine on the night of the murder, but says she was telephoned in the middle of the night. Is this true—and if not, why would she lie? We believe she was lying, and that she was in fact on staircase nine at the time of the murder. NOTES: From the evidence of mud and dirt on her coat, she may have climbed over the dons' garden wall and up the drainpipe to staircase nine. This would give her means and opportunity to set the trap, and she has a motive—Chummy was buying essays from her, which she hated, and she recently discovered that someone else on staircase nine knew about the cheating. She has been behaving suspiciously, and if she is a climber she could have set all the traps—we must consider her one of our best suspects.~~ RULED OUT! She was at Maudlin, but she did not commit Chummy's murder—and our own evidence, combined with Harriet's and the lack of tracks in the snow, rules her out of Donald's.

I was nervous as we pushed on the door to Michael's rooms—would it be unlocked?—but it swung open quite smoothly, and inside the space was quiet and dark. Daisy clicked on the electric light and it illuminated a sitting room exactly like Bertie's: a sofa in front of a fireplace, with a window to the left and a desk to the right. The window looked out onto the dons' gardens, and Daisy went to it and peered out nosily.

"The snow's covered everything," she said. "Bother!"

I was looking around the room itself. It was rather untidy—or, rather, it was tidy, but quite dirty. There were wisps of dust and dirty smudges on all the surfaces. I saw a little scrap of a label—B-O-C-K,—I read—on the floor. I nudged Daisy, and she picked it up, narrowing her eyes. She tucked it away in her pocket, but I was not sure whether it was a clue, or merely a bit of waste paper. It looked as though this room was Moss's lowest priority. It also did not look at all festive. You would hardly know that Christmas was almost here. There was no tinsel, or boughs of greenery, not even a present. Michael really was poor—no wonder he lived at Maudlin.

There was a stack of books above the desk, all quite scholarly, and some framed pictures of short, brown-haired people with snub noses who I supposed must be Michael's family. I looked at them and thought how alike everyone seems to become, in pictures. I am always being told that Chinese people all look the same, but to me, English people are just as similar.

I began to flick through the papers on the desk. Then I saw something that made my heart jump in my chest.

"Daisy!" I said. "Look, this is one of the essays Amanda wrote for Chummy! This means *Michael* must be the person who knew about what was going on!"

Daisy leaped up and came over to me. "How odd!" she said. "So it is! But if Michael was the person who found the essays, why hasn't he reported them to the Master yet? Why are they still here?"

"Perhaps he was going to, after the holidays?" I suggested. But there was something about that which did not sound quite right to me. Michael was so sensible and grown up. Why would he hold something like this back?

"You don't think he was blackmailing Chummy?" I asked uncertainly.

"He does need money," said Daisy, turning and waving at the room. "Look at everything—old and second-best! It could be that. But if he wanted to blackmail Chummy, then he'd have even *less* reason to kill him, or Donald. He doesn't stand to gain by their deaths, does he? Oh, perhaps he thought they weren't behaving like good Maudlin students! Remember how he shouted at Bertie?"

"Daisy, that's unlikely!" I said, raising my eyebrows and going back to flicking through the books. Then I froze. "Ssh!" I hissed. "There's someone outside . . ."

We both listened, and heard the unmistakable clumping sound of PC Cross walking down the stairs and out into the snow. He must have finished his questioning! Everyone would be back in their rooms soon. We had to hurry!

Daisy turned away from the desk and quickly began rooting about in the fireplace. Her hands went black to the elbows and her nose was smudged. At that moment, she did not look ladylike at all.

"Something might be here," she said. "Fireplaces are excellent hiding places, I've been told."

"Aunt Eustacia will murder you if you come back all covered in soot," I said. "Hurry, Daisy—he could be back any minute!"

"Aunt Eustacia loves snooping as much as I do," said Daisy. "Never mistake that. And anyway, perhaps everyone will go straight to Midnight Mass—Bertie always does, at home." She sounded calm. "Nothing, nothing . . . wait! What's this?"

She sat up. In her hands was a little book. It looked quite black at first, but as she wiped at it we saw that it was titled with dim gold letters.

"It's a Bible!" I said.

"Odd," said Daisy. "Why would someone hide a Bible in a fireplace, so close to Christmas?"

"Perhaps Michael has renounced religion?" I asked. "He is at university, after all."

"Hazel, no one renounces the Church of England," said Daisy, raising her eyebrows at me. "That would be—oh, I can't explain, it just isn't *done*."

"I suppose you'd know," I said.

"I would," said Daisy. "Let's see. Why would Michael hide this?" She opened it and began flicking through. "No, it's perfectly ordinary. Nothing written on it, no pages missing."

"Look at the title page," I said. "Perhaps it's stolen too."

Daisy's eyebrows went even higher. "If you like," she said. Then her face changed. "Hazel!" she said. "It *is* stolen! Look at this, how funny! It's *Chummy and Donald's* Bible! Their name's here, handwritten on the title page—look, *Melling*. It's one of those special family Bibles with the family tree in the front—we've got one at Fallingford. Look, there's Chummy's and Donald's names, and their parents's, and—" She stopped.

I got a shiver down my spine, a wriggling feeling all along my skin. "And?" I asked.

"Their grandfather had a brother," said Daisy. "A younger one. He got married young, to a Sophia Lamb, and they had a son, Henry Melling. *He* married someone called Amy Butler, and *they* had a son called Henry Michael Melling in May 1905. They divorced just after this Henry Michael Melling was born, look, in 1905. Hazel, how old would you say Michael was?"

"Thirty," I said.

"What if—what if Amy Butler began going by her maiden name again, after the divorce? She'd have called her son the same thing. And she wouldn't have wanted to call her son by her ex-husband's first name, either, so she might have begun calling him by his middle name."

"*Michael Butler,*" I breathed. "If it is him—that makes him Chummy and Donald's cousin!"

I suddenly realized something that I should have noticed long before. Family had been running through this case, just as much as climbing. I remembered Daisy saying *Christmas is quite the worst time for family*, Aunt Eustacia telling us about how an entail *sends all the relatives wild, imagining what would have to happen to leave them in control of the money*, and Michael himself saying *Christmas is the worst time for family. Makes me glad it's only me and my mother—no one else to argue with.*

"Hazel, look at this family tree—there aren't any other relatives living. Now that Chummy and Donald are dead, everything goes to this person, this Henry Michael Melling. We said Michael didn't have any motive. But this gives him all the motive in the world! We know how rich Donald would have become, if he'd reached his twenty-first birthday. He didn't, by a few *hours*, and neither did his brother, Chummy. That means that Donald couldn't buy that mine of his, and Chummy couldn't start spending any of the money either. *All* of it goes to this Henry Melling. And if Henry Melling is Michael Butler—why, it explains the whole case!

"Haven't we kept saying how oddly *undirected* the pranks, or murder attempts, really were? Donald and Chummy were climbing together. They were *both* near the stone when it fell. They *both* drank the mistletoe. Either of them might have been pushed into the pond—they looked the same in their black caps and gowns. And although it was Chummy who fell down the stairs, Chummy who was coaxed out of his rooms, it really wasn't out of the question that Donald might have come out of his rooms in the middle of the night to use the bathroom, and fallen. We assumed, because Chummy died first, that he was the real target and we had been wrong about Donald being the victim—but if it was *both* of them, everything makes so much more sense! It didn't matter who died first, only that they *both* did, and before Christmas. I suppose that when mistletoe and the pond didn't work on Donald, Michael went out to get cyanide—they couldn't both fall down the stairs! Remember when we saw him in town on Monday? That must have been the moment when he got the poison, and the cake as well! Do you know, while we were shopping on Monday, I observed Cambridge's chemists'—just as a precaution, you understand. A detective never knows what may be of use."

"And?"

"There's a *Bocking* chemist's on Rose Crescent," said Daisy. "Licensed to sell poisons. Doesn't that fit with the bit of paper I just found? Now, let's see, what about the Bible? Michael must have found the Bible when he came across the essays that Amanda had written for Chummy—of course it would have been in Chummy's rooms. Michael would have realized who he was, and what he needed to do to get the money. Of course, he couldn't destroy the Bible, he'd need it later, to prove who he was. But he realized how dangerous it could be to him if it was discovered. If he'd turned Chummy in, Chummy might have connected the missing Bible with the missing essay, and realize who Michael was. So he hid it up here. It makes sense!" She thrust the Bible into my hands.

"But, Daisy," I said, clutching the Bible in both hands in my excitement. "We've still got a problem. Michael doesn't climb! He couldn't have got up to Chummy's window, or all the way up the stairs without being seen! It doesn't work, Daisy. It has to be a red herring."

"Bother!" cried Daisy, sitting back on her heels. "Oh, bother! Pipped at the post! You're right, Hazel. We can't get around that fact. The trap had to be set by a climber. And Michael doesn't climb. At least—"

"Excuse me," said a voice. "What are you doing in my room?"

VII

We both wheeled about in horror. It was Michael Butler. He stood in the doorway, looking puzzled and not particularly threatening. His hair was uncombed and he was wearing a smoking jacket. There was even a small pen smudge on the end of his nose . . . his short nose. Snub, like Donald's. His hair, just a few shades lighter than Chummy's. I had said that all English people look alike to me. It was only now I saw that I had stumbled upon the truth without even realizing it.

If Michael was Chummy and Donald's cousin, he would get all their money. It was the sort of motive that made more sense than anything. Money matters. Although I did not understand that when I was young, I have seen it clear as anything many times since Daisy and I began to be detectives. Not having it makes you want it fiercely, and having some of it makes you hungry for more and more. Michael was not rich—this room proved that.

But could someone kill their own family to get it? I thought about my little half-sisters. I think my mother expected me to hate them, because they are only half my blood, but the truth is that the *half* does not matter. They are my sisters, the only ones I know, and I could not love them any more than I do. But if I had grown up not knowing them? Perhaps I would care less then. And if I was not me, but Michael Butler, who was cold to the students he looked after and shouted at people when they stepped in front of his bicycle in the street?

All that thinking, though it takes a long time to write, happened in only the few seconds it took for Michael to step forward, out of the doorway, toward where we were standing.

"What are you doing in my rooms?" he asked again. His voice was calm and chiding. We were naughty children, and we were about to be sent away.

But then he caught sight of the Bible in my hands. I saw his face change.

"How did you find that?" he asked. "Have you been snooping? Did Bertie put you up to this?"

"Bertie didn't put us up to anything!" Daisy burst out before she could stop herself. "We were tidying the grate, and we found it. You ought to have a woman about, this room really isn't clean."

Michael turned to me. "Give it here," he said. "Come

on. I don't need anyone to tidy up after me."

"Of course you do!" said Daisy, playing for time. "Look around! There's dust and dirt everywhere. The sofa, the grate, the windowsill. Even on your coat!"

And as she said that, something fell into place in my head. I remembered the marks Alexander had found on the windowsill of James Monmouth's rooms. I thought of how dirty climbers' shoes and coats became—how dirty Amanda's coat had been. And I looked at Michael. Thirty was not so old for a grown-up. He might still be able to climb. And what had he said on the day before Chummy was murdered? *At least it'll all be over on the twenty-fifth.* At that moment I knew that whether or not it seemed *possible* that Michael was the murderer, it had to be true. All the evidence was here.

"Daisy!" I said frantically, stepping back from Michael.

"Hazel," said Daisy. "Quick!"

I knew exactly what she meant. I turned and threw the Bible at her. I am not a good throw at the best of times—things tend to go soaring into the air and then flop down a few feet away from me. All my games teachers despair over it. But this time my throw was true. The Bible shot from my hands into Daisy's.

As soon as her hands clasped about it she was on the move. She took two running steps toward the window and leaped up onto its frame. We had left the window open when we stepped away from it, and I was glad of that now.

For a moment Daisy balanced on the sill, and then she jumped forward again and landed with a thump in the snow of the dons' garden.

"Hey!" cried Michael. "Where are you going?"

He shoved past me to the window, and I backed away.

"She's going up the drainpipe," I said. "She's going to take the Bible and drop it onto Maudlin's roof. You'll never get it then."

It was a guess—but the sort that was easy to make. I knew Daisy. I knew exactly what she would do.

"She is *not*!" cried Michael—and in a flash he was up on the sill as well, leaping out of the window and throwing himself at the pipe.

He was a climber, after all.

VIII

I rushed forward, heart thumping, to crane out of the window. Daisy has spent many years putting me in danger for the sake of the Detective Society (or at least, so it feels) but now, for once, she had decided to save me by throwing herself in harm's way, and I found myself desperately wishing that she had not.

I could see her climbing up the pipe, gripping with knees and fingers like a monkey. She is good, and fast—but so was Michael. His arms were stronger, and I could see him gaining on her. The few seconds' lead she'd had was rapidly shrinking. The pipe rattled and clanked. Of course, that was the noise Amanda had heard on the night of Chummy's death. Michael might have gone up it carefully, but while he hurried back down to James's rooms, after he had surprised Chummy, he would have had to go too quickly to be quiet. It was another thing I ought to have realized.

"Come back!" hissed Michael. "Come back here!"

He was so quiet that it made me tremble. I knew that he did not want to be heard, and that meant that he hoped to catch Daisy without anyone knowing. I wanted her to shout too, but she did not make a noise—and then I realized that she had the Bible clamped in her teeth.

So I began to yell.

"HURRY!" I shouted. "GO ON, DAISY! HE'S CATCHING UP!"

I was terribly afraid that I was being too quiet. Just as in bad dreams, my voice sounded smaller than it ought—but then a head popped out of the window just above me. It was Bertie.

"I say!" he called down. "What's up?"

I pointed. "Daisy!" I gasped. "Michael!"

I could not explain. I wanted to run up the staircase to them, but at the same time I did not want to move. Michael reached out a hand and grabbed at Daisy's foot. He missed. Then he tried again.

"I say!" called Bertie. "Be careful! What— Butler, what are you doing? Careful, that's my sister!"

It must have been awfully strange for him, seeing Michael Butler climbing, just like us seeing a mistress suddenly doing a handstand. That was what Chummy must have felt too, when he looked out of his window and saw Michael there: utter shock and horror. Once he had tried the window, and it had stuck, he would have gone running out of his rooms in a state of outrage. Michael knew about the essays, and now Michael was looking in through his window. He would have wanted to have it out with him at once—he would not have been expecting the trap at all.

"BERTIE!" I shouted, and at last the terror I felt came through in my voice. Bertie looked down at me, and I saw him understand.

"SQUASHY!" he cried. He almost swung out of his window too, but then he checked himself. I realized what he had—that the drainpipe might not take all three. It was creaking more and more.

Michael swung at Daisy again. This time his hand caught her foot. She kicked out at him, and he let go, cursing. They were more than three quarters of the way up now, their figures receding in the dark. I could only make out her white socks, and flashes of his white dress shirt. Daisy must have used that moment to gain a few more inches, because she seemed to edge out of reach. It maddened Michael, and at last he lost all self-control.

"COME HERE!" he bellowed, and he swung furiously, letting go of the pipe with his arms, so he was merely clinging on with his legs.

I saw Daisy's socks kick out again, hard. She was only hanging on by her arms, she must have been, and for a moment she swung out wide, perilously close to dropping.

“Stop that!” Bertie shouted, leaning out of his window, and he swiped at Michael.

Then Michael Butler gave a yell, one without any words in it. His arms cartwheeled—and then, like a stone, he fell.

Part Eight
Peace on Earth

He did not make much noise when he hit the ground. The snow covered him up like a blanket. I jumped out of the open window and into the dons' garden.

I stumbled, and felt the cold rise up my legs. Then I was running—slowly again, the way I do in dreams. The snow clumped around my shoes, heavy as mud. Although snow looks so light and lovely, in the dark of that night it did not feel that way at all.

I was there beside Michael first. He had fallen forward, on to his front, and he had missed the bushes at the base of the building—he was lying in a flat, wide patch of snow. His leg was at a horrid angle. He reminded me of the snow angels that Daisy and Bertie had made last year, when it snowed at Fallingford on Boxing Day.

"Mr. Butler?" I whispered. "Mr. Butler?"

I put out my hand, and suddenly I was back at Deepdean

again, in the Gym. I had thought that evening dark, but this was darker. If Michael was dead, what would that mean for Daisy and Bertie? Would they be to blame?

But then Michael Butler groaned. "Help me!" he said. "My leg!"

"Don't move!" I said. "They're coming. It'll be all right."

I did not know *who* was coming. I only hoped someone was. It was fearfully strange and backward, to be sitting in the snow comforting a murderer, but there seemed nothing else to be done.

I felt a hand on my shoulder. It was Bertie, and Daisy was next to him.

"I hope you're hurting!" said Bertie angrily to Michael, squeezing Daisy tightly to him. "You almost killed my sister, you cad!"

"I was quite all right!" said Daisy. "Bertie, stop exaggerating. Ow!"

I saw that there was a scratch on her leg, bleeding into her sock. "Are you sure you're all right?" I whispered.

Daisy glanced at Bertie and then leaned down to me. "He nearly caught me," she whispered back. "Hazel, it wasn't very nice. But don't tell Bertie that. He worries."

"Here," said Bertie to Michael. "What were you *doing*?"

"He killed Chummy and Donald!" said Daisy. "He's the one who's been setting all the traps, so he could inherit their money. He's their *cousin*—a secret one!"

"What?" cried Bertie, wheeling round to gape at us both. "Not really?"

"Of course!" said Daisy. "Hazel worked it out first, actually. Which is odd, because usually no one can beat me at detection. Here, Michael—or Henry, or whatever your name is. Did you always know who you were, or did you only work it out when you found the Bible?"

Michael groaned again, but this time I got the impression that he was putting it on.

"Answer her!" said Bertie. "Or I shall kick you."

"I shan't," said Michael. "I'm not going to say anything."

"I don't think he *did* know," said Daisy. "I think it was a surprise. But once he'd worked it out . . . well, I suppose he got the idea of pranks from Chummy." I could see Daisy recovering, becoming Daisy again. "He hoped that if both deaths looked like accidents—a fall down the stairs and a poisoning—he'd get away with it. But he reckoned without us! We've got the wood, and the poison label, and the Bible. *We've got him!*"

"Hello? Are you all right?" called a voice, and George and Alexander came panting up to us.

"What happened?" asked George. "Here, what's Michael doing on the ground?"

"He fell," said Daisy. "He was chasing me. He can climb—*he's* the murderer!"

"Well, why's *Hazel* sitting in the snow?" asked Alexander, above me. "Come on—"

I felt arms around my shoulders, and I was pulled to my feet in a rush. I buried my face in Alexander's coat. *I love Alexander*, I thought before I could stop myself. Then I almost drowned with embarrassment. How stupid of me, when I knew he never would love me back. What a silly, Hazel-ish thing to think. I could feel the tears leaking out of my eyes, smearing the good wool of his coat, and I was dreadfully embarrassed. I was glad it was so dark. But there had been a moment when I thought that Daisy might die. And I could not have borne that.

People were shouting all around me. Moss and Mr. Perkins had arrived, and Alfred, and PC Cross must have been called back, because he was there with the doctor, who had just arrived to examine Donald's body.

Then I was being led away, through the snow. I was suddenly somewhere much lighter, and there was a cup of tea in my hands, and someone was saying, "Hazel? Hazel?"

I blinked, and looked up. I was in Bertie's rooms, sitting on the sofa in front of a roaring fire. The lamps were lit, and the candles on the Christmas tree were burning. They made the tinsel glitter, the fronds of it floating gently, like fur or feathers. It all looked wonderfully festive. I glanced at the clock ticking on the mantelpiece, and saw that it was one o'clock in the morning. It was Christmas Day, I remembered. Christmas, in Cambridge, with snow on the ground—and two murders at Maudlin.

Alexander was sitting on one side of me, and George on the other, and Daisy was kneeling in front of me, peering into my face.

"Hazel!" said Daisy. "Buck up! You're quite all right. Now, come on. Don't you want to tell everyone about how we solved the case?"

"Is Michael all right?" I asked thickly.

"Quite all right," said George. "Apart from a broken leg

and broken ribs. He's been carted off to hospital, with PC Cross's sergeant guarding him. He won't get away!"

There were quite a lot of other people in the room, I saw now. There was Bertie, propped up against the mantelpiece, and Amanda, slumped in Bertie's desk chair. Amanda might be fierce, and bitter, but she had tried to go back to Maudlin when she thought Bertie was in danger—she would have put herself in harm's way for him, and I knew that made her a good person. Alfred was slouching on the other side of the sofa, and beside the fireplace (beginning to blaze up, Moss had just finished lighting it, and was still kneeling next to it, brushing off his hands) stood PC Cross.

His round, pink face was frowning in distress, and he was clutching his official notebook as though it was the last thing keeping him afloat in a storm.

"I've never had a murder case before," he said, to no one in particular. "It's quite a joke, at the station. Never at the right place at the right time."

I thought that whatever talent PC Cross had, Daisy and I had quite the opposite. These days, we never seemed to be able to go anywhere without finding a body there to meet us.

"Well, you're making up for it now," said Alfred.

I looked at him, and wondered whether he knew how close he had come to being accused. Then I saw a twitch at the side of his mouth, and knew that he did. I hoped he would be all right, now that there was no Chummy to torment him.

"I don't understand," said PC Cross, and he swung his gaze around all of us. "I don't *understand*. What happened? How did Mr. Butler end up hurt as well? What was he doing climbing buildings in the middle of the night?"

Daisy opened her mouth. So did Bertie.

"He was trying to get away," he said, before she could say a word. "I think he was trying to escape over the roofs. But his hands must have slipped in the cold. It's icy, you know."

There was a pause.

"Yes," said Daisy. "Hazel and I went into his room because we were playing hide-and-seek, to take our minds off things, you know. But while we were hiding, we found something quite odd: a bit of a label from a chemist's, and a Bible that had Mr. Butler's name in it, and Chummy's, and Donald's. They were all related to one another! We were still looking at it when Michael came in. He got awfully upset. Then he seized the Bible from Hazel and dived out of the window."

"*Related?*" repeated PC Cross.

"Yes!" said Daisy. "Michael was their cousin."

She said it so innocently—it really did sound almost as though she had only come across the information by mistake. For all that we are older now, Daisy is still just as good as she ever was at sounding like a silly little girl.

PC Cross frowned. There was a pause.

"Goodness!" said George. "Michael killed Chummy and Donald so he would inherit their money!"

PC Cross's mouth opened, and I could see understanding dawn across his face. Daisy and George winked at each other, very slightly.

"He set up the trap for Chummy!" said Alexander, jumping in to help. "He must have been setting all the traps—the dangerous ones, I mean. We didn't know he could climb. But he must have set the fishing line by climbing up the pipe after Chummy had gone out that evening. *That* was why no one heard any feet on the stairs, of course!"

Moss gasped. "I knew I hadn't heard anyone climbing the stairs!" he said. "Just someone on the landing. I couldn't understand it—I thought it had to be Mr. Donald. Oh, poor boy!"

I felt terribly sorry for him. He really had been fond of Donald.

"And he could have climbed up the pipe again to leave that cake outside Donald's rooms yesterday afternoon, after we'd all gone," Alexander went on. "While it was getting dark, so no one would see him."

"I hear it's quite easy to get cyanide," said Daisy. "Er. I mean. Not that I know. All you have to do is go into a chemist's and say you need to poison wasps. If you went round all of the chemists' in Cambridge I bet you'd find one who recognized Michael. In fact, I saw one the other day that matches the label we found. What was it called, Hazel? *Bocking's?*"

"Miss Wells," said PC Cross. "Rest assured that I shall be making a tour of Cambridge chemists' as soon as it is light, even if it *is* Christmas Day. Give me that label, will you?"

"What's going to happen to Michael?" I asked.

"If the evidence does stack up, he will stand trial," said PC Cross. "Don't you worry, Miss Wong. We'll get our man. Do you know, I wonder whether . . . I thought the other officers were mocking me, about never being at a death. But perhaps they were only jealous. This murder business . . . it isn't a very nice thing, is it?"

"No," I said, and for a moment I did not feel grown up at all. "It isn't."

PC Cross left the room, and Moss went with him. The rest of us all sat around and stared at the flames of the fire and the candles on the Christmas tree. We were quiet, at first. Then we began to talk.

"So," said Bertie. "Butler was a climber. I ought to have guessed, really. Some of the dons are, or they were, in their student days. But he seemed so grown up!"

"Daisy and Hazel worked it out, really," said George. Alexander smiled at me and my insides lit up at the sight.

"It was all of us!" I said. "We worked together."

"*Worked together?*" asked Bertie. "Squashy! Have you been playing games again?"

"Of course we have," said Daisy. "Treasure hunts and so on. It is Christmas!"

"You are awful," said Bertie. "You shouldn't play games, Squashy. Not with death. It's—it's not funny." He leaned slightly toward her, so that their shoulders were just touching, and then he brushed her hand with his. "But I'm glad you're all right," he said. "I told you I'd look after you, didn't I?"

"I don't need looking after!" said Daisy. "You are silly, Squinty." She took his hand, and squeezed it with hers. They seemed closer than they had ever been, and I thought that for some families, Christmas was a nice time of year after all.

"So, Michael set the pranks as well?" asked Amanda. She looked tired, but less cross than I had ever seen her. Some of the tension had lifted from her shoulders, and I saw how nervous she had been about being mixed up in Chummy's death. "I really did think it was Chummy!"

"Yes!" said Daisy, turning away from Bertie. "He did them all—I mean, all the dangerous things, in the last few weeks. You see, we realized that it didn't make sense if the target was only one person. But when you realize that the culprit didn't care who was hurt, then it works perfectly. Chummy had been pranking Donald in a harmless way all term, and that's where Michael must have got the idea from. Of course, I don't know everything, but I can guess.

"The climbing accident started things off, didn't it? Well, Bertie said that it was a well-known route. Perhaps Michael overheard Chummy and Donald talking about making the attempt. Then all he had to do was to go on ahead and loosen the stone—he didn't have to worry about which of them it would injure. And if someone else was hurt . . . well, that didn't matter to him. He really isn't a very nice person!

"Next was the bucket on the door. Michael climbed up to the top landing using the pipe and set the trap in Donald's rooms. Easy, for a climber."

"And the same for the mistletoe," said George, butting in. "Daisy Wells, you're taking all the credit. Michael climbs up, slips into Donald's rooms, and crushes some of the berries from the sprigs hanging up into a decanter of port. He assumed that Donald would drink it—and if he didn't, Chummy would. All he wanted was to make them ill enough that when one of them was pushed into the pond he wouldn't cry out or struggle. At least he stopped us younger ones drinking the port. He wasn't all bad."

"Shush," said Daisy. "You're interrupting my dénouement. Michael must have realized that Chummy was suggesting everyone drink the bad bottle at the party, and decided to drink it as well, so that he didn't look suspicious."

That made me feel rather unwell. I thought about how much Michael had gambled—and what he had lost.

"And then the pond," Daisy went on. "He lay in wait in the dark, until Donald went by. But if Chummy had happened to go by first, he would have pushed him in as well. It didn't *matter*. Which brings us to the stairs. I think Michael must have been getting frustrated by then. Nothing was working. No one was even seriously hurt. The good thing was that everyone simply thought they were pranks, but the bad thing was that Chummy and Donald were still alive. And he had to kill them both before Christmas Day if he wanted to be sure of getting *all* the money.

"He must have planned the fishing line trick in advance. The room downstairs was being done up. He took a moment when the builders were there to knock that nail into the skirting board. Then everything was ready to be used whenever he wanted.

"He heard Donald and Chummy arguing that night—we know because he went upstairs to tell them off. He heard Chummy climbing out of the window—I wonder if he even heard Chummy locking Moss into his rooms—and he knew it was the perfect chance. He climbed up the drainpipe into Chummy's rooms so he wouldn't be heard, went out of the door, and set up the fishing line. Of course, he had some because he was a climber. Easy. Then he climbed back down the drainpipe into the empty room and waited, to make absolutely sure that he heard Chummy when he came back in. Remember what Amanda said, Hazel, that when she arrived she saw *all* the lights on the staircase on?"

"Yes!" I said. "I thought of that! There shouldn't have been anyone in that empty room. And according to Michael's alibi, he should have been asleep by then, with his light off."

"But he wasn't!" said Daisy, nodding. "He was in the empty room. He waited until he heard Chummy coming back and closing the window above him. Then he climbed back out onto the drainpipe and up to Chummy's rooms. He shoved that bit of wood across the window, so it wouldn't open outward, and then he tapped on the glass. Chummy saw Michael and he was horrified. I wonder whether he realized then that Michael was the person who'd stolen the essays. He must have been angry, too. He went to the window and tried to open it, but of course it stuck. So Chummy, in a terrible funk, spun about and rushed out of the door to go to Michael's rooms downstairs—tripping over the fishing line and falling."

"*That's enough*," said Bertie, standing up. "Can't we talk about something else? Today, although you all seem to have forgotten it, is Christmas. We have a holiday to celebrate!"

"I suppose," said Daisy. "Just because you asked so nicely."

I realized all over again how odd the English are. No matter how bad things get, they can always make light of them.

Then the Master of Maudlin arrived, with Aunt Eustacia rushing in behind him like an avenging angel. I was glad that so much had happened that he was not likely to remember banning us. But although Aunt Eustacia was angry, at that moment she felt safe, and clean, and clear. I wanted to wrap my arms about her, but of course I did not. Alexander, George, and Harold were sent back to St. John's for Christmas, along with Bertie and Alfred. Maudlin was closing until the next term—Chummy and Donald's party was cancelled and all of the students were being sent away. Amanda, Daisy, and I were going back to St. Lucy's. I found that I was utterly glad.

Once we arrived back, Aunt Eustacia called us into her book-lined study and grilled us on every detail of the case. She wanted to know everything: what we had done, why, and how. We did our best to shield the Detective Society, but she had a way of worming through all of our evasions to get at the truth, and I have the uncomfortable feeling that she really ended up understanding almost the whole story. She is Daisy's great-aunt, after all.

"We *had* to step in!" Daisy kept on saying. "It happened right in front of us! We couldn't simply ignore it!"

"Hmm," said Aunt Eustacia. "You do seem to be making a habit of this sort of thing. What is it about you girls? Really, Daisy, if your parents . . ."

Daisy turned pale.

"Well," said Aunt Eustacia. "Never mind that, eh? You both seem largely unscathed, and that is a wonderful thing. We shall still have Christmas, after all, but now I think you ought to go to bed. You've been up half the night. I can see Hazel yawning."

I was glad to go, but when we got back to King Henry's rooms, I discovered that I was still thrumming with nerves, unable to sleep. Daisy and I stayed up for at least another hour, talking through the case.

"It is odd!" said Daisy. "I know it's Christmas, but it doesn't *feel* as though it is."

"I know," I said, and I could feel myself frowning. Two bodies did not feel very festive.

"Oh, Watson! These cases always do get to you, don't they?"

"I'm all right," I said. "I ought to be used to it by now."

"But that's the best thing about you, Hazel," said Daisy.

"Everything matters to you. You *bother* about everyone. Sometimes it is terribly annoying—your obsession with Alexander, for example . . ."

I felt my face heat up. "Don't—don't tell him, will you?" I whispered. "He'll laugh at me. And anyway, he likes *you*."

"Why ever should he laugh?" asked Daisy, her face surprised. "You're *Hazel*. You're the best person I know. Don't I keep telling you so? He ought to be honored. I don't know why he keeps on mooning after me, either. I keep on trying to warn him off by being rude to him. Do you know, I'm sure I don't understand this love business. What is it about me that he likes? And what is it about *him*, for you? Don't you mind that his sleeves are always too short?"

"No," I said, burning with awkwardness. "I don't know! Let's not talk about it."

"All right," said Daisy, sighing. "Sometimes I do think that I shall never understand people."

I woke up late on Christmas morning to bright sunlight. Daisy was sitting on my bed, her golden curls falling in waves about her face, eating a Chocolate Orange.

"Merry Christmas, Hazel!" she said. "Here, have some of this."

I took a segment, and let the sweet tang of it soak into my mouth.

"Merry Christmas!" I said, looking around at our bedroom. There was only a little sprig of holly tied to the end of Daisy's bed. It did not feel very Christmassy at all. I had my present for Daisy, carefully wrapped—I had left it in the sitting room after Daisy had got into bed the night before. I hoped it would be enough.

Then I noticed something.

"Daisy," I said. "Where did you get that chocolate?"

"From the living room, of course," said Daisy casually, biting down on another segment. "Father Christmas—or rather, Uncle Felix—has clearly been here in the night."

I got up in my bare feet and nightdress and rushed into our living room—and was met by the most perfect scene.

The fire was blazing, and in front of the fire guard were propped two bulging stockings. I could see bars of chocolate and fudge, packets of Turkish Delight, and tangerines in silver foil. Next to them were piles of presents, beautifully wrapped in tissue paper and ribbon. The room was festooned with green, spicy boughs, and breakfast was laid out on the low table next to the sofa: muffins and bread ready to be toasted, and eggs and bacon still steaming.

It was like magic.

"Oh!" I gasped. "It's beautiful!"

"Merry Christmas, Hazel," said Daisy, coming in behind and laughing at me, and we rushed forward together to open our presents.

"Yours first," said Daisy, and she handed me a square wrapped package. I opened it to find a notebook with gilt edges and a beautiful leather cover. "For the next case," she told me proudly.

I gave her my makeshift fingerprint kit. "You are clever, Hazel!" said Daisy with delight, when she opened it. "We shall be able to behave like real detectives now!"

Next were two parcels marked: *For Daisy and Hazel, from Lucy*.

"Miss Livedon!" said Daisy. "Or—she'll be Mrs.

Mountfitchet soon. Really, how can one person have so many names?"

They both contained Austrian-style hats, absolutely beautiful grown-up ones. Mine was red, and Daisy's was blue.

"There's something else in here too," said Daisy. "Oh!"

They were police manuals, official ones. *For you to learn proper procedure*, Miss Livedon had written on them.

Next were two books of logic puzzles. Both said, *With love from George and Alexander* on their frontispieces. I opened mine first, and got a little burst of joy, but then I saw that Daisy's was exactly the same.

There was a box of chocolates for me from Bertie, and for Daisy there was an absolute heap of puzzles and games. Some were labelled *From Mrs. D* and *From Chapman*—but they were all in Bertie's scrawly handwriting, and neither Daisy nor I were at all tricked. My father had sent several large parcels—improving, leather-bound books for both me and Daisy (he is quite sure that she needs to be improved), and a Fortnum's cake for each of us. On the label of mine he had written *Merry Christmas! Your real present is at home.* I was puzzled—but more presents were waiting.

Hetty had sent two small pocketbooks, hand-embroidered, with notes. *I miss you both*, she wrote. *Come and see us again soon!*

And finally we opened Uncle Felix's presents. I had a

beautiful leather-bound set of Dickens ("Ugh," said Daisy. "Such long books. I can't think how you can sit still long enough to read them, Hazel! But if you like them . . .") and three glorious one-guinea notebooks.

Daisy looked at them silently, and then she opened her parcel. She had a set of Margery Allingham mysteries, and a large wooden box that opened out into a detective kit. It was a real one, with little bottles and brushes for taking prints, and pots to put evidence in.

"Oh," I said. "It's beautiful."

"So are your notebooks," said Daisy.

"I shan't use them until the one you gave me is full!" I said. "I really like it much better."

"Well," said Daisy, "Uncle Felix's kit is much nicer than yours. But—you know, I do think I prefer yours as well. It's much more portable."

I burst out laughing. Daisy cannot lie to me even when she tries.

"Merry Christmas," I said to her.

"Merry Christmas to you too," said Daisy. "Detective Society forever."

After we had dressed, we went down to Aunt Eustacia's study and found Uncle Felix there. He seemed taller and handsomer than ever, his monocle screwed into his eye and his gold hair slicked back fashionably. Miss Livedon was with him, looking different again from the last time we had seen her. This Miss Livedon glowed with happiness, and I suddenly saw what Uncle Felix must see when he looked at her. She had a tiny diamond on her finger that sparked when she moved it. I looked at it, and felt odd. It was not just Daisy and I who were changing. Even the grown-ups were at it.

"Daisy, Hazel," said Miss Livedon, nodding at us, and then Uncle Felix winked at us and said, "I hope you liked your presents."

"Oh yes! Thank you!" we both said.

"I'm sure Aunt Eustacia has already told you of the change in our circumstances," said Uncle Felix. "We have an important request for you. Will you act as our bridesmaids? Of course, it's not up to your usual mysterious standard, but I hope it's a case you'll enjoy nonetheless."

"I suppose we can make the time," said Daisy. "Although you ought to have *told* me before now!"

"What, you didn't guess?" asked Uncle Felix.

"I did," I said. "At least—I'm not surprised."

"Then Hazel ought to be head bridesmaid," said Uncle Felix.

"We'll *share* it," said Daisy, glaring at him.

"By the way," he went on, "we swung by the local station on our way in. Wanted to hear the latest about the bit of trouble you had at Maudlin. Seems that idea of yours about Bocking's paid off, Daisy. PC Cross asked them to open up first thing this morning, and there was a Charles Melling in the poison book. It's a fake name, of course—the man knew Butler when he was shown a photograph. Said he was told he wanted to destroy a wasps' nest. You've got Butler concealing his name—proves intent, and proves he knew about the family connection. It'll be an easy conviction."

"Really, Daisy!" said Aunt Eustacia. "How many of these cases have you been mixed up in now? It hardly seems healthy."

"But I'm healthy as anything," said Daisy, folding her hands together primly. "It's all coincidence, Aunt E. Hazel and I can't help it if adventure happens to fall into our laps."

"Adventure!" said Aunt Eustacia. "Really! Well, at least it's all done now. Run along and get ready for church, girls. We'll go to the late-morning service. But first I want to grill your uncle's new fiancée without children about."

"At least she's honest about things," said Daisy to me afterward.

"She's exactly like you!" I said, and laughed at Daisy's upset face.

After church we had a treat for Christmas dinner: we were all invited to St. John's. Aunt Eustacia led us through Cambridge, dressed like a queen in purple. Then came Uncle Felix, Miss Livedon on his arm. They could not stop looking at each other and smiling. I think they hardly noticed where they were going. Then came Amanda and her friend Harriet, Amanda looking gladder and brighter than I had ever seen her. The terror of the essays had been lifted from her, and I was glad. I thought she would be better now. Daisy and I brought up the rear, both wearing our new hats proudly. Daisy's looked lovely with her fur coat—at last, I thought, we both looked quite grown up.

We walked through Cambridge in the snow, its bells tolling out Christmas Day in never-ending chains of sound. There was King's College Chapel, looking almost familiar now, there was Senate House, with its gargoyles and curlicues, and there was St. John's itself. Alexander had been to the Christmas service at St. John's Chapel with Bertie, though Harold and George had not. They had all come to the lodge gates to meet us now, and as I saw them my heart drummed.

Poor Bertie! I thought, as I looked at him. It must be hard for him. He had come to Cambridge to forget Fallingford, and now it had happened again.

But then Harold turned to Bertie, and Bertie smiled at him—and I saw something else I perhaps ought to have seen from the beginning.

"*People*," said Daisy to me resignedly, as they led us through the quad to Harold's rooms. "Really! Even Bertie's caught it."

I decided then that Bertie really would be all right after all.

Then Daisy turned—to George. "Escort me, if you please," she said, holding out her hand.

"Of course," said George, bowing and winking at her. She took his arm and they walked in together, and Alexander and I were left alone. I saw him gaze after Daisy, and then look at me. "May I?" he asked.

He held out his arm, and I put my hand on it, just the way I had seen Daisy do. It felt terribly strange, and not particularly comfortable, but all the same I loved it.

"Hazel," said Alexander. "George said . . . well, never

mind. Daisy . . . you know her. Do you think she'd ever—?"

"No," I said, glancing up at him. He looked so sad that my heart ached. "Not ever. I know Daisy."

"Well," said Alexander, and he sighed. "I suppose some things aren't meant to be. It'll be all right, eh?" He squeezed my arm, and I squeezed back. Suddenly I saw that there was something else that Alexander and I shared. It was not perfect at all, but that did not matter.

We walked into St. John's College together, following the others along the snowy quad path to the dining hall. I heard the noise of dinner long before we walked through the main doors—the clatter of plates being set down, and dishes served—and as I smelled the delicious things in front of me, my mouth watered.

Then the doors were thrown open for us, and inside was a scene from a painting, a dining hall even grander and more ornate than Maudlin's, all stone and stained glass, with an enormous tree in the corner, decorated and lit. On the long wooden tables turkeys gleamed like chestnuts, bowls of cranberry sauce and piles of potatoes and stuffing and roast vegetables. Christmas crackers were laid out at each place, and students were filing in, wearing their formal caps and gowns. Aunt Eustacia was at High Table with the St. John's dons, and Uncle Felix and Miss Livedon.

"Are you sure you're all right, Hazel?" Alexander whispered to me as we walked to our places next to Daisy and George.

"Yes!" I whispered back. "I am."

And I really was. I thought this Cambridge Christmas was the most wonderful I had ever had.

After dinner we were allowed to spend the evening with the boys. Daisy and George had a marvellous time. George had a book of real crimes with him, and he read them out to Daisy, so they could decide how they would have solved them. Before long, they had unpicked the Maybrick poisonings and proved Franz Müller innocent. I saw that Daisy was delighted to have found someone who thought in the same strict, logical way that she did—but she really was not in love in the slightest.

Alexander and I were playing Snakes and Ladders. After our conversation, I found I had terrible difficulty looking at Alexander directly. I kept feeling Daisy's eyes on the two of us. I decided that I hated being in love. It was far too awful and uncomfortable.

"Are you enjoying yourself, Hazel?" asked Alexander after a while.

"Yes," I said, blushing. "Why?"

"You've been acting oddly," said Alexander. "You've changed since the Orient Express. You do still like me, don't you? I'd understand if—I mean, we don't have to write anymore—"

"Of course I still like you!" I said, wishing like anything that Alexander was not so honest. "I like you an awful lot."

"I do too!" said Alexander happily, his American accent coming through more strongly than usual. "You're a real pal, Hazel. I'm so glad that we can be friends. Some of the fellows at school are stupid about it, but I know that it isn't like that at all."

My mouth had gone dry. "No!" I squeaked. "Not at all."

Daisy looked over at me, and I saw her eyebrows lift. Then she went back to talking to George.

And that is nearly all, except for one more thing. On Boxing Day, all around Cambridge, posters appeared. They were hand-lettered, and they appeared to have been stuck up overnight. They read:

THE JUNIOR PINKERTONS
WOULD LIKE TO ANNOUNCE
that they are NOT the best detective society in Cambridge.
That honor belongs to ANOTHER SOCIETY,
whose quick wits
SOLVED A VERY IMPORTANT CASE.
The Junior Pinkertons ADMIT DEFEAT
and humbly REQUEST A REMATCH.
BEST OF THREE?

When we saw them, I could not help laughing. It was the best Christmas present I could imagine.

"You see?" said Daisy, peeling one off the wall and clutching it triumphantly. "I *told* you we were better."

Daisy's Guide to Cambridge

Once again, Hazel has asked me to write an explanation of some words she has chosen. I must admit that, for once, I do see her point—there is a frightful lot of slang about in Cambridge, and even I needed to brush up on it a bit. I have also included some Deepdean words, although if you do not know what those mean by now there is really no hope for you.

Backs—this is the bit of Cambridge that is by the river. It means the backs of the colleges, as the fronts of them face the city.

Bags—a sort of trouser, quite baggy, that students wear. They are rather ridiculous.

Bedder—this is a word for a person who looks after the students' domestic things in a Cambridge college, rather like a maid would. Of course there is an odd word for them at Cambridge.

Blab—this means telling a secret that you should not. Only sneaks blab—I would never do such a thing.

Bluestocking—this is a word for a scholarly woman, who studies instead of getting married. Although I do not want to get married, I am not a Bluestocking. I am a detective.

Bunbreak—we have this every school morning at 11 a.m. We are given biscuits or buns and allowed to run about outside for ten minutes exactly. The best bunbreak is on Saturday, when we have squashed fly biscuits.

Bursar—the person in a college who looks after the money. It is rather like being a treasurer, but more academic.

Buttery—a place in college where you can buy food and drinks.

Cam—the name of the river that flows through Cambridge.

Chelsea bun—a lovely sweet bun, with raisins and sticky syrup in it. It is a specialty of Fitzbillies tea rooms in Cambridge, and an excellent bunbreak treat.

Christmas cracker—a brightly colored paper tube with a joke and a paper hat inside it that two people pull apart for fun at Christmas time. It makes a little popping noise as you do it, which is why it's called a cracker.

Chump—an idiot. Someone who does not deserve to be in the Detective Society.

Dais—a raised platform in a hall where the most important people sit, so that the less important people can see them at all times and feel small.

Decanter—a glass jug with a stopper that holds wine once it has been poured out of its bottle. Grown-ups say that this makes the wine taste nicer, but I am not sure.

Don—the word for a professor or teacher at Cambridge, rather like a mistress for university students.

Dorm—the place where we stay during school terms, since we cannot go home.

Entail—a way of inheriting money that has nothing to do with wills—it simply passes to the oldest living man in a family. It is very unfair.

Heir—a person who is set to inherit money. You say it like "air"—which may well be all that some heirs get, if the older generations have blued all the family's money.

Livery—another word for uniform, a very official sort.

Master—a special word for the person who runs a college.

Pash—this is a word that means being in love with someone, but politely and not romantically. For some reason, everyone behaves as though it is perfectly acceptable for one girl to have a pash on another, but not all right to be in love with her. Logically, I cannot see much difference.

Porter—this word can mean two things. It can be the person who carries your trunk at a station, or it can be the person who sits at the entrance of a college and watches who comes and goes.

Po-faced—this means to be stiff and dull. I am never po-faced.

Poison book—chemists have these in their shops. When you buy deadly poison you have to note your name down in a poison book, so there is a record in case you decide to kill someone with it.

Sent down—another way of saying expelled.

Shrimp—the littlest girls in the school, almost babies, really.

Spiffing—marvelous or fantastic.

Wizard—another way of saying spiffing or excellent.

AUTHOR'S NOTE AND ACKNOWLEDGMENTS

I grew up in Oxford, at Pembroke College, in the 1990s (my father was the Master). It was a wonderful and very odd place to be a child, and I am so grateful to all the students and staff who looked after me. I couldn't write a college book without thinking of them and it, and borrowing quite a lot of its geography.

I dropped Maudlin and St. Lucy's into the Cambridge landscape quite abruptly. Apologies to Cambridge residents for getting rid of Queen's College, moving a bridge, and reassigning most of Mill Lane. As a consolation, though, Fitzbillies, Heffers, and the Market Square are quite real and unmoved from their 2018 locations—you can visit all of them, and I think you should.

I've been fairly historically accurate in this book. Tinsel and Chocolate Oranges had both been invented by 1935, as had Christmas crackers. The Night Climbers are absolutely real too—I read a brilliant book called *The Night Climbers of Cambridge* by Whipplesnaith (not his real name) to get a lot of my details. I think he'd have been friends with Bertie.

For Alfred's background I am indebted to my friend OB. I'm grateful to Alex Strick from Inclusive Minds for putting me in touch with Habeeba Mulla, who helped me make sure that George and Harold were properly represented. The facts of Harold's and George's lives were built by Shompa Lahiri's excellent book *Indians in Britain*. Did you know that in 1927 there were 1,800 Indian students at British universities, and that in 1936 a London doctor called Mangaldas Mehta was knighted for services to medicine? I've named George's father after him. George, though, is named for a less pleasant bit of British history: in 1903 George Edalji, a British Indian, was sent to prison for a crime he didn't commit. One of the people who helped release him was Arthur Conan Doyle (you might know him better as the author of *Sherlock Holmes*).

The more historical research I do, the more I remember that immigration isn't a recent invention, and it's not a bad thing. Alfred, Hazel, Alexander, Harold, and George belong in 1930s England just as much as Daisy and Bertie do, and I wouldn't want to write a historical book that doesn't reflect that reality.

In fact, the biggest invention in this book (apart from the murder) is the weather. In 1935 Cambridge had an extremely mild winter, with no snow at all. But I couldn't write a Christmas book without it. Call it artistic license.

And now, the part where I thank people. My publishers, Simon and Schuster, have once again done a fantastic job—thanks especially to my editor, Alexa Pastor, for taking on the series so brilliantly. And, of course, thanks to my illustrator, Elizabeth Baddeley, for another beautiful cover and maps!

Thank you to my agent, Gemma Cooper, who continues to support me and the books tirelessly—you've fought for them and me for five years now, and I never stop being grateful to you for your kindness and care.

Thank you to my family, especially my mother, Kathie Booth Stevens, who is always there when I need her and who I love very much.

Thank you to my friends for looking after me through the writing process. There are too many of you to name, but especially Non Pratt, Louie Stowell and Karen Lawler, Katherine Woodfine and the rest of the Crime Club, and Katy, Mo, Ruth, Sibeal, Beth, Harriet, and the rest of Team Cooper. Thanks to Charlie Morris and Wei Ming Kam for giving me much-needed feedback on drafts, and for being generally great.

Thank you to my partner in crime, David Stevens. You make me feel so lucky. I'd dedicate a whole library to you if I could.

And finally, thank you to all my fans. You are who I write for, and knowing you love my books is the most marvellous thing about being an author. Detective Society forever!

Robin Stevens

London, January 2018